The Altogether Unexpected
Disappearance of Atticus Craftsman

www.transworldbooks.co.uk

The Altogether Unexpected Disappearance of Atticus Craftsman

Mamen Sánchez

Translated from the Spanish by Lucy Greaves

Doubleday

LONDON · TORONTO · SYDNEY · AUCKLAND · JOHANNESBURG

TRANSWORLD PUBLISHERS
61–63 Uxbridge Road, London W5 5SA
www.transworldbooks.co.uk

Transworld is part of the Penguin Random House group of companies
whose addresses can be found at global.penguinrandomhouse.com

First published in Great Britain in 2015 by Doubleday
an imprint of Transworld Publishers

Originally published in Spanish as *La Felicidad es un Té Contigo*

Copyright © Mamen Sánchez 2015
English language translation © Lucy Greaves 2015

Mamen Sánchez has asserted her right under the Copyright, Designs
and Patents Act 1988 to be identified as the author of this work.

A CIP catalogue record for this book
is available from the British Library.

ISBNs 9780857523235 (hb)
9780857523242 (tpb)

Typeset in 11½/14pt Bembo by Kestrel Data, Exeter, Devon.
Printed and bound by Clays Ltd, Bungay, Suffolk.

Penguin Random House is committed to a sustainable
future for our business, our readers and our planet. This book
is made from Forest Stewardship Council® certified paper.

1 3 5 7 9 10 8 6 4 2

The Altogether Unexpected
Disappearance of Atticus Craftsman

Chapter 1

Inspector Manchego's office wasn't, strictly speaking, an office. Rather, it was an open room divided into several square cubicles by thin plasterboard panels, which were of course themselves very practical: each occupant was free to arrange their own collage of clippings, photographs, urgent messages, Christmas cards, police reports and lists of restaurants that delivered. The layout was reminiscent of the changing cubicles in certain shopping centres where, owing to a lack of ceilings or any kind of soundproofing, one inevitably hears tremendously indiscreet comments about the different types of fruit and salami that the female anatomy might resemble when squeezed into over-tight trousers. The difference was that here in the office, instead of fashion disasters, other kinds of issues were aired, more along the lines of violence and abuse, armed robbery, thefts from cashpoints or street brawls. Words like 'allegation', 'prosecution', 'court case' and 'prison sentence' jumped from one cubicle to another like fleas in an infested mattress.

He wasn't called Manchego either, but the inspector, whose real name was Alonso Jandalillo, fancied that he might share the immortality of Don Quixote de la Mancha's heroic deeds as well as his name – despite the fact that to date his résumé contained nothing of note. To this end he had adopted 'Manchego' as an alias for the two or three field operations he had taken part in. Those three syllables sounded particularly good accompanied by the background noise of a walkie-talkie.

Sometimes, for he was a man of action in spite of the belly he had been cultivating of late, he lamented the sedentary lifestyle he now led. On turning fifty, he had retired from patrolling the streets of Madrid and had been given a cushy desk job in a neighbourhood police station. But he missed the adrenaline rush he used to get from driving his police car, blasting the siren and intimidating other drivers over the loudspeaker: 'Move aside, lady, chop chop, get that van out the way, we're on a top-secret mission.'

So, when Mr Marlow Craftsman and his interpreter, Mr Bestman, dared to invade the three square metres of which Manchego was lord and master, both wearing tweed jackets and waistcoats, expensive shoes and grey overcoats, and carrying black leather briefcases, they renewed his faith in his profession. A profession he loved even though most of the time it caused him nothing but stress.

He felt the urge to get up and greet them, but stopped himself just in time. A police inspector isn't a business-man, he remembered, he doesn't shake hands, doesn't smile, doesn't even interrupt the mechanical rhythm of his typing. He might, as a maximum gesture of courtesy, remove the cigarette from his mouth, tap it a couple of times on the edge of the ashtray, clear his throat and say: 'Please, take a seat.' Then, only once his visitors' eyes are at the same level as his and there is no way they can intimidate him by look-ing him up and down, he might lift his head and say: 'How can I help you?'

Marlow Craftsman was about sixty years old, judging by the expression lines around his ratty little eyes. He was as pasty as cold meat, had skin the exact colour of cooked ham and his lips were so thin that they seemed to have been drawn on with a pen.

The interpreter was somewhat younger but equally pink. He had more hair, of the salt–and–pepper variety, and he wore reading glasses.

'Allow me to introduce my employer,' said Bestman in grammatically flawless but acoustically horrendous Spanish. 'Mr Marlow Craftsman, of Craftsman & Co.'

The inspector put on his best blank face. He got it just right. Judging by the dramatic emphasis that Bestman had placed on the name, followed by a lengthy pause to give it time to sink in, the man sitting across from him was in all probability a bank baron. The firm sounded like a bank. One of those banks that have been in the hands of the same family of English aristocrats for over a hundred and fifty years. For there could be no doubt that those two specimens were sons of the Perfidious Albion; hence their air of superiority and their Hamilton watches, a sharp observation that later, when Manchego looked back on the scene, he would have occasion to feel rather proud of.

'Ah ha,' he replied without saying more, given that he didn't have the faintest idea what that name meant.

'Mr Craftsman has come from London to report the disappearance of his son Atticus. Since the young man's last-known residence is number 5, Calle del Alamillo, we have been sent by Scotland Yard to initiate proceedings here, at your station, which is the closest to his address.'

'Scotland Yard sent you?' This sounded promising.

'Not exactly, Mr Jandalillo . . .'

9

'Inspector Manchego,' interrupted the policeman.

'Not exactly, Inspector Manchego,' repeated Bestman. 'They simply advised us to come here.'

'I see.'

'The situation is that Atticus Craftsman has shown no signs of life for three months. The last time he made contact with his father was via a telephone message on the tenth of August.'

'Could I hear the message?' asked Manchego.

'It's in English,' replied the interpreter as he opened his briefcase and took out a state-of-the-art smartphone.

He pressed various buttons, then lifted the device to the inspector's ear and held his breath. Manchego heard a nasal voice, as if the speaker had a cold, and a rhythmical sound in the background, a kind of lament or prayer, and the strumming of a guitar. Of course, he didn't understand a word of what the speaker was saying, but he could tell that it wasn't a call for help because there was no distress in the tone of voice. That evening, on remembering this detail, he would congratulate himself once more for being such a gifted investigator.

'What's he saying?' Manchego had to admit that his lack of English was an issue he really had to address.

'He says, word for word, "Leave it to me, Dad. I've got it all under control."'

The inspector automatically shot an inquisitive glance at Mr Craftsman. He, in turn, had his pink ratty eyes fixed on the inspector's.

'So,' Manchego asked, 'what's he referring to?'

The interpreter translated. Mr Craftsman replied.

'My employer says that he is probably referring to the work he was undertaking in Madrid.'

Manchego leant back. After all that, this was just another case like all the others. Dirty dealings with drugs and the settling of scores.

'*Mister Crasman*,' he reprimanded, with the best English pronunciation he could muster, 'is your son involved in drug-trafficking?'

'No, God no!' responded Bestman without even translating. 'The young Mr Craftsman, like his father here, his late grandfather and all his paternal ancestors dating back to the eighteenth century, is in the publishing business.'

'I see,' said Manchego.

'He is a respectable young man, educated at Exeter College, Oxford, with an outstanding academic record and an impeccable career. He has never been involved in any kind of shady business whatsoever. He is the victim here, not the suspect.'

Inspector Manchego took a long drag on his cigarette. Yes, he had made a wrong move, but, as he explained to the Englishmen, it was important to explore each and every possible cause of a disappearance, even the most unlikely.

'We have to proceed by ruling out options,' he declared.

'Mr Craftsman is leaning towards the possibility of a kidnap,' replied the translator.

'Why?' Manchego wanted to know. 'Have you received any calls demanding a ransom? Do you have any proof that the young man has been retained against his will?'

'The truth is, no, we haven't.'

'In that case let's stick to the facts and not get sidetracked, gentlemen.'

It was important to always maintain a dominant position over the Englishmen, Manchego said to himself. He opened a program that contained the templates for reports, selected the 'open new document' tab and wrote 'Crasman Case', although he later changed this to 'Craftsman' at the translator's insistence:

> The complainant, Marlow Craftsman, reports the disappearance of his son, Atticus Craftsman, thirty years of age, one metre eighty-seven tall, well-built, blond hair, green eyes, slight limp from an old rowing injury . . .

He stopped and frowned.

'Rowing?'

'Precisely. A snapped tendon.'

Manchego imagined the young man in a rowing boat on the River Thames. Muscular back, strong shoulders, brawny arms, but what about his legs? You hardly used your legs, he thought. He made a mental note: 'Investigate the function of the legs in rowing.'

> . . . The young Mr Craftsman's last-known address was: right-hand flat, second floor, number 5, Calle del Alamillo, Madrid, and he last made contact with his father on 10 August 2012 at 8 p.m., London time.

He hesitated for a moment, then typed a final sentence:

> There are no indications that this case is connected to drug-trafficking.

'Very good, gentlemen,' he said after drawing breath. 'I'll process the report today and the investigation will get under way as soon as possible. You can expect to hear from me in due course.'

He made a move to get up and see them out, but on

seeing that the two men remained seated he returned to his chair straight away. Mr Craftsman was giving instructions to his translator. A lot of instructions.

'My employer is surprised that you don't require any further information.'

Manchego raised an eyebrow.

'Here we do things straight down the line. It takes as long as it takes. We don't accept payments, or bribes, or anything like that to speed things along, as you will surely appreciate.'

'What are you talking about?' said Bestman, astonished. 'We mean DNA samples, photographs, bank details, pager, the registration number of the car he was driving when he was last seen . . .'

The inspector cleared his throat. He turned in his chair. He counter-attacked.

'So you were concealing the fact that *Mister Crasman* was driving a vehicle when he was last seen.'

'We weren't concealing anything,' protested Bestman. 'You're the one who didn't ask.'

'You wouldn't be insinuating that I don't know how to do my job, would you?'

Dominant position, Manchego reminded himself, dominant position.

'Of course not.'

'Then tell me once and for all everything you know about the case. And I warn you that if I find that you're hiding any important information from me, you'll both become objects of investigation yourselves.'

The Englishmen exchanged a few words under their breath. Then they opened their briefcases simultaneously and each took out a folder that they placed in front of Manchego's computer. It would be a long night, thought the inspector, groaning inwardly; he would have to read all this to be able to write the report.

'This folder contains all the information in English and this one has everything translated into Spanish,' explained the interpreter.

'Very well.'

'Since we don't have a DNA sample from the young Mr Craftsman,' added the Englishman, 'perhaps it would be of use to take a sample from my employer, his father.'

Manchego scratched the back of his neck. He had never been in a situation like this in his life.

'You'll have to wait a moment,' he announced.

He got up and hurried out of the office. He went out into the street, crossed at the lights, entered the Adelina pharmacy and asked for some cotton buds. He paid in cash. He returned to the station, went into the cubicle where the two men were waiting for him, intrigued, and said:

'Right then, *Míster Crasman*, open wide.'

Chapter 2

Atticus Craftsman vividly remembered the sound that the tendon in his knee made when it snapped, right in the middle of the boat race against Cambridge, and the noise of the oar hitting the water. For the seventh year running, thanks to his injury, Oxford University took second place in the competition where second meant last. The rivalry with the light blues was just one of hundreds of ancient traditions at Oxford, along with the striped ties they wore, the oath – sworn on the Bible – not to chew gum in the Bodleian Library, strawberries and champagne on Christ Church Meadow, or the fact that students were not allowed to walk on the grass in the college's central quad, with the resulting inconvenience of having to walk all the way round the outside simply to get from one side to the other.

All those rules had seemed shocking to begin with but, after surviving the first year, the students not only devoutly adhered to them but also ultimately perpetuated them, as the rules came to form part of the collective spirit of the student flock.

Nor had Atticus forgotten what he felt when he first saw

the commemorative plaque that hung on his bedroom door: 'Here resided the famous author J.R.R. Tolkien.'

It was no coincidence. Marlow Craftsman had made it very clear to the rector of the college that his son Atticus must be allocated the room in which *The Lord of the Rings* – in his eyes one of the most representative works of universal literature – was conceived. His wish had been granted without delay, in view of his status as patron of the college and benefactor of the library. Before Atticus, the room had been occupied by his elder brother, Holden, who had conceived his first son Oliver there. This displeased their mother, who would have preferred a white wedding and no baby on the way. Marlow himself, his father Dorian and his grandfather Sherlock, a founding member of The Apolaustics, had also lived in that room, and it had come to be as sacred to the Craftsmans as the old custom of naming their children after the lead characters of great novels.

As Atticus stood forlornly at the door to his new life, however, he felt none of the pride his father had spoken so much about. Instead, he felt an unbearable tightness in his stomach because he knew the plaque demanded of him an intelligence and creativity that he lacked – utterly.

So, after a few days of worrying about not being able to do Tolkien justice, he put a Chelsea sticker – his favourite team – over the silver rectangle and signed up for football, punting and rowing, sports in which he excelled.

He also got a job as a guide at the university museum, even though he didn't need the money and the uniform was a kind of ridiculous medieval costume, because the girl of his dreams, who did need the money, worked at the ticket desk. This was the best way he could think of to get close to her without arousing suspicion.

The girl's name was Lisbeth and that day, the day of the

snapped tendon, she was watching the boat race from the bridge with a dark blue scarf tied around her neck. When Atticus's boat lost its rhythm she walked away from the river, disappointed, with her arm around a boy from Lincoln College.

Atticus spent the six weeks after the operation on his knee recuperating at the family home in Kent. Although his father insisted on calling it a 'farm', it was really an expanse of land where they grew nothing but grass, and more of a country retreat with its Victorian mansion, gardens, lake and ducks.

They had a mahogany library which held over eight thousand leather-bound volumes, some of which were genuine treasures. It was Atticus's favourite place to spend the lonely afternoons of his confinement, watching the rain on the windowpanes, remembering Lisbeth, stoking the fire and dipping into those books which, until then, had seemed like nothing more than decoration. He discovered ancient philosophies, avant-garde ideas, priceless etchings, black-and-white postcards from places that no longer existed, shocking perversions, saintly lives, Byron, Keats and Beckett . . . all these mixed together in both the library and his mind as a sweet-and-sour concoction.

Weekends at the house were lively. His parents returned from London, their friends came to visit, Holden brought little Oliver in a sling on his back and the library became a lounge where they drank tea and talked loudly.

On Sunday afternoons, Atticus would feel strangely anxious as he waited for them all to bundle back into their cars and disappear down the chestnut-tree-lined drive. Only then, finally, could he regain control of his army of stories and poems.

★

While his knee healed, his mind expanded and his spirit absorbed feelings that belonged to other people but became his own.

He returned to Oxford a different man. A braver one.

He went to find Lisbeth at the museum, whisked her away from the ticket desk and led her through the cobbled streets of the city centre to his college's small chapel, which was always empty. Once inside, he closed the door, lifted the cover on the piano, played 'Bridge Over Troubled Water' in memory of the fateful day of the boat race, played 'Raindrops Keep Falling on My Head', stroked the soft skin of her hand, touched her hair and her face and asked, 'Do you want to see my room?'

They slept in each other's arms in the narrow bed. Female visitors were not allowed in Exeter College, but the porter, Mr Shortsight, was inclined to turn a blind eye – he knew how to feign deep sleep in the armchair in the porters' lodge and, what's more, enjoyed hearing the nocturnal sighs of forbidden lovers. The only condition, and all the students knew this, was that they had to make sure their clandestine visitors left before dawn. The head porter came on duty at seven o'clock sharp, with his distance glasses on and a list of infractions in hand.

Lisbeth was a light sleeper. She woke up before Atticus. She was sitting up against the pillow, waiting for him to open his eyes, when she found herself face to face with a man who looked about eighty, smoked a pipe and was accompanied by a tiny Hobbit. He said good morning, walked from one side of the room to the other, buttoned up his waistcoat and vanished.

'I think I just saw Tolkien's ghost,' she whispered to Atticus.

He silenced her with kisses.

Anyway, it must have been true that the ghosts of old professors wandered through those rooms. There were inexplicable gusts of air, whispers in the night and stifled bursts of laughter, and on some mornings the grass in the quad was covered in footprints.

The graduation ceremony was solemn and formal, with students in caps and gowns, tourists convinced they had jumped back in time and bells pealing wildly and joyfully.

Saying goodbye was heartbreaking. Many friendships, many projects, many loves would come to an end now that they were graduating.

Lisbeth returned to the small island of Guernsey, lost in the English Channel. Atticus set off with a rucksack on his back to travel the world: he visited Europe, Arabia, India, Istanbul. He then settled in London, near Knightsbridge, two blocks from the offices of Craftsman & Co, where he started working for his father. Little by little he left behind the sweet memories of his first love and swapped them for ones with different flavours: sharp, spicy, rich and exotic. He bought a classic Aston Martin, just like James Bond's, in order to return punctually, every Sunday, to the library at home in Kent, where his thousands of alphabetically arranged books and a roaring fire awaited him. He needed nothing more.

Until one day Marlow Craftsman called him into his office.

Chapter 3

'Atticus, son, we have an unpleasant issue that requires an urgent solution. I need your help.'

By that point, young Mr Craftsman had turned thirty. He had his life laid out, solid friendships, a healthy sum in the bank, an enviable physique and the freedom to go where he liked without a care in the world, with no other duties than attending to his pleasant work at the publishing house from Monday to Friday, his lovers on Saturday and his books on Sunday.

'Come, take a seat,' his father told him, pointing to one of the office's two leather chairs.

Atticus felt as comfortable there as in the living room at home. Portraits of the same men hung on the walls, there were photos of the same family in silver frames and his boss was the same hero who had banished his nightmares when he was a little boy. He was tempted to put his feet up on the mahogany desk, but his father's worried expression stopped him. He opted for a more formal posture: legs crossed at the ankle and a hand on his chin. Just like his grandfather Dorian in his portrait.

'You see, Atticus,' began Marlow before changing

smoothly from father to boss, 'first and foremost I want to thank you for your work. You've become an important part of the company and I'm very proud of you. As you know, when Mr Bestman retires next year you'll be named development director.'

'Um hmm,' nodded Atticus, who frequently received the same information from his father: congratulations and the reiteration of his next promotion as a prelude to a delicate assignment. He was sure that the surprise would come next.

'Good.' Pause. Cough.

'Um hmm?'

'It's an unpleasant matter.'

'Yes.'

'It requires an urgent solution.'

'Right.'

Marlow drew breath. He got up. He started pacing around the office.

'I'll start from the beginning,' he said. 'To bring you up to speed,' he added. 'The matter dates back to 2006.' Pause. Cough. 'Therefore, as you will have deduced, the problem arose six years ago. Although at the beginning it wasn't a problem, it was an investment.'

He really was struggling to get going. Atticus felt an urge to get up from his chair and shake his father like a snow globe, to see if he could make it snow once and for all.

'Back then the business was expanding healthily,' Marlow explained. 'We were opening offices in several European capitals. One of these, as you know, was in Spain, in Madrid.'

Atticus nodded.

'Mr Bestman had a visionary idea.' He frowned. 'He thought that to support our book sales it would be advisable for Craftsman & Co to also publish small literary magazines in each country, so as to promote our titles.'

'Very astute,' Atticus acknowledged.

'We rolled out those projects and I must say that, to date, they have more than fulfilled their purpose. As you must understand, they don't make a lot of money but they are valid tools. Some, like the German magazine *Krafts*, have even come to be considered among the most prestigious literary publications in the country.'

Marlow went back to his desk. He let himself fall heavily into his chair.

'All bar one, that is.'

That afternoon, after the meeting, Atticus Craftsman felt the need to drink alone. He went into a pub and ordered a cold pint. He downed it in one. He burped.

His briefcase contained the documents his father had given him. It certainly was a thorny issue, hence Marlow's initial reluctance to spit it out. For Atticus it meant climbing a rung of the career ladder, there was no doubt about that. The issue called for someone experienced, in whom the company could place complete trust. But it also meant a significant change to his routine. He would be forced to leave England for an indefinite period and defer other matters that currently occupied all his energies.

He ordered another pint.

The task, after all, was simple. Unpleasant, yes, but simple. He would have to travel to Madrid and close down *Librarte* magazine, fire all its staff, hand out redundancy cheques, shake hands, put up with tears, explain the reasons behind such an extreme decision in the nicest way possible, and lay all the blame on them: they were responsible for the economic losses, the lack of foresight, the irreparable damage to the Craftsman brand, etcetera.

'There is one more detail you should know,' his father

had said between a pause and a cough. '*Librarte* magazine has only five employees. Five. And it so happens, son, that they are all women.'

How hard could it be, thought Atticus in the pub. Even so, for some strange reason, he felt the urgent need to inject alcohol directly into his veins. Four pints later he stumbled home. Perhaps that's why he forgot to pack many of the essential items that he would soon miss in Madrid.

Chapter 4

Inspector Manchego had managed to convince his friends that *mus* was a country bumpkin's card game. Due to, he said, the use of chickpeas as counters. Someone suggested that they could swap them for something else, like pebbles, jacks or sugar cubes – something easy to find in the bar or nearby – but Manchego insisted that they hadn't left their village, put up with hardship and made their way in the capital only to ruin everything on account of a game like *mus*. He also banned them from ordering tumblers of wine or tapas like Russian salad. Lousy bunch of yokels. As for him, he intoned solemnly, he was going to learn to play poker and drink whisky. There were, at first, some dissenting voices, but the guys soon got into the swing of meeting up to play poker on Thursday evenings. What Manchego didn't know was that his friends took turns to stand on the corner so they could see him coming and raise the alarm, allowing the others to quickly hide the Spanish deck of cards, gulp down their wine, choke themselves on croquettes and squid before, very seriously, welcoming him with the chips laid out and their poker faces on.

They went to all this trouble for two reasons; firstly,

because they were genuinely fond of him, and secondly, because he was the only policeman in the group and in their neighbourhood it was every man for himself against thieves, drug addicts, loan sharks and parking fines. Manchego had helped all of them get out of fixes or protect their businesses. And he didn't ask for anything in return, they reminded themselves, except this obsession with poker, the poor guy, and in the end it was no skin off their noses to make him happy.

So, regular as clockwork, that Thursday shortly after nine o'clock, Macita, Josi, Carretero and Míguel (yes, with an accent on the 'i') were waiting for him with the whisky on ice.

Manchego turned up with an odd kind of look, a half-smile, eyes sparkling. He greeted them, as usual, with slaps on the back. Then he sat down, spreading his legs wide.

'*Guess what*,' he said, wiggling his eyebrows up and down to signal suspense.

He had news.

'I've got a case,' he continued, before any of them had a chance to come out with something stupid like 'You got a raise' or 'They finally installed your broadband.'

'Drugs?' asked Josi.

'Maybe, Josi, maybe. I don't rule anything out, you know that,' he replied, pleased with the shrewdness of his friend, who owned a garage and was his star pupil. 'But no. On this occasion it seems not. It's an international affair that goes beyond our borders.'

'Immigrants, say no more,' decided Macita, who ran a grocery store and was obsessed with how many shops run by Chinese immigrants were springing up. 'Those people sleep on their feet,' he liked to say. 'I've seen them with my own eyes, swear to God.'

25

'I'm investigating the case of a missing person,' Manchego revealed. 'A stuck-up English aristocrat has lost his son and is looking for him. He came to the station yesterday. Scotland Yard sent him.'

He poured another round of whisky.

'I'll prove it,' he announced.

He took his mobile out of his pocket and dialled a number. They listened carefully.

'*Manchego espikin*,' he said. '*Not in jospital*,' he added. Whoever was on the other end of the line must not have understood the phrase that Manchego had written on a scrap of paper, so the inspector repeated it again.

'Manchego,' he repeated. '*Polís, Espein. Yes, yes. Not in jospital*.' And then for the third time: '*In jospital not*.'

His friends looked at him, intrigued. No one dared ask anything.

'I have just informed *Míster Crasman*, the aristocrat, who is an important businessman from London and, by the way, a friend of the Queen, that his son has not been admitted to hospital.'

He leant back and stretched out his legs.

'When investigating a disappearance,' he explained to his admiring audience, 'the first thing is always to be sure that the missing person has not been the victim of an accident or a violent robbery. To do so, we use the special police line to contact all the hospitals across Spain. There are thousands. We give them the person's details and wait.'

'And nothing,' twigged Macita.

'Nothing?'

'They didn't find anything, I mean.'

'Correct. He isn't in hospital anywhere.'

'Then *Míster Crasman* will be relieved,' Josi thought to suggest.

'Not at all, Josi. Think about it,' Manchego corrected him. 'When a missing person turns up, even if he's seriously injured in hospital, that's the best news possible. It's much worse not knowing where or in what condition he is. If he's not in hospital that could mean he's dead, at the bottom of a well, for example. Or kidnapped.'

His tone of voice was different when he said that last word; he stretched it out in a loud whisper.

'And you're sure it's nothing to do with drugs?' insisted Josi.

Chapter 5

Marlow Craftsman was lying down, engrossed in reading *The Waste Land*, pursuing the Holy Grail, imagining empty cemeteries and other poetic cruelties when he was assaulted by the sound of the phone ringing on his bedside table.

He lifted the receiver.

The voice of Inspector Manchego, drowned out by the cheerful tinkling of ice in glasses, the laughter of barflies and background music, caused him the same pain as a blow to the head. The man was shouting unintelligible words in a devilish language.

'Not in hospital?' he was finally able to decipher.

He drew breath. He exhaled slowly while pressing his fingers to his temples, exactly as indicated by an Eastern relaxation technique. Obviously, before Marlow Craftsman went to the police he had called every single hospital in Spain, with the help of two secretaries at his publishing house, two women whom he swore to secrecy about the investigation. They had found nothing. They had also called police stations, prisons, hotels and other public places he imagined might give some clue as to the whereabouts of his son. To no avail. Later he checked that Atticus hadn't hired a car or a yacht, hadn't taken a flight, a train or a ferry. One of the secretaries suggested checking campsites as well, but Marlow assured her that the only reason his son would be found in one of those odious places was if he had been kidnapped, and that would move their little investigation up to a new level: one for which they would need to seek professional assistance.

Following the logic of this argument, Marlow had gone with Charles Bestman, his right-hand man, to Scotland Yard, where a friendly police inspector had insisted on transferring the dossier to Spain because, he said, 'missing person cases are best dealt with in situ.'

Mr Bestman spoke perfect English, French, German and Spanish, so he would easily be able to act as interpreter.

Charles Bestman was also startled when the telephone rang after ten o'clock at his home on Chelsea Gardens. He was already in his pyjamas. He checked the time on the grandfather clock in the living room. It was never wrong. It had belonged to his own grandfather and had survived air raids, the division of family inheritances and other domestic disasters, yet continued to give the time with perfect accuracy.

'Darling, who on Earth could be calling at this time?' his wife Victoria asked from the dressing room.

Charles lifted the receiver. He listened in silence.

On the other end of the line he heard voices, the clinking of glasses, background music. He listened more carefully. His pulse accelerated. If the young Craftsman had been kidnapped, as he suspected, then sooner or later he would get the dreaded call demanding a ransom. 'For the moment, the hostage is well,' they would tell him, 'but if you don't pay us immediately we'll cut off his ear. Bring us the money in a suitcase, don't tell the police.' Then they would give him directions to a bit of disused land on the edge of the city, tell him not to take any weapons, not to pull any tricks. And then, worst of all, he would have to give Marlow Craftsman the bad news.

'Who is it?' he asked after a few suspenseful seconds.

Nothing.

He put a finger in his right ear and pressed the telephone to his left. The voices were speaking Spanish. There was no doubt that it concerned the kidnapping of Atticus Craftsman.

'Hello?'

He was able to make out a phrase over all the noise. He didn't recognize the voice of the person speaking, but he understood straight away that it was someone connected with the police.

'And you're sure it's not something to do with drugs?' he heard the man say.

He heard the echoing sound of a whisky bottle being uncorked, followed by the gurgling of the liquid as it was poured into a glass.

'Manchego, you've left your phone on,' said a third person.

'Your turn to deal, Macita, get on with it,' he heard Inspector Manchego say, then the call ended.

Chapter 6

Wherever he went, Atticus Craftsman was in the habit of carrying his small collection of erotic books with him. They were five volumes bound in red leather with no names printed on their spines. They weren't very large editions, taking up about the same amount of space as his wash-bag. They contained no prologues, introductions, footnotes or indexes of names or dates – just naked text, no more no less.

That was, really, his only perversion. He had never watched a pornographic film, never bought a dirty magazine and he didn't like looking at websites with sexual content. He wasn't depraved or into weird stuff. However, he felt inexplicably unable to go anywhere without his small travelling library.

Wrapped in tissue paper, those five books were the first things he took out of his suitcase as soon as he closed the door to his room behind the hotel porter. He placed them on the bedside table, in strictly alphabetical order as usual, moving the phone and the lamp slightly to one side: Duras, Lawrence, Miller, Nabokov and Sade. Five ways of understanding female sensuality.

'You can't learn that stuff from books,' Lisbeth had warned him on one of their secret nights in Tolkien's room. 'They're just fantasies that have come out of the dirty minds of authors. They've got nothing to do with reality.'

Atticus had rescued each one of the books from oblivion. At some point, one of his relatives, male or female, had acquired, read and hidden them among the thousands of books in the library in Kent. What better place to bury a guilty conscience? The strange thing was that all five of them were exactly the same size, were printed on the same paper, as fine as cigarette paper, and had the same impeccable binding. Perhaps they had all been a single, exciting gift for who knows who.

The fact is that they had finally ended up in his hands. Almost by chance.

Lolita was the first. He found it one rainy Sunday afternoon, when the pain in his knee was still unbearable, and it served as a comfort. It distracted his mind, relaxed his body and filled his dreams with shameful scenes in which Lolita had Lisbeth's face. Then came *The Lover*, more torturous, more violent, turning some of his dreams into nightmares.

It was then that he realized the two books were exactly the same size and style. He hitched himself up with the crutches, hobbled over to the shelves as best he could, and pored over them, from right to left, until one by one, like red fireflies, the other three novels jumped out at him. Lisbeth said that you couldn't learn how to love from books, but she moaned and contorted her small, satisfied body thanks to Miller and Nabokov, believing all the while that Atticus was responsible for such delirium.

The tale of the young Craftsman's skill in the bedroom spread like wildfire through the corridors of the all-female colleges. His fame soon became legend. Women sought his gaze, followed him through darkened side streets, pressed him into corners, devoured him. On one occasion, a young student asked him, with all the seriousness in the world, to make love to her in his rowing boat. They navigated the Thames by night, moving back and forth to the rhythm of the oars.

He said nothing to Lisbeth about those occasional amorous encounters. After all, she was the one who most benefited from all the new experience he was gaining.

At the end of his third year, Atticus could have written his own erotic novel with a combination of what he had learnt from books and discovered in real life. If he didn't, it was out of respect to Tolkien. The ghost of the old professor attended each and every one of those lessons in love in absolute silence, without ever frightening the pupil's many teachers. Tolkien may have been wide-eyed with surprise, but his respectful tolerance made him, for better or worse, a secret accomplice. It would have been improper to tell the world about Tolkien's voyeuristic tendencies.

Once he had unpacked the books, Atticus removed a small electric kettle from his suitcase. It was a pain to take it everywhere, but it was worse to have to wait for room service to bring him hot water. He needed a cup of tea every forty minutes; he had it calculated down to the second.

He always travelled with two or three boxes of Earl Grey, even though people assured him you could buy it in most countries, because he was truly terrified by the idea of ending up without his cure-all remedy. This wasn't a new habit. He'd arrived at Eton a frail thirteen-year-old boy, constantly struck down by flu, headaches and poor digestion. He was lucky enough to fall into the hands of Dr Hamans, who hailed from the Netherlands and was writing a thesis on the curative properties of herbal infusions. He adopted Atticus as a guinea pig and managed with Earl Grey what no one had with conventional medicine: he transformed the fragile boy into a mighty oak. If Atticus had a stomach ache, he prescribed a hot cup of tea. If his head ached, the prescription was for cold tea; if he fell playing cricket and scraped his skin, a squirt of tea on some cotton wool was enough to clean the wound; if he got a fever, compresses soaked in Earl Grey would bring his temperature down. The treatment worked with astounding efficiency. Atticus grew thirty centimetres during the five years of his secondary education, didn't fall ill once, was chosen as captain of the cricket team and came top in six subjects.

Hamans wanted to study the case in depth at a medical school in London with a grant from Twinings, but Marlow refused to let his son be used as a lab rat. In the end, he only allowed him to donate a few blood and tissue samples, which, unfortunately, Hamans studied furiously for months without obtaining any conclusive results. Atticus, mean-while, remained convinced that tea cured everything and developed an addiction to Earl Grey that was more psychological than physical. He decided to take his kettle everywhere, just as some women travel with their hairdryers.

Alone in his room, he plugged in the appliance, filled it with water, waited until the light came on and then cursed himself for having packed in such a rush, with four pints inside him and his head all over the place. He had forgotten the mug. His mug.

He wasn't an obsessive. Nor a fetishist. But he felt the same devotion to that mug that other people feel towards their pets. The mug was called Aloysius, in honour of Sebastian Flyte's teddy bear in *Brideshead Revisited*, and Atticus had got an artist in Kensington to stamp the name in black letters on the white porcelain. He took a glass out of the small cupboard that housed the minibar. He poured boiling water over the teabag. The glass steamed up. How irritating. He burned the tips of his fingers when he touched it.

Then he unpacked the rest of his luggage: three business suits, six made-to-measure shirts, three pairs of wool socks, six pairs of Ralph Lauren boxer shorts, two belts, a Burberry overcoat that would be completely useless judging by the May sunshine, two pairs of Italian shoes, a scarf – how absurd – his cufflinks in their box, six linen handkerchiefs, four ties (all striped) and his wash-bag, which contained his cologne, shaving foam, mouthwash and dental floss.

At the bottom of his suitcase, folded in two, was his old pillow, his travelling companion since he was seven years old, patched, threadbare, its stuffing almost all gone. It was very clean, though, with a faint and pleasant scent of soap. He quite literally couldn't live without it.

The only time he was unfaithful and was forced to sleep on a disgusting pillow in the bed of one of his occasional lovers, he suffered the consequences in the form of severe muscle strain – that was only relieved by hot tea compresses and the loving care administered by the nice girl to whom the pillow belonged.

He placed his pillow on top of the hotel's one. On the pillowcase, in large red letters, was embroidered the words 'Property of Atticus Craftsman', and the telephone number of his parents' house, which, fortunately, hadn't changed in the last twenty-three years. It wasn't an eccentricity, as he explained to the surprised women who had shared it with him: the pillow was quite simply a question of health.

He took a look around the luxurious room of his Madrid hotel. It was large and light, classic and airy. It had two

35

windows that looked out over a wide avenue lined with chestnut trees. It was two in the afternoon on a sunny Sunday in late May. His stomach demanded a sandwich, preferably smoked salmon and cream cheese with herbs. He asked himself if it would be possible to find such a delicacy in Madrid, in addition to the shade of a tree in a green space resembling Hyde Park under which to eat said sandwich.

With this hope visible in the form of a smile from ear to ear, he went out into the street and began walking.

Chapter 7

Berta Quiñones, the poor thing, hadn't slept a wink all night. She had been up since six in the morning, passing the time until it was late enough to call the girls, thinking about how she was going to give them the bad news, while she put a wash on, mopped the kitchen floor, watered the plants and vacuumed the carpet.

This wasn't her normal Sunday routine. Berta was the polar opposite of a compulsive cleaner. When she didn't have to go to work, she forgot about everything and everyone, stayed in bed well into the morning, alone and relaxed and happy. Then she would make milky coffee, go out to the balcony, treat the empty street to one of her best yawns and spend the rest of the morning reading novels.

In her case, solitude had been a conscious and appropriate choice. Of course, like all literary spinsters, in her youth she too had lived her very own story of unrequited love. You bet. The truth was – and Berta felt somewhat ashamed when she admitted it to herself – that the boy of her dreams never even suspected that Berta loved him. They never exchanged a single word. They only saw each other from a distance and he only lifted his head to look at her once in the five years that the romance lasted, so in all likelihood he never gave a single thought to the girl with messy plaits and glasses that he once caught looking at him from the balcony of her house, the first in the village, opposite the telegraph office.

Because she didn't dare ask him his name, she borrowed a hero's name for him: Robin, like the prince of thieves who stole from the rich to give to the poor. She also invented a soft voice, expert hands, bravery worthy of a fictional character, smooth lips, long kisses and a clearing in the woods where she could love him, in secret, far from the curses of witches or the spells of fairies.

Robin used to arrive with the postbags promptly every morning at eight o'clock. Berta would be waiting for him, curled up at the small window in the attic room, two dreamy eyes behind her glasses, and would watch as he stopped the 2CV – a white steed covered in dents – next to the post office. He would go in, come out, rev up, speed off.

Berta would feel her heart exploding and have to stay still for a few minutes until her legs stopped trembling and she was able to gather the strength to stand up, collect her books from the floor, and run down the stairs, out into the street and all the way to the square, where her schoolmates would be waiting for the teacher with their homework ready.

Her mother complained that she had her head in the clouds. 'Quite the contrary, Mrs Quiñones,' the teacher assured her. Berta's head was anywhere but in the clouds.

She was a walking library. She had read so many books, dreamt so much, had imagined Robin so many times as the protagonist of those wonderful stories that fiction and reality had become muddled.

She was given a grant to go and study in Madrid: documentary maker cum laude, philologist, doctor of literature and language teacher, a genius.

Six years later, when Mr Bestman, Craftsman & Co's development director, interviewed her in an elegant office, he spent a long while examining her CV. He asked her three or four trick questions: what did she think of Harold Pinter, had she read Yeats, and what was her opinion on the Latin American boom and its twenty-first-century legacy. 'Do you think that Mario Vargas Llosa will one day be awarded the Nobel Prize?'

After half an hour of intense conversation with the Englishman, Berta became the brand-new editor of *Librarte* magazine. She left her work at the university library and reached the conclusion that you never know what life will throw at you.

By then she had turned fifty and lost all hope of crossing paths again with 'Robin' who, according to a friend, had disappeared from the village with three million pesetas' worth of stamps, the dirty thief, and the telegraph operator's daughter, the filthy whore. She remembered the sweet-and-sour mixture of fear and happiness she had felt on her first day at *Librarte*'s small office: the sense of expectation before she met her colleagues, those four women with whom she would share both joy and pain, mid-morning coffees, the pitfalls of daily work, successes, failures and – why not? – maybe even true friendship that extended beyond the office. On her way to work she bought four potted dwarf roses and placed them next to the four computers on the four desks in the main room with little labels that said: 'Welcome to your new home.'

The office, ninety square metres on the top floor of an old building on Calle Mayor in the city's historic centre, had previously been the home of a romantic young couple – Berta guessed this as soon as she saw the way the light filtered in through the lace curtains. As well as a tiny office that used to be a bedroom – you could still make out the shadow of a headboard, a grey outline on the white wall – there was a square room with two windows, which now contained four desks facing each other in pairs, a corridor that led to an old-fashioned bathroom with a built-in bath, and an ancient kitchen, no more than a cubbyhole but which was still in good use, with the kind of stove and oven her grandmother used to have.

Apart from the desks, the only furniture was a pine bookshelf, still empty as yet, and a formidable photocopier, the size of a fridge, which took up most of the wall space next to the door. Maybe a nice coloured throw, thought Berta, or a crocheted cloth with tasselled edges, might disguise it as a side table.

Soleá had been the first to arrive.

'Soledad?' Berta had asked her as she hesitated between a warm kiss on the cheek or a firm handshake.

'It's Soleá, like the kind of singing,' she had replied in an accent that conjured up her native Andalusia: Granada, the Albaicín neighbourhood, her family's white-washed house, a garden of wild oleander, steep streets.

She was very young, very petite, very tanned. She had recently finished her degree in Journalism, and she wanted to conquer the world.

'One day I'll write a novel,' she told Berta. 'I've got the plot, I just need to get my ideas straight and focus a bit, Berta, because this huge city still makes my head spin.'

Then came María. She arrived with a worry clinging to her chest.

'This is my daughter,' she said. 'Her name's Lucía and I promise I won't bring her to work again.'

But she did bring her again, she certainly did, in a cot, in her pram, with a fever, with a cough. Lucía become another member of the team, like the office mascot. Berta installed a white rocking chair for her in the corner of her own office. In the little kitchen they heated up bottles and purées; in winter they knitted her pink scarves. One year later, María announced that she was expecting twins. She was off work for six months because she spent the last two months of her pregnancy in bed, at risk of going into labour prematurely, but Lucía still occupied her space, her rocking chair, her corner. Almost every morning, at nine o'clock sharp, Lucía's father, Bernabé, would arrive carrying her, knock on the door, swear to Berta that he was going to get someone to help, that it would be the last day he left Lucía with them, that he knew that she ran a serious office, not a nursery, but there he would be again the next day.

Manolito and Daniel weighed five and a half pounds each when they were born. They wouldn't feed, they became lactose intolerant and they caught chickenpox two weeks after Lucía, which meant a whole month of spots and tears, calamine lotion, antihistamines, scabs and itches. They swapped the rocking chair for a mattress. Berta had to step over the children in order to sit down at her desk. That was when she found she had an incredible aptitude for singing as she worked and telling stories between invoices.

'If we women don't help each other out, who knows who'll help us,' she repeated as a mantra to appease her colleagues' complaints.

The third to arrive was Asunción. She was huge, and on a diet.

She greeted them all with a hug and the first thing she said to them, before sitting down at her desk, was that she didn't have a health problem or diabetes or any of that, it was the menopause, which had hit her something chronic, and the hot flushes were killing her.

The last to arrive was Gabriela. Please, call me Gaby, you know, like the clown. She was the only one to notice the flowers.

'You're in love, my girl.'

'Stupidly in love. Up to my eyeballs.'

They all went to her wedding, eight months after the magazine launched.

Gaby in radiant white, the gorgeous groom, the church full of flowers. Lucía carried the *arras*, thirteen coins the groom would give to his bride, and Asunción caught the bouquet.

'You next, Asunción.'

'God help me,' she said, flushed. 'I've already been married and divorced.'

The last six years had flown by. Berta turned off the vacuum cleaner, washed her coffee cup, sat down at one end of the sofa and picked up the phone. Remembering that first morning, she called them in the order they had arrived: Soleá, María, Asunción and Gaby, her best friends. She couldn't put it off any longer, she had to give them the news.

'I know it's Sunday,' she said to all four in the same apologetic tone. 'But we need to have a meeting. Come to the office at eleven. No, María, this time you can't bring the kids.'

Chapter 8

A few days after the unsettling call from Inspector Manchego, Marlow Craftsman decided that, much to his regret, it was time to tell Moira that their son had been missing for three months. He had put off telling her up until then because he still harboured hope that the issue would be resolved before Christmas. That was looking increasingly unlikely. Whenever Moira asked how Atticus was getting on in Spain, Marlow would reply with something like: 'Fine, dear, just fine.' And because he was a man of few words, she would be satisfied, roll over in bed and fall fast asleep.

Only when November came and she began the torturous preparations for Christmas did Moira become more insistent. She wanted details.

She needed to know how many nights Atticus would be staying in Kent, what day he would arrive, if he would be bringing guests this time, if he was still vegetarian, if he had changed cologne or still liked the one he had used all his life, and, above all, the exact time and date of his departure, because she planned on giving Atticus's room to Holden's parents-in-law, who were going to spend New Year's Eve with the Craftsmans that year.

Moira always wrote everything down in her enormous black diary, from the cards they received to the presents they sent to the amount of beef they should order from the butcher's in Sevenoaks.

The uncertainty was killing her.

Marlow took a hot cup of Horlicks on a silver tray up to Moira, who was in bed. The maid always prepared it before she went to bed herself, and she tended to dissolve half of one of her own tranquillizers in the drink because she figured that Mrs Craftsman was partly responsible for her symptoms. That night, Marlow, unaware of any such scheme, added another two tablets of diazepam with the good intention of making it easier for Moira to take the bad news he was about to give her.

The dose proved excessive, of course.

'Moira, dear,' Marlow began softly while he stroked her back. 'I'm afraid I have to tell you something about Atticus.'

'Atticus?' she mumbled.

'How to tell you this, my love . . . Don't be frightened, try to see the bright side of it. For a few days now, well, we haven't known where he is.' There, he had said it.

Moira made no comment. She remained lying on her side with her face pressed against the pillow.

'He's probably somewhere without any mobile phone reception, you know how Spain's a mountainous country, with a lot of sea round it, and because he's an adventurous type he's probably decided to take a holiday. I can just imagine him, dear, on board a fishing boat, or on a snowy mountaintop, or perhaps on one of those islands that the Spanish still own off the coast of Africa.'

'Africa?'

'Yes, sort of near Mauritania.'

Silence.

'But he'll be back soon. He would never miss Christmas at home. He's a good boy, our Atticus. And just in case,' he added very quickly, 'I've informed the police. They're busy looking for him, Moira, and they assure me we'll have news soon.'

More silence.

'For the moment, we know he isn't in hospital, which is reassuring. He hasn't been in an accident, thank God. There haven't been any accusations either, so he hasn't got into any trouble. He's simply disappeared. Without a trace. Just like that time, do you remember, when he was twenty and went off on that gap year. We didn't hear from him for months. We didn't worry then and we aren't going to worry now, Moira, because there will be a reasonable explanation for all this. I, for one, am not in the least bit alarmed. He's a grown man, he can make his own decisions, he doesn't need to ask our permission. If he wants to climb aboard a tuna-fishing ship, that's his choice. If he wants to become a hermit and live off insects, then so be it. It's his life.'

Moira started snoring. The overdose had done its work. In all probability, thought Marlow, she wouldn't remember anything the next day. Shame, because it had been an excellent speech for a man of so few words.

Calmer and fully convinced by the strength of his own argument that there was no cause for alarm, he got into bed as well, pulled the tartan blanket up to his chin and fell fast asleep.

Chapter 9

Contrary to Berta's initial fears, Soleá and Asunción actually got on a treat. When she saw them for the first time, one next to the other – one young and wild, the other mature and serene – she had pictured an impossible tandem bicycle with broken brakes and flat tyres. The words 'Staff Writer' were written on both of their contracts after the phrase 'Job Title', but each one had her particular way of understanding the role. While Soleá spent all day out wandering the streets in search of stories to tell, Asunción enjoyed working in the office and the careful task of calmly writing reviews, features and profiles.

From the very first day they had divided the work according to their interests: Soleá went to the opening nights, presentations and festivals; she elbowed her way into interviews, her photos came out blurry and her articles were light-hearted. Asunción read, took notes, compared, wove strands together. Between them, in the end, they always managed to season their articles to perfection.

They met with Berta once a week to organize the contents of the next issue. Each one presented her list of suggestions and Berta analysed them with the neutrality of King Solomon. She was always astounded by what her two writers came up with.

'Do you really want to write about the African tribal music festival, Soleá?'

'It's free, Berta, half of Spain will be there.'

'In the Monegros Desert?' Berta blinked, coughed and nearly always gave in.

'And you, Asunción, want to write an article about the aesthetic perversions of Surrealism?'

'There were heaps of them.'

'That I don't doubt.'

Then they shared the work out by sections: film for you, books for you, museums for you, events for you, music for you, art for you, and so on. The order of ingredients in the cocktail varied every week so that everything got covered.

Berta was the one who gave the green light to what they wrote and controlled the budgets, organized their trips, hired photographers and always managed to find four or five advertisers who would cover most of the costs of each edition. Normally these were film companies, mobile phone networks, discount warehouses, restaurants and hotels. It was company policy that *Librarte* couldn't accept advertising campaigns from publishing houses other than Craftsman & Co, and this seriously limited Berta's possibilities for finding clients.

María took care of the administration of the small business with the same attention to detail that she applied to her accounts at home. 'It's easy,' she would say. 'You just have to get the balances to tally and Bob's your uncle.' She collected the receipts that Berta signed in countless files and folders. She kept every ticket, every receipt and every note in shoe boxes, which she covered with crêpe paper and cellophane. A different colour every year. She also bought train or bus tickets for the writers (*Librarte*'s finances had never, to that day, been buoyant enough to allow a plane journey), printer ink, toner cartridges and other items of stationery.

She was astonishingly thrifty in the office, as she was at home: they recycled the paper, they got the last drop of ink out of each biro, they turned the lights off as soon as the sun came out, they shut the computers down every night, they didn't switch the heating on until well into November and they never turned the air conditioning on, because María claimed that on top of being expensive it was unhealthy and unnecessary. This was most probably because she had grown up in a village near Toledo and experienced such heat as a child that she had become immune to the ravages of the thermometer.

Therein lay the root of most arguments in the office, be-cause while María was happy with a fan and cold water to combat the heat, Asunción suffocated with hot flushes and sweated buckets.

Berta had to mediate: she gave María the month and a half of annual leave that she begged for on account of the school holidays and, in return, allowed Asunción to turn on the air conditioning for the last half of July and all of August, and learnt to disguise the resulting spikes that showed up on the electricity bill.

As for Gaby, she alone constituted *Librarte*'s technical team. No computer program could refuse to do what she wanted. She was capable of finding the documents that mysteriously disappeared from Soleá's desktop or resuscitating Berta's Mac when she burst in panicking about what she called 'the sudden death of that piece of junk'.

She imported and exported photos and archives, was a whizz with Photoshop, used InDesign, Quark and Adobe as if they were physical tools, knew how to turn proofs into

PDFs and could get into the others' laptops from the comfort of her own home.

She had studied Graphic Design in Paris when that sounded like outer space to people on the Iberian Peninsula, and she had found the love of her life in the boy who sat next to her in class, an Argentinian whom everyone addressed using his surname: Livingstone, because they had forgotten his first name.

Franklin Livingstone had grown up in Santa Fe, in the province of Córdoba, on a farm with green, fertile land, lulled to sleep by gaucho songs, eating steak and drinking bitter maté. Hence his unpolished character, his leathery skin and his rough hands. His mother, who hailed from a well-off Buenos Aires family, had imagined a glorious future for him: on the thirtieth floor of a Manhattan skyscraper, a successful businessman, prestigious lawyer, famous architect or ruthless banker. But none of these dreams of hers had come true. At university in Boston, more bored than he had ever imagined possible, he discovered that his cowboy's hands were made to caress more interesting things than the current accounts of his future clients. Women and paintbrushes, in that order, began to take up most of his time.

To his mother's horror, he left business school and enrolled in art school. When he finished, he got a grant to travel to Paris, the city of light and art, and became one of the pioneers of digital design, which his mother naturally thought was a load of mumbo jumbo.

There he met Gaby, bright as a button, full of hopes and dreams, with everything ahead of her. He started to work the old magic on her, like they used to do in Córdoba back in his grandparents' day, with presents and sweet nothings.

He painted a portrait of her in oils in which he emphasized her lynx's eyes staring out from the other side of the canvas. What greater proof of love was there than those months of work, holding in his mind's eye the image of the colour of her skin, the softness of her curls or the curve of her chest? She was always catching him looking at her from his desk, sometimes using a pencil to measure the distance between her eyes, or the length of her neck.

When the portrait was finished he invited her to see the hovel where he lived, a student room in a building in the fifteenth arrondissement. It was there that their love story began, with an artist's attentiveness. Or rather, two artists: him the brush, she the paint.

Sometimes Livingstone would come to the office mid-morning. He would bring the girls cakes, flowers, ice cream or *alfajores*. He would say to Gaby: 'See you at home, princess.' And it still made her legs tremble.

They had been married for over five years. They wanted to have children. It wasn't happening.

'Right when you least expect it, Gaby, you'll see,' Berta consoled her.

But every month, Gaby emerged from the office bathroom with a sour look on her face.

'You'll see,' Berta would assure her once more, 'right when you least expect it.'

Chapter 10

Inspector Manchego started to lose his balance on his second whisky. When he was out of earshot, Josi assured the others that Manchego was simply out of practice.

'He's always been more into sangria than spirits,' he told the others as soon as the inspector left the game. 'In the garage at his parents' house we used to get a big tub, fill it with half red wine and half Fanta, add a good splash of vodka – not that you could taste it in so much liquid – plenty of ice and plenty of sugar. We'd open the door and they'd be queuing up outside. We were the life and soul.'

'Did you used to drink out of a *botijo*, a *bota* or a *porrón*?'

'*Porrón*, Macita, what a question! Manchego used to drink straight from the jug. Back then, he had some stamina . . .'

The street was dark and empty. The streetlights and the pavement were moving a bit, as if the ground had been paved with waves. Manchego had lost forty euros, Christ on a bike, what bad luck, his four kings had been beaten by the four aces that Carretero pulled out of his sleeve at the last minute.

He was walking home so he could get some air, with

his standard-issue gun tucked into his belt, just in case. He had bought one of those made-to-order harnesses that combines braces with a gun holster, and although he knew he shouldn't drink when he was armed, he justified it to himself, saying that they weren't allowed to use the siren without good reason but all his colleagues used it to get out of traffic jams. It was a trade-off. He was very conscientious when it came to the siren.

He heard footsteps behind him. He tensed up.

A guy with headphones overtook him on his right.

He kept walking.

He heard footsteps again. He stopped. The footsteps stopped too.

Manchego grabbed on to the trunk of a flimsy tree. It was his anchor.

Up ahead, between the cars, someone was moving. A shadow.

'Who's there?' Manchego shouted.

Silence.

He lifted his hand to his belt. He checked the gun was in place.

'Who's there?' he repeated. 'Don't do anything stupid. I'm a police officer. I'm armed.'

A strong, rough-looking man stepped out into the light. He was moving from side to side, in time with the street. He must have been on the same boat as Manchego. He stopped a few centimetres away from Manchego.

'Got a light?' he asked.

'Don't do anything stupid, mate,' replied the inspector. 'I've just warned you that I'm armed.'

'I'm only asking for a match, officer.'

'Inspector, if you don't mind.'

'Inspector.'

Manchego took a lighter out of his pocket. He removed a pack of cigarettes from another. He offered the man one. They smoked together. They talked.

'If I had to investigate a disappearance,' said the man after listening carefully to the case of Atticus Craftsman, 'I'd start by interrogating the people who knew him. Then I'd search his house.'

'The problem is that without a warrant I can't bust the door open. It takes days for the papers to come through.'

'He could be dead inside the apartment,' the other man warned.

'He could be.'

'And there's no other way of getting in?'

'Not legally.'

'But . . .'

'Well,' pondered Manchego, 'if someone, let's say a burglar, happened to break in to steal something and just at that moment a plain-clothes police officer happened to be passing by . . .'

'Improbable.'

'Highly.'

'I'm a locksmith.'

'What a coincidence!'

The street swayed. It had been nasty whisky.

They said goodbye and promised to meet again at the same tree one of these days. The man's name was Lucas. He picked up a scrap of paper from the ground and wrote his phone number on it.

'Call me when you like,' he told Manchego. 'The guy's probably dead inside the apartment, anyway,' he reminded him.

Chapter 11

Soleá never answered her landline. It was hopeless. She unplugged it when she was at home, otherwise she would have to let it ring endlessly. She hated the idea of having an answering machine. She considered it an invasion of her private life and argued that answering the phone was the same as opening the door and inviting someone in.

'Just imagine,' she said, 'for example, that you're eating a bowl of cereal in front of the telly and the bloody phone rings. Do you have to make room on the sofa for the person who comes barging into your house, plonking themselves between the spoon and your mouth, between your ears and the end of the film?'

'And what if it's important?'

'They can wait.'

'And if it's urgent?'

'Look, Berta,' assured Soleá, 'ninety per cent of the time it's only urgent or important for the person who's calling.'

'But I'm your boss, Soleá, I need to be able to contact you.'

'Then get me a mobile. But a company one, Berta, because my salary won't stretch to any more bills.'

Already resigned to the bad-tempered response she was going to get, Berta dialled Soleá's mobile number and waited for her to wake up. It was exactly nine in the morning. On a Sunday. Thank goodness she wasn't standing next to Soleá, because that girl was perfectly capable of shoving the phone down her throat.

At the fourth or fifth ring she heard a sleepy voice on the other end of the line. Soleá was whispering.

'Berta, I'm going to kill you.'

'Where are you?'

'At the squat on Calle Zurita.'

'What?'

'It's nothing to worry about, love, my night just got a bit complicated. I went to the opening night of that play I told you about, at the Triángulo, and it was raining when I came out, and the first thing I saw was this place. I came in and there was a guy from back home who played guitar really well. A sort of recital. It got late and in the end I fell asleep on a pile of sleeping bags.'

'Doesn't it smell of pee?'

'Oh, Berta! Shut up!'

Without giving Soleá time to come up with an excuse, Berta told her about the urgent meeting. At the office at eleven. Soleá didn't argue. Berta had never given her such an unequivocal order before.

Berta was lucky to catch María still at home. She had been up since seven because the kids were light sleepers and the sound of the lift always woke them up. They were about to leave for a day out in the countryside. They had the picnic ready: tortilla de patatas, breaded steaks and Russian salad. María had spent Saturday afternoon cooking, ironing, washing up, mending trousers, bathing children, heating soup and tidying. She planned on spending Sunday relaxing, lying on a rug all day, in the shade, while the kids played on the swings. She had even packed a DVD so she could park them in front of a screen – thank God for laptops – while she had her siesta.

Bernabé usually played football on Sundays and then went to a bar for lunch with the team. He would come home when it got dark, sit in front of the telly until María and the kids got back and invariably ask to have dinner early, because on Mondays he worked the early shift at the café. His was a hard life.

'And what do you expect me to do with the kids, Berta? Just put them in a cupboard?'

'Haven't you got a neighbour you can leave them with for a bit, sweetie?'

'No, my love, I haven't. I've got a gossiping witch, a drunk and a madwoman. That's what I've got.'

'But you do pay peanuts for rent, María.'

'I suppose I do.'

In the end she convinced Bernabé to take them to football with him.

'Tie them to the goalpost, Bernabé, do me a favour.'

Berta's tone of voice made it clear that something very serious had happened at work. María imagined the worst, and started shaking. Her life would go to pieces if she lost her job.

Asunción answered straight away. She told Berta that she had been awake for a while, reading. The boys were out and about as usual. She wasn't expecting them back until lunchtime.

'I'm actually glad you rang,' she confessed. 'Sundays make me feel sort of gloomy. I'll go to ten o'clock mass near the office so I can be there at eleven on the dot. Shall I bring croissants?'

Gaby was the most difficult. In a whisper she explained that she was ovulating – 'Spot on, Berta, your timing's impeccable' – and that she had to lie down for at least half an hour after intercourse. As intercourse hadn't taken place yet, she would try to wake Franklin up gently, wearing no underwear, to see if they could resolve the issue in fifteen or twenty minutes.

'But the earliest I can be there,' she said, 'is quarter past eleven. That's the minimum for a nice romantic quickie. You understand, don't you, Berta?'

Chapter 12

Asunción stopped weighing herself the day she hit eleven stone. Her determination to spend her time thinking about more interesting things than the fluctuations of her impressive body mass was not exactly a coolly calculated decision. It was in fact the result of having smashed to pieces the solar-powered plastic scales that her sons had given her on Mother's Day.

'You've got to start looking after yourself again, Mum,' they had pleaded with her. 'Go out, buy new clothes, get your hair dyed . . . It's six months now since Dad left. You have to get over it, move on.'

Although they were only fifteen and seventeen, they had dealt with being abandoned much more bravely than she had. And let's be clear, their father had betrayed them too. He had promised at the altar to care for them responsibly and lovingly, to protect and educate them. He had agreed and consented and sworn on his wedding day that he would love them until death did them part. And, in the end, it wasn't death that did them part but an air hostess from Barcelona.

Asunción had been suspicious about her husband's

frequent stopovers, two a week, but he had explained that he was opening a new branch in Ciudad Condal and asked her to be patient. Because until the office was up and running, he would have no choice but to fly back and forth like a boomerang.

And then, after twenty years of cuddling up to her in bed, he started acting strangely.

Until one evening, at eight o'clock, the doorbell rang. Asunción went downstairs to answer it. She was already wearing her pyjamas, slippers and woollen dressing gown. She had made a cup of tea and was halfway through reading *The Red and the Black* in French with her feet up. The kids were about to come home from football training, the chicken was in the oven, the table was set, the romantic music was on and the vanilla-scented candle was lit.

At the door stood a tall, tanned woman squeezed into an Iberia uniform. If this had been wartime, it would have been a military uniform and she would have been bringing Asunción the news of her husband's death in active service. But this was peacetime, unfortunately, and the woman came bearing no more and no less than her family's death certificate.

'Can I come in?' she asked with the sickly sweet air of someone accustomed to dealing with the oddities of the human race.

'It depends.'

'You're Asunción, aren't you?'

'That's me.'

'I'm your husband's lover.'

The soul weighs nothing. A Hollywood producer pretended it did for a good film title. It doesn't weigh anything because it isn't of this world, like love or pain. It holds the qualities that draw human beings a little closer to God.

All the same, Asunción clearly heard the sound her soul made as it thumped to the floor. It sounded like a stainless-steel pan bouncing down the kitchen steps.

'Come in. Have a seat.'

The air hostess told her how everything had started with an innocent game of: 'Could you bring me another Coke, please, could you bring me a pillow, please, can I have a blanket, I'm cold.' How there was a magnetic force of attraction that had destabilized the flight. How they started to meet in secret, in hotels and on beaches, until they decided to buy a flat between them. How that secret would have to come out in a couple of months because, she told Asunción, 'I can't zip my skirt up any more and I'm going to go on leave, because flying is dangerous for the baby.

'I've come because he can't bring himself to tell you,' she said, lowering her eyes. 'He says you're going to get divorced, that he doesn't love you any more. That it can't go on any longer. But at this rate the baby will be born without a father, I can tell. Or his bigamy will mean we'll both end up in the news. He's capable of marrying me without divorcing you.'

Then came the shouting, the weeping and the gnashing of teeth. The hell. The kids suffered, did badly at school and got into trouble. The house fell apart, the rent became too much to pay and Asunción had to look for somewhere else. She lost control. She withered.

Until one Sunday, the sixth of May, at ten in the morning, those two problematic teenagers had the bright idea of spending their money on a set of automatic, digital, solar-powered scales to give to their mother, who hadn't got out of bed in six months. Said inanimate object became a tiresome conscience that stared at her with its plastic eyes from the bathroom floor. 'Weigh yourself,' it taunted her, 'weigh yourself and you'll see how being abandoned, on top of everything else, makes you fat.'

So, when she plucked up enough courage to lug her spare tyres on to the contraption and confirmed her suspicions that she was closer to eleven stone than the nine and a half she'd weighed all her life, and she confronted the dishevelled, ageing woman who stared back at her from the mirror, she finally decided to take control of the situation. Bloody scales, bloody mirror.

She rewrote her CV, explaining that she had been out of work for the last fifteen years due to family circumstances beyond her control, and went to get a reference from her old boss, who she found looking as worn out as she felt but still sitting in front of the same desk in the same office as fifteen years ago, when Asunción fell pregnant for the second time and they said goodbye with tears in their eyes.

'There's an Englishman who's getting a team together for a literary magazine. You might be interested. It pays bugger all.'

She dyed her hair, painted her nails, went along to Mr Bestman's casting and passed the exam with flying colours. She had spent fifteen years totally dedicated to literature; she'd never studied it formally, she admitted, but she was a voracious reader. As hooked on books as she was on sweets. A real bottomless pit for authors and genres. She didn't mind if it was Lorca or Ezra Pound, the Brontë sisters or the Brothers Grimm. 'It all goes down the same way, Mr Bestman. Ask me what you like because I've got it all covered.'

So she got the job as staff writer for *Librarte*, and returned to the land of the living a stone heavier. She slowly became less afraid, left her insecurities behind her, regained her hope and banished her insomnia. The only thing that remained, to her dismay, was that cruel, accusing, tenacious and cellulitic excess weight that there was no way of shifting, however many fad diets she went on and however much soya milk she drank.

'Look, Asunción,' the doctor had said. 'It's down to your metabolism. It'll pass, don't worry, it's to do with the menopause. You'll also notice hot flushes, loss of libido, high pulse rate, vaginal dryness, incontinence, irritability, joint pain, digestive problems and changes to your body odour, among other things.'

'What am I going to smell of?' asked Asunción, terrified, contemplating her own Kafkaesque transformation from woman into cockroach.

But faced with such an awful diagnosis, Asunción, who had become a veritable Joan of Arc in her battle against her recent emotional ebb, decided to fight tooth and nail against the extra weight.

She didn't manage it. She lost the battle. She wept inconsolably. Her mascara ran. She looked at herself again in the mirror, a weeping monstrosity with hair like a mop, and shouted: 'That's enough!' She reminded herself of the old nanny she and her brothers had as children, who came from Malaga and used to scream just as forcefully whenever they pushed her too far.

She lifted the scales above her head and threw them against the bathroom mirror. Bloody scales, bloody mirror.

That day she was cured, definitively. She became a happy plump woman who, thanks to the menopause, smelt of motorcycle oil unless she drenched herself in perfume; she hoped this was only temporary. She helped find work for immigrant women in the parish. She cooked for her sons. She considered her boss, Berta, to be her best friend and was capable of saying things like 'I've already been married and divorced, thank God' without tears betraying her apparent bravery.

So, when Berta called at nine in the morning that Sunday in May, six and a half years after her first living death, Asunción was reminded of the day the air hostess rang the doorbell. She felt the floor trembling beneath her feet and heard the clang of her soul falling down the kitchen steps. She went to church for ten o'clock mass, crossed herself, knelt and used all five senses to pray. She sent a distress flare to the Lord.

'Father, if it is Your will, take this cup away from me. Don't let me lose my job, dear God, please, I beg you. Let Your will be done, but please could that will not be to leave me in the street, if possible. I understand that wars, famine and all that take precedence. If You're too busy, ask one of the saints to help me. One who doesn't have many devotees. San Pantaleón or San Lamberto or San Vito who, with a name like that, will surely get me out of this fix.'

Once she had placed her trust in God, Asunción crossed the street and ordered a dozen croissants, some *tortel* cakes and five *ensaimada* buns to take away, because, as they say in Spain, bread helps you swallow your sorrow. She guessed that Berta would have already put the coffee on.

Chapter 13

What took place at exactly quarter past eleven that Sunday morning in the *Librarte* office wasn't a meeting between five civilized women, but rather a coven of merciless witches who resorted to the dark arts and black magic in an attempt to dodge the misfortune that was set to descend upon them.

They arrived one by one, in the usual order: Berta, Soleá, María, Asunción and Gaby. All terrified, all trying to disguise the real extent of their anxiety with exaggerated gestures. They normally greeted each other with a simple 'good morning', but that Sunday they hugged and kissed one another as if they were at a school reunion and hadn't seen each other for twenty-five years. They breakfasted on Berta's coffee and Asunción's pastries, and talked about children, books and theatre opening nights to pass the time until the awful moment when they had to confront reality.

In the end, Berta had no choice but to talk. She explained that she had called them at such an ungodly hour – sorry, girls – on a Sunday because she needed to give them some terrible news. It couldn't wait until Monday because, after thinking long and hard about it, she had arrived at the conclusion that, perhaps, between the five of them, they might be able to come up with a way to sort things out and avert disaster.

'The disaster is the magazine getting closed down, right?' grasped María.

'It seems so.'

Sounding shriller than usual, Berta explained how Mr Bestman himself had called the previous afternoon to inform her of Mr Craftsman's imminent visit.

'The big boss? Marlow Craftsman?'

'No, my love. His son.'

'What son?'

Berta had to give the girls a run-down of the Craftsman family. She told them about the aristocratic grandmother; about Marlow, the managing director; about Moira, the elegant wife; about Holden, the rebel; and about Atticus, the designated heir, who at that moment must have been landing in Madrid with their redundancy letters neatly stacked in his briefcase.

'According to Bestman, the magazine's losses are inexplicable, enormous and too great for the company to absorb,' Berta told them, devastated. 'What's more, he says that *Librarte* hasn't managed to make a name for itself among Spain's literary publications, that it has no renown and no credibility. That hardly anyone reads it and that, instead of promoting Craftsman & Co's new titles, it has the opposite effect; in other words, it gives them a bad reputation.'

Their hearts sank. Gaby fanned herself with recycled paper. Asunción had a hot flush. Tears rolled down María's face and Soleá exploded:

'He can go to hell!' she shouted with the combined fury of all her Gypsy ancestors lined up one behind the other.

Then the silence solidified, taking on the consistency of

sticky jelly. It collected in the mouths of all five women and stopped them talking. They were suffocating.

'We have to think of something,' said Asunción, whose tongue was, miraculously, the first to work its way free.

'Otherwise, we can expect hard times,' said Berta.

'Or maybe great expectations,' replied Asunción with the last scrap of humour she was able to dredge up.

That reference to Dickens seemed to flick a switch inside Soleá. She stood up and drew breath. She shouted:

'I've got an idea!'

The others looked at her in surprise. The coven had only been going for fifteen minutes and they were already getting started on the witchcraft. Of course, the chemistry that united those five women made for an explosive concoction.

Soleá lowered her voice, as if it might have been possible for someone from outside their office to hear her criminal plans, and made a gesture for her colleagues to move closer. She drew them into a circle around her and then talked about her beloved Granada and its old poets, and about El Albaicín, nights perfumed with jasmine and mint, the lime-white caves, families gathered around grandmothers, secrets that everyone knows but no one talks about, forbidden liaisons and broken hearts, traditions, settling of scores, Gypsy curses.

'I'm going to tell *Míster Crasman* something that my grandmother told me when I was a little girl. A secret no one knows, which can't fail to pique his interest. Then I'll take him to Granada and keep him distracted until you lot think of something better.'

In the centre of the circle they stoked a raging fire, and on the fire bubbled a cauldron into which they all spat curses. Soleá's idea made sense. It could, at least, give them time to come up with a better, more civilized and less esoteric plan, one that would convince Marlow Craftsman and Mr Bestman to keep *Librarte* going for a few more years.

'While you entertain Atticus Craftsman, we'll go through the accounts, we'll talk to advertisers, booksellers, printers and the distributor. We'll square the expenses and get the business in good health so that we can press on, if you'll pardon the pun. When we're done, the right decision will be to keep the magazine going: closing it down won't be an option.

'I want you all here at nine o'clock sharp tomorrow,' said Berta, drawing the meeting to a close. 'And you, Soleá, make yourself look gorgeous.'

Chapter 14

Atticus Craftsman had felt like a man of the world ever since, at the tender age of twenty, he had travelled round half of Europe with only a backpack and the contents of his savings account. His grandmother had opened the account for him when he was a boy and, to his surprise, he discovered that it contained over twenty thousand pounds. Grandmother Craftsman had apparently spent her life transferring a small amount every month to each of her grandchildren, envisaging a bleak future for the family business. Her fears were unjustified: Marlow Craftsman had proved to be an excellent administrator and the publishing house was financially robust. For someone who had survived the crash of 1929 and two world wars, however, economic stability and world peace were two possibilities as remote as time travel or an alien invasion. As a big fan of Jules Verne, Grandmother Craftsman struggled to clearly delineate between reality and science fiction: she had never accepted the validity of Darwin's theory of evolution nor, of course, the Big Bang theory, and she was not convinced that a man had walked on the moon as the Americans would have everyone believe.

In the end, thanks to Grandmother Craftsman's scepticism, Atticus was able to fulfil his dream of travelling to the Near East, exploring Arab countries, submerging himself in the Dead Sea, visiting the Holy Land, and sailing into Istanbul on board a cargo ship, with Asia on one side and Europe on the other.

He returned from his trip with no money, no Earl Grey, and absolutely no desire to eat lamb ever again, be it spiced, with rice, boiled, roasted or stewed. In fact, he gave up meat altogether. It wasn't a life choice, he explained to his mother, it was indigestion.

Ten years had gone by and he still couldn't bear the idea of lamb with cumin. Or the prospect of leaving the comfort of his London flat or the family home in Kent. He had grown accustomed to sleeping between clean sheets, bathing in hot water, dressing like a dandy and eating solely organic produce. He hadn't the slightest desire to leave England again.

So, when his father entrusted to him the task of travelling to Spain for an unspecified length of time, Atticus was overcome with an irrational, shameful fear of the unknown. Yes, it was absurd – Spain was a modern, developed, European country – but it was a real fear none the less. He felt a knot in his stomach, as if the heart of darkness awaited him, and he could almost hear its unsettling, dull, rhythmical pounding coming towards him through the dry leaves.

It was only May, but Atticus couldn't believe how hot it was when he stepped out of the hotel at two o'clock. The heat smothered him, flattening him against the pavement. And, along with the exhaustion from his early morning flight, it skewed his vision of reality. To start with, the light was so blinding that it stung his eyes, and however much he screwed them up he felt as if he was sweating between his eyelashes. Everything looked liquid, undulating, mirage-like.

He undid the top buttons of his shirt and he rolled his sleeves up to his elbows. His feet were burning inside his woollen socks. He was strangely bewildered.

He found a bar in a shady alleyway, a few streets away from the hotel. It reeked of fried food. He went up to the bar. He noticed that the floor was covered in toothpicks, napkins, seafood shells and other unidentifiable detritus.

'I'd like a salmon and cream cheese sandwich, please,' he said in Spanish with an unmistakably English accent.

The three or four men who were sitting at the bar stopped talking. The barman looked at him as if he had told a joke.

'Sorry, sir,' he explained, 'but that's not the sort of thing we do here. We're more traditional. More like *pinchos* and *tapas*, if you get me.'

One of the customers, the one nearest to Atticus, came to his aid. He told the barman: 'Bring him some garlic prawns, Paco, see what he makes of them. And a nice cold beer.' Then he positioned himself ten centimetres from Atticus's face.

'Here no salmon, no nonsense,' he said loudly. 'Here beer and prawns, amigo.'

And he slapped Atticus on the back.

At five o'clock, after six litres of beer, four portions of Russian salad, two of Manchego cheese, three of tortilla, four of fried squid and two plates of ham that he didn't try on account of his being vegetarian, Atticus managed to drag himself away from his new friends and went out into the liquid heat.

His head was spinning and his stomach felt heavy and

70

slow. The sensible thing would have been to go back to the hotel, drink some tea and wait for his body to assimilate the concoction of saturated fats. When he got to the end of the street, however, he found himself at the entrance to the Parque del Retiro and noticed that his feet were leading him into the inner-city woodland.

In London – in Hyde Park for example – he would have found some shade, grabbed one of those deckchairs they have all over the place and settled down for a nice snooze with the background noise of children playing and the quiet company of squirrels. But there was no one dozing peacefully on the grass in El Retiro. The noise was too much for an aching head like his. There were musicians, shouts, races, skates, bicycles, tourists, suspicious-looking vendors, oriental masseurs, tellers of predictable fortunes, mounted police, jugglers, tramps and countless circus performers, each as astonishing as the next. In the midst of the chaos, Atticus glimpsed the murky water of a lake covered in little rowing boats. His rower's instinct led him to the Municipal Sports Club, where some half-decent looking sculls were kept. He went to enquire and was told that at this time of day he wouldn't find anyone except the caretaker's cat. It was suggested that he should come back another day, at another time, when he didn't reek of alcohol. He was standing with his back to the water and didn't notice the girls who ran up to the jetty, fleeing from a group of guys who were trying to splash them.

'Out of the way, gringo!' shouted a bare-chested boy when it was too late for Atticus to avoid a shower of dirty water that soaked him from head to foot.

'Get in, blondie!' one of the girls shouted to him.

In the boat were five voluptuous young women with their wet T-shirts clinging to their bodies. Behind them, three or four boats full of eager young men were trying to catch up with them, surround them, besiege them and splash them again. The girls were laughing, they had wet hair and they were chattering wildly.

Atticus took control of the small craft. He grabbed the oars, put his hundred thousand hours of training into practice and was able to row the girls safely to shore, to the surprise and disgust of the louts in pursuit. The girls then took the opportunity to mock the other rowers, wring out their hair and T-shirts, share cigarettes and chewing gum and invite Atticus to spend the rest of an unforgettable afternoon with them.

They were part of a large, carefree group who had decided to set up camp in the Retiro until the police threw them out. They were students who didn't appear to have homes or families and wanted nothing more than a good time. They had bottles of rum and Coke, guitars and drums and an exam the next day that none of them planned on turning up to, because, as they explained to Atticus, they belonged to the Complutense University Anti-Exam League: an association created by students from various faculties who were fighting for the complete eradication of all testing because they believed that it bred competitiveness and failure.

'So, in protest, we've decided not to take any more exams,' said the very guy who had drenched Atticus in lake water. 'We oppose the system because it's unjust and unequal.'

'The day will come,' added another guy, 'when exam rooms are deserted and classrooms are empty. Lecturers will lose their jobs and the government will be forced to change the law.'

Ignoring the fact that all those dreamers were going to

fail comprehensively and get into a whole heap of trouble the following day, Atticus declared that he was absolutely in favour of their revolutionary proposal. This gave him the right to share their drinks, campfire, and fumbles on the grass. Atticus couldn't remember anything after about nine o'clock that evening. He never knew what police threats chased him and his new friends out of the park at midnight, along with the other drunks, homeless people and crooks who were lying about on the grass, or what vehicle he got into later, or which dive his friends abandoned him in, or how he found his way back to his hotel.

The next thing Atticus knew, he was waking up naked on the messy bed of his luxury room with a headache that all the Earl Grey in England wouldn't shift. He had apparently slept alone, because there were no signs of a female visitor. Nor a male visitor, thanks to God and all the saints in heaven. It didn't appear that either of his kidneys had been removed during the night – there were no stitches down his sides – or that he had been raped, or beaten, or robbed. The most probable scenario was that he had made it back to the hotel under his own steam, although in a truly lamentable state, and that, incredibly, he had been able to remember his room number before passing out on the bed.

After recovering his physical composure and his dignity with a cold shower and plenty of cologne, Atticus, between throbs of pain, slowly remembered where he was (in Madrid), and why (on business), and about the meeting he had arranged with a certain Berta Quiñones at ten o'clock that morning.

He looked at his watch. It was a quarter to eleven. He cursed alcohol and swore he would never again touch a drop as long as he lived. In a flash of inspiration, he thought to blame his tardiness on the time difference between Madrid and London. Better to look like an idiot than a drunk, he said to himself, and with typical British foresight he ordered a taxi on the telephone in his room.

Chapter 15

A week and two days had passed since Marlow Craftsman's visit to Manchego's office, and the inspector had to admit that the investigation had ground to a halt. After ruling out hospitals, prisons, hotels and all other logical possibilities, the matter was starting to acquire an air of mystery. He had interrogated all five members of *Librarte*'s editorial team but this had proved fruitless. They had all corroborated Berta's version of events. They said they hadn't heard anything from Atticus Craftsman for three months, and although this was somewhat puzzling, it was a real relief because the company director's son had apparently come to Spain with the intention of closing the magazine down.

'As I'm sure you'll understand,' Berta Quiñones had explained, 'we've kept as quiet as mice these last few months. The truth is, Inspector, that while they're still paying our salaries we'd rather not investigate Mr Craftsman's whereabouts too closely. He's a grown man, after all, and perfectly free to do what he likes.'

Manchego opted to call Bestman this time, instead of Marlow, so he could speak in Spanish. Explaining the disappointing results of his search was going to be rather complicated and would require a good deal of diplomacy.

He got through to Bestman at his London office, where he was sheltering behind several bilingual receptionists, all of whom Manchego informed who he was, what he was investigating and the difficulties he was having in tracking down Mr Craftsman.

'Mr Manchego,' said Bestman finally.

'Inspector.'

'As you like.'

Bestman didn't seem to be in a good mood.

'I'm sure I don't need to reiterate how crucial it is that our conversations remain confidential. The fact that we are unsure of the whereabouts of one of Mr Craftsman's sons is a delicate matter that we must handle with the utmost discretion.'

'Of course,' replied Manchego. 'My lips are sealed.'

'In that case,' Bestman clenched his jaw slightly, 'I would appreciate it if you would refrain from sharing your professional concerns with all of Craftsman & Co's receptionists. It would not be entirely advantageous for this matter to become the talk of the office nor to go beyond its walls and enter the public arena. It would not be good for the business.'

'I understand,' said the inspector, backing down.

There followed his ineloquent presentation of the facts: no news, no leads, no line of investigation . . .

'Trying to find *Crasman* in Spain is like looking for a needle in a haystack,' concluded Manchego. 'That's what it is.'

On the other end of the line, Bestman was cringing at the mere thought of having to pass on that information to Marlow. He made a mental note of the phrase 'a needle in a haystack'.

★

When he hung up, Manchego acknowledged that he was at a dead end. The next stage should be to look for evidence in the apartment on Calle del Alamillo. He would ask for a warrant, but he knew that the judge was unlikely to give him permission to bash the door down without a weighty reason. Not to mention that with Christmas, New Year and Three Kings Day coming up, there was little chance of his request being dealt with until the middle of January.

Perhaps the moment had come to skirt round the edges of legality, he said to himself. In films, when the State machine moves too slowly and danger is imminent, the hero usually takes justice into his own hands.

The greatest danger, he understood, was precisely that he might get taken off the case. Christ on a bike, if Bestman and Craftsman's patience ran out they might take the case out of his hands and hire a firm of private detectives instead.

He couldn't let that happen. He hadn't waited half his life for a case like this to come his way only to screw up now thanks to a sluggish, overloaded legal system and the haste of a couple of Brits who lacked the requisite stiff upper lip.

While he was contemplating this, adrenaline set his mind racing and merged the nebulous image of Bestman with that of a stranger, a flimsy tree and a couple of cigarettes. He remembered having had an odd conversation about the Craftsman case with a man who claimed to be a locksmith. He put his hand in his pocket. He still had the scrap of paper with a phone number and a name: Lucas.

He dialled the number.

'Hello?'

'Lucas,' he said authoritatively. 'We need to meet.'

Chapter 16

When Soleá wanted to make someone fall for her, she wore her short floral skirt, her close-fitting shirt and her high-heeled espadrilles. She let her black hair hang long and smooth down her back, with a natural wave either side of her face. She put lengthening serum on her eyelashes and applied lipstick that was midway between the colour of blood and red wine.

She knew her assets and defects like the back of her hand: she would have liked to have been taller, with wider hips and a fuller bust, and been able to dance like her grandmother Remedios and sing like her brother Tomás. But she recognized that her blue eyes and her plump lips, inherited from her mother, and the golden skin of the Montoya family mixed with the perfect oval of her Heredia face were God's gift to her. Soleá knew that she could dance and sing well, at least well enough to attract attention outside Granada's El Albaicín neighbourhood.

In the past, women like Soleá used to get married very young, then have a handful of beautiful children and spend their lives surrounded by cooking pots and guitars. That was enough to make them happy. Now, however, thanks to television, the internet and the foreign students who had moved into the new part of the city, with their sandals and hairy legs, their accents and modern ideas, things had changed significantly. Girls went to school, had dreams, wanted to see the world.

Grandmothers crossed themselves when one of their granddaughters started talking about university and languages, career opportunities and economic independence.

'And when are you going to get married?' they would invariably ask.

That said, the women were still more understanding than the men. Most of the men tried to squeeze girls' desire for freedom out of them with kisses and promises of undying love. A lot of young women succumbed to the onslaught, fell in love, capitulated and delegated the fulfilment of their own dreams to their daughters.

However, it was Soleá's father, Pedro Abad, who had most encouraged her to fly the nest.

'Study. Train. Get out into the world.'

He knew straight away that his daughter had itchy feet and had set her sights high. He walked her to school every day, then to the Faculty of Philosophy and Arts and then he accompanied her to Madrid, for her MA in Journalism. They looked for a nice place for her to live, in an old neighbourhood with steep narrow streets; they rented a tiny apartment, filled it with geraniums, assured themselves that it was a respectable area and parted with floods of tears.

When Soleá got her first job as staff writer for an arts magazine, Pedro Abad went back to Granada and told everyone. Grandmothers fanned and crossed themselves, but that night, by way of a celebration, the youngest women in El Albaicín doubled the ingredients in their stews.

They never openly admitted it, but Soleá's success was

the success of all the Heredias and Montoyas, and the Amayas and the Cortéses; it was shared by their daughters and granddaughters. This was perfectly clear to Soleá when she saw the hope shining in their eyes every time she went home. Which is why the prospect of losing her job filled her with such dread. She wasn't worried on her own behalf because she was young and clever and would surely find another job before long, but she felt bad for those girls who would be angry and hurt. Because, as Soleá was only too aware, drama was a permanent resident of El Albaicín. Joys and sorrows were shouted to the four winds. There were no secrets there. They were carried far and wide.

'Mum, I've got to tell you a big secret.'

Manuela was in the courtyard of her house in Granada when her phone rang that May Sunday. Soleá's father was a *payo*, meaning he wasn't a Gypsy, but the Gypsies thought he was all right. He had been born in Granada and worked his whole life in the fruit business, and made a reasonable living from selling oranges. He had inherited the business and his parents' house and had fallen in love with Manuela when he was a boy, playing chase with her and her cousins through the streets and squares.

'Oh, my Soleá!' Manuela replied, covering her face with her hands. 'You're not pregnant, are you?'

Soleá really hated getting her mother and grandmother involved in *Librarte*'s business. She had always preferred to keep them at a distance from the life she led in Madrid, from her investigative articles and her desire to write a serious novel one day. However, circumstances had changed and she knew that if she wanted to keep her job, at least for a few months until Berta found a more permanent solution, she had no choice but to tell the two most important women in her life about the idea she'd been pondering for years.

'Do you remember Granny Remedios's old chest?'

'The one where she keeps your grandfather's things?'

'That's the one.'

'Of course.'

'Well, we're going to have to open it, Mum. It's a matter of life or death.'

Wearing her short floral skirt, her close-fitting shirt and her high-heeled espadrilles, Soleá looked at herself in the full-length mirror. She took a deep breath and crossed herself. She ran out of the house. The others were waiting for her at the office on Calle Mayor, all shaking with fear.

'Did you speak to your mother?' Berta asked as soon as she opened the door.

'She's with us,' Soleá replied. 'She's going to help us.'

Relief spread like wildfire through the other women. The plan was in action. All they had to do was wait, feigning innocence, for the unsuspecting Atticus Craftsman, who would arrive any moment with his air of superiority, his leather briefcase and his redundancy letters, ready to give them their settlement, their redundancy pay, a slap on the back and then, definitively, the boot.

Chapter 17

The taxi pulled up in the middle of Calle Mayor, bringing the traffic to a standstill. It deposited Atticus with the same lack of haste as an old lady crossing the street – and with utter indifference to other drivers' insults and honking horns.

As the crow flies, the building that housed the *Librarte* office wasn't too far from his hotel; it should have taken about fifteen minutes to get there. However, as soon as Atticus entered the narrow streets full of old-fashioned shops – with their awnings, wooden signs and their tired appearance – and saw the barbers' shops, second-hand bookshops, and the bars from whose ceilings pigs' trotters were hung up to dry like laundry, he felt as if he had fallen down a black hole and gone back fifty years.

He breathed in a heady combination of morning smells: fried food, cigarette smoke, ripe fruit and the exhaust fumes of buses. He rather liked the mixture of Spanish aromas. Strange. He was hungry.

He rang the bell. The spyhole went from opaque to glassy. The door opened.

On the other side of the door was a middle-aged, plump,

smiling woman who hugged him as if he were a prodigal son returned to the fold.

'Come in, Mr Craftsman, make yourself at home,' she said genially. 'I'm Berta Quiñones. The girls and I have been waiting for you. Have you had breakfast?'

'I haven't, as it happens,' replied Atticus, somewhat surprised by such a reception.

'Fantastic!' shouted a second older lady who was fatter than the first, and even more cheery. 'So you won't say no to a good cup of hot chocolate with *churros* and *ensaimadas*, am I right?'

Her name was Asunción. She told him that the buns were delicious, made with plenty of butter and filled with angels' hair jam. She showed him how to eat the *churros* properly, by rolling them in sugar and then dunking them in the hot chocolate several times before eating them.

'Go on, try it.'

The other three women were significantly younger. They surrounded him and observed him attentively while, still holding his briefcase, he ate the gloriously tasty, crispy *churro*.

The prettiest of them, a tanned beauty with blue eyes, came slightly closer than propriety allowed. She said:

'You've got chocolate round your mouth, *Míster Crasman*.'

And she held out a white handkerchief that she removed from her own pocket.

On top of the photocopier, which was covered with a crocheted cloth, sat the rest of their breakfast. As well as the *ensaimadas* and *churros*, there were 'saint's bones' marzipan rolls, almond pastries and aniseed doughnuts.

Atticus let the five women spoil him.

'If you're too hot, I can put the air conditioning on,' said María.

After half an hour, he was so full he felt like the Big

Bad Wolf with rocks in its belly, and everything Berta was saying was making his head spin. She had already brought him up to speed with the office and everyone who worked there:

'She's got three gorgeous children, she's single, she's fat because of her menopause not because she's ill, and I live near here with my cat. This one paints better than Picasso, that one writes better than the angels themselves. María is like a little ant: always saving, saving, saving. Gaby is cheerful as a lark and Soleá . . . is the apple of my eye. An amazing girl, Mr Craftsman, clever as a hare, sharp as a fox, the life and soul of this magazine.'

Berta seemed like a mother to all of them and the office felt like a family home.

'Do you smoke, Mr Craftsman? It's illegal, you know, to smoke in the workplace, but given that you're the boss I should think we can make an exception.'

'You can call me Atticus.' The Englishman had no option but to concede in the face of such a show of affection. 'If it did please you, my ladies,' he added, because Atticus had a purely academic knowledge of Spanish. He tended to use expressions he had learnt from seventeenth-century books like *La vida es sueño*, *Lazarillo de Tormes* or *Don Quixote de la Mancha*, which were set texts at Oxford University.

They had prepared Berta's office as carefully as his Aunt Mildred, if she were still alive, would have prepared the guest bedroom of her house in Portsmouth. And like her, they had hung new net curtains in the window, placed a glass of ice-cold water in front of him, left a silver frame empty on his desk ('for you to put your favourite photo in'), and arranged a vase of wild lilacs.

Atticus thanked them wholeheartedly for their kind gestures. Then, excusing himself with a charming smile, he

84

shut himself in his new office, put his feet up on the desk and fell fast asleep.

An hour later, on the other side of the door, the girls were unable to bear the worry of waiting any longer, so they turned off their computer screens and started talking in whispers.

'What do you think he's doing in there? I haven't heard a peep for ages.'

'He must be studying the case.'

'Don't you think it's weird that he hasn't asked us for documents, account books or anything?'

'I reckon he'll call us in one by one in a bit.'

María was the most pessimistic of the five of them. She had made up her mind that nothing could be done, that no strategy would work. The man had come to fire them and that was what he would do. Their fate was sealed.

Soleá, on the other hand, had complete faith in her plan. She was just as nervous as María, but her impatience had less to do with the probable outcome of their situation and more to do with her excitement at entering into battle with the Englishman.

'I'm going in,' she said when it had gone twelve thirty. 'I can't stand it a moment longer. All this waiting is killing me.'

'Go for it, Soleá, go get him!' said Gaby, egging her on.

Berta got up and walked over to Soleá. She grabbed her by the shoulders and looked her straight in the eye. She said:

'We're counting on you. On you, Soleá, no one else. It's up to you to sweet-talk him.'

'Don't worry, I'm not going to let you down,' she replied solemnly. 'Anyway, he's not bad looking,' she admitted.

'He's hot,' said Asunción.

'He's scorching,' added María.

'Go get him!' said Gaby again.

Then Soleá knocked on the door. Twice.

They heard the sound of furniture scraping inside Berta's office. The silver frame slammed on to the desk. Atticus Craftsman cleared his throat.

'Come in,' he said.

And Soleá disappeared into the darkened room without looking back. Into the lair of that blond, handsome, green-eyed wolf.

Chapter 18

Never, for as long as he lived and even if the continents cast off from their moorings and formed a new Pangaea, would Atticus Craftsman forget Soleá Abad Heredia's entrance into his new office on Madrid's Calle Mayor.

That woman cut through his body and soul like a knife.

If he hadn't been so polite and British, he would have allowed himself to completely lose his cool instead of falteringly trying to conserve it, stumbling against furniture, knocking over the glass of water, stuttering and limping. Howling with wolfish desire.

She was a witch, there was no doubt about that. In fact, they all were. Five witches in a coven, preparing concoctions and love potions in their copper cauldrons. How else to explain why he, a man of the world, educated at Oxford and with a mother as devoid of emotion as his, felt such an animal reaction to a beauty like Soleá?

The girl had eyes like a cat's, blue as the sea, as round as the full moon. And she waved her hands in circles, her fingers opening and closing like fans in front of the innocent victim of her enchantment.

Her hair was black, pitch-black. And it came down to her

waist, with a wave at some indefinable point between her neck and her middle. She smelt of orange blossom and she moved with the grace of a fine thread in the breeze.

Soleá didn't let him get a word in. She planted both hands on the desk and, leaning forward, showed Atticus the curve of a pair of round, firm breasts.

'You just stay there, *Míster Crasman*, and listen to this story I'm going to tell you. It's a family secret. Something that absolutely no one knows, but I swear it could change everything.'

And so Soleá began telling him about a dream she'd had:

'I wanted to write a novel based on this story . . .'

She told him that once, when she was a child, she had been shut in the attic as punishment for doing something naughty. There, she had started pulling away the moth-eaten sheets and brushing the dust off old furniture from her grandparents' house.

'I found a wooden chest and broke the lock to open it. Inside there was a military uniform, with a beret and everything, an old pistol, some ruined boots. It had belonged to my grandfather, my mum's father, who died in the civil war. At the bottom, tied with a red ribbon, I found a pile of papers: letters, documents and poems. Mostly poems, *Míster Crasman*.'

'Was your grandfather a poet?'

'No,' replied Soleá, shaking her head. 'That's the thing. My grandfather was a cattle trader, nothing to do with poetry. But,' she went on, 'according to what my Granny Remedios says, out in the fields they often used to meet a skinny lad with a big round head who spent his days sitting on a rock and writing. They would share food and talk with him. The lad was called Federico and he was born in Fuente Vaqueros, that's what he told my grandfather.'

At this point, Soleá paused for dramatic emphasis.

'Are you telling me that your grandmother has un-published García Lorca poems in her attic?'

'That's what I'd write my novel about,' said Soleá. 'I remember reading one of the poems when I was a girl, and the refrain stuck with me: "*Luna de cascabelillos, luna gitana, bata de cola.*"'

'Very Lorca,' the Englishman admitted.

'The tricky thing would be convincing my grandmother to let us see them. When she found out I'd broken the lock on the chest, she went crazy. It was fifteen years ago, but my ears still hurt from how hard she pulled them that day,' she recalled. 'She hid the chest somewhere else. I never knew where. And I haven't seen it again since.'

'But . . .' Atticus lifted his hands to his blond mop of curls. 'By Jove, your grandmother could be rich!'

'She doesn't care about that,' Soleá pointed out, hammering her blue eyes into the centre of his heart. 'She'd rather die poor than live with the shame.'

'What shame?'

'What other shame could there be, *Míster Crasman*?' said Soleá, lowering her voice as if about to reveal a terrible secret. 'Lorca was gay.'

After such a revelation, Atticus Craftsman was left in no doubt that people from the south of Spain were so nuts they were off the map. If the poems Soleá was talking about really did exist, he was looking at a literary find of incredible proportions. He wouldn't say anything to his father for the moment, because if the great Marlow Craftsman found out that there was even a remote possibility of getting his hands on some unpublished Lorca poems, he might well show up in Spain with his team of lawyers, advisors and shareholders and turn Atticus's life upside down. What's more, it was highly likely that this story would turn out to be a farce, and that the pastoral scene with the goats and the poet were inventions and the papers were utter bull.

Soleá had suddenly fallen silent. She was looking at him with her bewitching eyes, waiting for him to make the next move. She looked like a Gypsy who tells people's fortunes and scatters rosemary in exchange for a few coins . . . you'll marry a rich man, you'll be cured of all your ills, you'll have an infinitely long life, as long as the lines on your palm.

Atticus understood that he had no choice but to investigate that story, however unbelievable it might seem. Firstly, because he couldn't spend the rest of his days thinking that once, in his youth, back at the beginning of the twenty-first century, an extraordinary woman had offered him fame and glory on a plate and he had turned her down because he didn't believe her. Secondly, because Soleá's spell had worked its way into all the veins and arteries of his British anatomy and had sown them with wild flowers. Beautiful flowers, but poisonous, like wild poppies. It was better to get to the bottom of the truth, or the lie, than have to look into the mirror as an old man and see a face filled with regret.

'What was your grandfather's name?'

'Antonio Heredia.'

'And you say he was a cattle dealer . . .'

'Exactly.'

'And he was homosexual?'

Oh, how Atticus regretted having pronounced that word without first considering the consequences or understanding that such a statement was a serious affront to someone who grew up believing that 'gay' was the worst insult possible. Atticus, who was perfectly accepting of everyone whatever their sexual orientation, watched Soleá's transformation in shock: her body grew rigid, her fists clenched, her eyes closed to a squint, her voice became hoarse, she turned the air blue.

'I shit on *all* your ancestors!' she shouted. 'Every last one of them! For fuck's sake! That's it, fucking Englishman, I've had enough of your fucking magazine and your stupid English face! No one disrespects Soleá Abad Heredia's grandfather, you better believe that!'

Furious, she thumped the table and shot curses from her cat's eyes.

Berta, who was of course listening through the door, appeared on the scene all of a sudden, alarmed by the shouting.

'What have you done to Soleá?' she accused Craftsman, who had gone into a state of shock.

The three other women followed their boss into Atticus's office. There really wasn't enough space for six deranged adults in the office, all gesticulating and screaming as if they had lost their minds.

In the midst of the chaos, Atticus heard some worrying accusations: harassment, sexual abuse . . . This was getting out of hand.

'He insulted my grandfather!' Soleá was finally able to make herself heard over the voices of her colleagues. 'God rest his soul!' she added.

The crime can't have seemed so serious to the others, as they gradually calmed down and lowered their voices.

'Shit, Soleá, way to scare us,' said María, embarrassed. 'We thought Mr Craftsman was trying to rape you.'

Atticus felt his legs shaking. He slumped into the office chair.

'All of you, please get out,' he finally managed to say. 'Except you, Berta. I want you to stay. We need to talk.'

★

91

The conversation that followed was a tense one. Berta listened to Atticus's monologue, unable to interrupt, while he gradually regained his composure. He started by explaining the motivation for his visit to *Librarte*, which, as she had surely gleaned from her conversations with Mr Bestman, was for no other reason than to close the magazine, although he was determined to study the problem in depth in the hope of finding some solution that would suit everyone involved. In the event of the magazine being deemed definitively unviable, which was the most likely outcome, the publishing house was willing to generously negotiate their redundancy packages.

However, due to unexpected circumstances – Craftsman said – he needed to go on a short research trip to the south of Spain. There, he would spend a few days resolving certain issues that he said were none of her concern – don't take it the wrong way, Ms Quiñones – so the fate of *Librarte* wouldn't be decided until his return. During his trip he planned to write a report on the reasons behind the magazine's failure. He therefore required, and please take note, account books, expense receipts, figures for revenue and overheads, lists of advertisers, the price of paper converted to pounds sterling, the results of the general media study, etcetera, etcetera.

'Ah, yes, one other thing,' added the young man. 'If I'm going to spend a while in Spain I would prefer to rent a small studio flat near the office. I don't like hotel life. It's very impersonal. I hope you'll be able to find something appropriate.'

'Of course,' replied Berta maternally. 'I know a little flat on Calle del Alamillo, next door to my place. We can stop by there later if you like and I'll show it to you. It's sweet.' At that moment the office door opened slightly, and Atticus saw the outline of Soleá's body appear, with her narrow waist, her small bust and her black hair.

'I'd like to apologize, *Míster Crasman*,' she said in a whisper. 'I lost my head because my family is sacred to me. I don't know if you understand, but it won't happen again. I swear I won't raise my voice at you again.'

Guessing at that moment that the lie he was about to tell would stay with him for the rest of his life, Atticus Craftsman was able to articulate the purest of truths:

'It was my fault, Soleá. It's because I'm English.'

Chapter 19

The result of the phone conversation between Inspector Manchego and Lucas the locksmith was a flawless plan for a forced entry, technically illegal, that would be of significant mutual benefit. The policeman promised to pay two hundred and fifty euros to the locksmith, who in turn promised to break and enter without arousing suspicion, to keep shtum and to duly carry on daily life without fear of future police investigations. They set a date for a couple of days later. Manchego handed over the money and they sealed the deal with a firm handshake.

The night in question turned out to be damp and unpleasant, as befits late November. They met on the stroke of midnight and it was unbearably cold. The inspector admitted to himself that perhaps it would have been better to meet at eight in the evening, as the locksmith had suggested, when it would have been just as dark, but when you're going to commit a crime, he thought, you should meet at midnight: the peak time for criminal activity.

The plan was simple. He would meet Lucas near the doorway, greet him with a quick nod so as not to arouse suspicion, and would keep watch in the street while his accomplice professionally and stealthily opened the door to number 5. Then he would wait on the corner until Lucas gave him a missed call on his mobile. This would be the signal that he was inside the flat, the coast was clear and Manchego could go in without fear of being seen.

Lucas arrived right on time. He had a relatively suspicious toolbox under one arm and was looking particularly criminal. His face was covered with a scarf and he was wearing a woollen hat, leather gloves and clothes that would have been perfect for a villain in any detective film.

Manchego thought it was a fitting get-up for a break-in, although he would have preferred a little more discretion, perhaps less sturdy boots or the odd item of clothing that wasn't camouflage print – Lucas resembled a cross between a biker and a poacher – but all in all his accomplice didn't look too bad.

He greeted him, as planned, with a subtle tilt of the head.

Lucas walked straight past Manchego as if he hadn't seen him. He went up to the flat, took out a home-made lock pick, thumped the door, and then kicked his way in making a hellish noise.

Lights came on in some of the windows. A very elderly neighbour called out in a shaky voice: 'Who's there?' and then threatened to call the police.

More blinds opened and a few faces peered out.

Inspector Manchego began to panic. This wasn't what they had planned. His break-in needed to be silent, prudent, innocuous; a quick in-and-out with no witnesses. Discretion was of the utmost importance, that's how he had explained it to the locksmith. What a bloody incompetent idiot, what a lousy shit of a thief.

'But you're a policeman,' the so-called Lucas had replied.

'If anyone hears us, all you have to do is show them your badge and say you happened to be passing by.'

'Yeah, OK,' Manchego had accepted, 'but it's better not to have to step in, if you know what I mean, unless strictly necessary.'

The old woman was now shouting: 'Police! Police!' Her shrill voice echoed off the walls in the narrow street.

All of a sudden, his mobile rang. That lout of a locksmith was calling, as planned. Just like he should have done if it had all gone smoothly, without anyone noticing.

'Christ on a bike!' shouted Manchego, answering on the third ring. 'You burst in like a herd of elephants, wake the whole street up and now you call – but don't hang up, you idiot.'

'We have to switch to plan B, Manchego. There are neighbours out on the stairs,' the locksmith replied, sounding unbelievably calm. Lucas had nerves of steel.

Inspector Manchego took out his badge and standard-issue gun and pushed open the door to number 5, Calle del Alamillo.

'Police!' he shouted.

The stairwell was narrow, the hallway dark. Several heads, all belonging to rather elderly people, were poking out over the wooden banister. Someone flicked the switch and a dim bulb lit up on the landing.

All of a sudden, Lucas's unmistakable form appeared, jogging downstairs with the toolbox under one arm and a couple of books under the other. As he passed Manchego he gave him a firm shove with his right arm, the one holding the books. The inspector stumbled. He hesitated for a moment, wondering whether he should point the gun at his partner in crime to make the scene more convincing or let him escape with only a verbal threat.

'Stop, stop, in the name of the law!' he finally exclaimed. And as the locksmith disappeared off down the street, he thought he heard him let out a laugh.

The neighbours congregated in the doorway, under the flickering light. All of them, seven in total, were wearing their pyjamas, dressing gowns and slippers, with their false teeth in and glasses on.

Manchego tried to calm them down:

'Show's over, ladies and gents, you can go home, the thief has left, he must've been a drug addict, he didn't have time to rob any of you. It's lucky that I happened to be having dinner at the taco place downstairs, I heard the shouts and came straight here. I'm in plain clothes, but I never take off my standard-issue, even to take a leak.'

'He broke into the second-floor right-hand flat!' screamed the old lady. 'The Englishman's place!'

The seven neighbours and Inspector Manchego made their way in single file up the two flights of stairs that separated them from Atticus Craftsman's flat.

'He's a young man,' the old lady explained as they went up. 'And it's strange,' she continued, 'he took the flat before the summer, spent a couple of nights here and then disappeared. We haven't seen him since May.'

The door was open; pulled off its hinges, mangled. Useless shit of a locksmith, thought Manchego. The light was on.

The flat smelt as if it hadn't been aired in a long while. It felt as if no one had opened the windows for months. The blinds were closed and the furniture was covered in a thin layer of dust.

On a wooden table, the only one in the flat, there was a pile of books, papers, folders and other jumbled documents. It looked as if someone had been working on them but had left in a hurry.

As for the rest of it, there were no signs of violence, the bed was made, the fridge was empty, the inspector didn't find a single body decomposing in a single wardrobe, no suicide note, no leads as to the whereabouts of the mystery tenant who, according to his elderly neighbour, had paid six months up front and his contract was almost up.

'I'd like to talk to the owner of the property.'

'That's me,' replied the neighbour. 'How else do you think I know about the rent? My son Gabriel uses the flat, but he's in London at the moment. He works for a bank.'

Manchego scratched the back of his neck.

'I see.'

'My late husband and I bought it, for our boy, you see.'

'And how did you meet the tenant?' He was about to say Craftsman's name, but stopped himself just in time. Doing so would have raised suspicions. He was supposedly there due to the purest coincidence and, as such, he needed to feign ignorance.

'My friend Berta Quiñones recommended him to me,' the housewife replied. 'She's a lovely girl who lives next door, at number 9.'

'I see.'

'He's English,' she added. 'Tall, blond, very handsome. Seems very young to be Berta's boss.'

'We shall have to inform him of the break-in,' said the inspector in the hope that the woman could put him on the trail of his missing person.

'The thing is, we don't know where he's gone,' she confessed. 'Neither Berta nor I have seen him.'

'He didn't give you an address or telephone number?'

'No. He didn't even say goodbye.'

'I see.'

Inspector Manchego spent another hour checking the

flat. He went room by room – kitchen, bedroom, bathroom, living room – opening drawers and closing doors, but finding no evidence that could further his investigation. The conclusion he came to was simple: Craftsman had rented the flat with the intention of staying there for at least six months, but had only spent two or three nights there. Wherever it was he had gone, he had taken his toiletries and all his clothes with him, with the exception of two pairs of woollen socks and an overcoat that was still on a hanger in the wardrobe, but he had left behind a pile of papers that, as far as Manchego could see, related to *Librarte* magazine's finances.

In other words, Craftsman had gone on a personal trip, since he had taken his cologne but left his work papers behind. This made Manchego think that the Englishman must have been planning on returning to Madrid to carry on with his work before long. And that didn't tally with his having disappeared for over six months.

So Marlow might be right after all: Atticus Craftsman had been kidnapped, and Manchego had to admit that there was genuinely nothing to connect him to drug-trafficking.

'*Not in the house, míster,*' he would say over the phone as soon as it got light. '*Not muerto in the house.*'

Chapter 20

Berta remembered it perfectly clearly: she had taken Atticus to see the flat after work that very Monday, at about half past seven, the same day they had welcomed him with hot chocolate and *churros*.

Because it wasn't far from the office to the flat on Calle del Alamillo, Atticus said he would rather walk than get a taxi. He took off his jacket and tie, rolled up his shirtsleeves and undid his top two buttons. He ruffled his blond hair (he sported an English haircut – in other words, a mop seemingly chopped at random), doused himself with cologne and, when they went out into the street, took a deep breath then coughed.

Berta walked beside him on the narrow pavement down the tiny streets to the old building where Señora Susana was waiting for them in her Sunday best. She was holding the keys to her son Gabriel's flat, ready to show them round the sweet, welcoming, cool space with two balconies, which was arranged with a grandmother's attention to detail so the Englishman would like it. 'Believe me, *Míster Crasman*, it's a real bargain.'

Tiny particles of dust caught the light and danced in the

still air in the hallway. Mingled with the smell of boiled vegetables was the aroma of Mediterranean pine, thanks to an air freshener that Señora Susana had placed on the landing, lest the inevitable stench of cabbage put the foreigner off.

But Atticus appeared immune to anything negative. That afternoon he had a certain something in his gaze, as if stunned or bewitched, and everything seemed fine to him. Fine that the fuses sometimes went and you had to push them back up with a broom handle. Fine that the pipes were made of iron and first thing in the morning the water came out the colour of pee. Fine that there was no lift, no doorman, no garage. Fine that the floorboards creaked and there was only a gas cooker. Fine that from time to time you had to order a gas bottle and connect it under the sink. All fine. Even the price.

Berta and Señora Susana decided to go and celebrate the deal at the bar downstairs. They said goodbye and hailed a taxi for Atticus, who still looked stunned and whose mind was clearly elsewhere: who knows in which corner of Soleá's undulating geography or the pools of her catlike eyes.

The two women were walking the two hundred metres separating them from their slices of tortilla when Berta stopped dead just as they were passing the El Alamillo taco place.

'What's wrong?' Señora Susana asked when she saw her go pale and stop dead in the middle of the pavement.

'Nothing, nothing,' replied Berta.

'You look like you've seen a ghost.'

And in fact Berta had seen something. No more and no less than a couple, a man and a woman, who should not have been there or anywhere else for that matter: the woman was María. The man was not her husband.

101

Berta felt feverish, as if she had the flu, and the back of her neck was throbbing. Señora Susana was discreet in her own way and, despite being a lonely old lady, decided not to ask any questions. Instead, when they got to the bar she started nattering about other things in the hope of soothing Berta's obvious agitation. All Berta wanted was to finish the tumbler of wine and run home to her books, where true love was still possible.

Four months earlier, on the sixth of January, Three Kings Day, a day she would never forget, Berta had gone out for a stroll around Plaza Mayor. The square was still full of Christmas stalls, and Berta had stopped to look at the ones that sold expensive, but exquisite, little earthenware figurines of shepherds and sheep. Her mind was set on finally buying another Melchior, because the little gold box that hers carried had broken ages ago, and even though she had fixed it with superglue you could clearly see the join. In spite of the cold, the square was full of families – the kids trying out their new bikes – and street musicians were playing carols on their accordions. There were also a few loved-up couples making the most of other people's boisterous happiness to enhance their own, wandering round the square holding hands and kissing under the colonnades.

Berta was leaning over a counter, struggling to decide whether she wanted a figurine with a red or blue cape, when she heard María's distinctive voice, high in the middle of a sentence and dropping at the end, right next to her, calling a man 'my love'. The man had his arm around her waist and his back to Berta. María was facing Berta, but was blind to everything but that unknown man's lips.

After a sloppy kiss complete with tongues and noisy slurps, María pulled away from her lover's embrace and found herself face to face with her boss's shocked expression. She jumped, raised her hand to her mouth, lowered her gaze and knew that the next day she would have some serious explaining to do. It would be as bad as if her own mother had discovered that, instead of spending Three Kings Day around the hearth with her family, María had slipped out in search of the wild adventure of a clandestine affair.

Indeed, the next day, at exactly seven p.m., Berta Quiñones, the same woman who had greeted each of them that morning with a little present wrapped in tissue paper – perfume, a hair clip, a make-up bag, 'which the Three Kings left by my fireplace for you because you've been so good' – asked them all to finish their work and go home.

'Except you, María,' she said, pointing at her with an accusatory finger. 'I want you to stay a bit longer, please, because I really can't get the accounts to add up. Let's see if you can explain them to me.'

María walked into Berta's office with her head down.

She was the first one to speak.

'Look, Berta,' she defended herself, avoiding Berta's questioning gaze, 'marriage, contrary to what you might think, because you've never been married, so you haven't been through these things, isn't a bed of roses, you know? In fact, it's the opposite: it's a bramble patch perched on top of a cliff. You've no idea how hard it is to not end up plunging to the bottom.'

'Sure,' said her boss as quick as lightning, 'and you've just smashed your head right open.'

'True, I have, but not just now,' acknowledged María. 'I've been living at the bottom of an abyss for a long time. What you saw yesterday, contrary to what you think, is probably the thing that'll save my marriage in the long run. I was dead, Berta, and now I've come back to life. Even my kids have noticed the difference: I'm the cheerful woman I once was, the woman who felt wanted and loved, who still believed she could be happy.'

'Cheating on your husband?' Berta threw at her.

'I'm not cheating on him,' said María, defending herself tooth and nail, 'quite the opposite. Whenever I sleep with my lover, I imagine I'm with Bernabé.'

Chapter 21

Sometimes María regretted having married so young. If she'd been more patient and less desperate to get out of Urda, she wouldn't have fled her parents' house at nineteen with the first outsider who happened to pass through the village. But she was fed up with her life, and that's what she told Bernabé on the riverbank – fed up of doing the chores at home, looking after her younger siblings, obeying her father's tyrannical orders and chivvying her zombie-like mother. Every day was spent rushing about, working like a slave, never stopping to wonder whether somewhere, not far away, there might be a better future.

'I'd like to move to Madrid, get any old job to start with, study accounting, because that's what really interests me, and then get a proper job, buy a flat and be independent.'

'Well, guess what, I've got a flat and a job,' replied Bernabé, 'but I feel lonely. I miss my family, my friends in Zamora, and I miss having someone who cares about me.'

The deal was simple: cheap board and lodging in return for hot food and clean clothes. Feelings were put to one side; I'll work, you'll study. If I need privacy, you'll go and stay at a friend's house. We'll share the bathroom and split the electricity bill.

It all worked well for a couple of months. By the third month, their clothes came out of the washing machine all mixed up, only one bed saw any use and the thing about having visitors stay over had stopped seeming like a good idea. María married at twenty and Bernabé at twenty-three. She achieved a lot. He achieved nothing.

During the first years of their marriage, María smartened the flat up and studied hard, worked as a waitress, a secretary and, finally, a book-keeper for a small company that sold office products. She slept five hours a night on average, only relaxed on Sunday afternoons and had no time for fun, friends or holidays.

Bernabé, meanwhile, settled down on the sofa in front of the TV, and watched nothing but football games. He forgot how all the domestic appliances worked and what all the cleaning products were for.

He was perfectly contented with his job at the café near their flat: he loved standing behind the bar, almost like a therapist or a confessor; he liked the regulars and the games of dominoes they played when he could escape from his chores for a while; he enjoyed making saucy comments to the girls who sometimes came in for a mid-morning coffee; he was fond of the lads who came to buy sandwiches, the seductive sound of the cigarette machine and the smell of toast for breakfast and grilled meat for lunch.

It had its downside too, of course. Primarily, the un-interrupted twelve-hour shifts, from seven to seven, the miserable salary and the complete lack of a career ladder. But he wasn't ambitious. He was happy enough with his routine life, his football game on Sundays, his beers in front of the telly and the unconditional love of María, his hyperactive wife, who was always cooking up plans that they never had the time or money for.

'This summer, if we manage to save a bit, let's go away somewhere, shall we? What do you reckon?'

'Depends,' he would reply, absorbed in the highlights of the match he had just watched. 'Where do you want to go?'

'To the beach. To the south. Somewhere really sunny.'

But that summer, instead of going on holiday, they had to deal with a complicated pregnancy that meant María, faced with the threat of premature labour, had to stay in bed for three months. The baby was determined to be born early and the doctor was equally determined that it would reach full term.

From her throne of white sheets, María gave Bernabé orders: 'Open the blind, close the curtain, put the washing machine on, make me a hot chocolate.' Until, after ten days, Bernabé told her the only lie of his life. He said he had a double shift at the café and, what with her on leave, money was tight, so he would make the sacrifice and work longer hours. 'María, it's for the good of both of you,' he said, and from seven to ten he went to watch the game at a friend's house.

Lucía was born two months premature, which coincided with an international football final, much to her father's annoyance.

'Typical girl,' he exclaimed when he held her for the first time.

A short while later, María got her job at *Librarte*. 'What a weird name for a magazine,' said Bernabé, and carried on eating his chips.

Then the twins were born on the only day of the year that, as luck would have it, no football was being played anywhere in the world.

And life got a lot more complicated for María.

The chaos into which her daily routine descended after the kids were born contrasted significantly with the early days of marriage. María no longer suggested going on holiday, nor did she dream that her husband, one day, might find a job that was better suited to their desperate financial situation. She got used to his trivial chat in front of the telly, his lack of ambition, his domestic habits and his apathy.

Sometimes she let herself think that if she hadn't left with the first guy to wander through Urda, she would still be a free woman. Then she was shocked to look in the mirror and come face to face with the spitting image of her mother, albeit a modern version: another zombie stuck in a rut.

But these thoughts weren't of any use to her. To banish them from her head she hugged her three kids, smiled kindly at Bernabé – who, at the end of the day, was a good person, a good father and a loyal husband – and pretended to be truly happy.

Until Barbosa arrived on the scene.

Chapter 22

César Barbosa was no male model. It's true that his cocky attitude, his leather jacket and the stubble that caressed his jutting cheekbones made him look particularly manly, and that his husky smoker's voice combined with a thick Madrid accent made him undeniably attractive to foolish women. But what had really driven María into Barbosa's hairy arms wasn't his voice or any of his questionable physical attributes, but the belief, lodged in the deepest recess of her girly imagination, that one day the hero from *The Bridges of Madison County* would come and save her from her tedious life.

María had identified so much with Meryl Streep's Francesca in that film – which Bernabé, who fell asleep in the second scene, had dismissed as boring, bland and unrealistic – that from that day on her outlook on life had taken a 180-degree turn. She clung to the idea that all was not lost, even if she was trapped in a dull, lifeless marriage, as intensely as her children dreamed of going to Disneyland.

All she needed to make her fantasy reality was a flesh-and-blood Clint Eastwood: someone who looked like a bad guy but had a heart of gold. Someone disillusioned when it came to love, with a past he would rather forget and an uncertain future. Someone who was willing to start a passionate affair with a married woman.

That man was César Barbosa.

He had no scruples when it came to wooing a woman: first he would let her talk at length about herself, because he knew that women like nothing more than to be listened to. Then, expertly, cunningly, he would identify her weak points. Finally, he would attack, aiming straight for the heart.

To a woman who feared loneliness, he promised undying love. To a woman who was smothered by commitment, an open relationship; to a woman who erred on the side of prudishness, a long courtship with plenty of respect; to a woman who suffered with sexual inhibition, a thousand and one nights of rampant debauchery; and to María, an extramarital adventure with all the trimmings.

Secret meetings, clandestine dates, hotels, parks and back seats, whatever you want, babe, we'll act out your fantasies, your deepest desires, as filthy as you like, you're so hot, you're too young to feel so old, you've got a heart-stopping arse, what a waste, come on, be generous, if your husband doesn't know how to value your body then let Barbosa enjoy it.

She accepted the invitation to debauchery, of course. She had spent months dreaming of that day.

'I want you to call me Francesca,' she said as she entered the room of the little hotel that would become their meeting place from then on.

And he shushed her with kisses.

César Barbosa was the type of guy who put his faith in the university of life and awarded himself a first. Who showily scorned degrees and prizes because he secretly coveted them but knew he didn't deserve them. Who believed he was an artist, with an artist's vices and thought that being an artist wasn't an affectation but a way of life.

He dropped out of journalism school through a combination of complete failure and expulsion, after six years of clowning around in the cafeteria. He adopted the title 'freelance photographer' to explain to his father why he should lend him the money for his first Kodak camera. Then he went out into the street in search of an image to can and flog to the papers for a fee that would finance his experimental artistic photography. He set up a studio in the attic of a derelict house. He called it a 'loft', and managed to trick a few aspiring models into posing nude for him. He did indeed sell those photos for a tidy sum, but he used a pseudonym. Later, he specialized in the underground movement and that was when he bought his leather jacket, from Portobello Road on a research trip to London paid for by a Sunday supplement, and some Dr Martens boots that he destroyed going up Guadarrama on a motorbike.

He got a dragon tattooed on his arm. Time went by, fashions changed and the underground movement emerged and went mainstream, but all the while César Barbosa refused to let go of his leather jacket.

'A few of us nostalgic types are left,' he often muttered at the bar. 'True survivors of a mythical time when we had The Cure, punk and Madonna's fingerless gloves.'

'And Bruce Springsteen,' the barman would reply, raising his glass. 'The Boss.'

In recent years he had done a few jobs for *Librarte*. He usually turned up at the office unshaven and reeking of stale tobacco, often wearing a sleeveless T-shirt to show off his dragon. The girls called him the Pirate behind his back, mainly because he had the same name as Captain Barbosa from *Pirates of the Caribbean*, but also because his cocky attitude and fondness for rum meant he was more than worthy of the nickname.

For two years María paid no attention to the Pirate apart from muttering timid pleasantries – 'morning, good morning, the invoice, thank you, we'll transfer the money in a month, goodbye, bye' – and when she did pay him some attention it was quite by accident, and thanks to a silly, embarrassing mistake, which she blamed on the children's tonsillitis. 'I swear I don't know what got into me, what a thing, come into the office when you can, César, and we'll sort it out.' She had paid him twice for the same piece of work: a photo shoot with a truly ugly author, what a joke, the poor thing's hideous.

'I didn't even notice,' he lied, because he awaited each pay cheque in cold sweats. 'In any case, I've spent it now.'

'Then you'll do the next job for free,' said María, ever pragmatic.

But César turned up at the office holding an envelope with the money, and he handed it to María with the same solemnity with which Sultan Boabdil handed over the keys to Granada to the Catholic Kings.

'Come on, let me buy you a drink,' the Pirate said then.

And he took her straight into a scene from *The Bridges of Madison County*. While Clint Eastwood showers in the upstairs bathroom, Meryl Streep takes an ancient flowery dress out of the trunk, plonks it on and looks like Laura Ingalls from *Little House on the Prairie* but fifty years older. Clint Eastwood stares at her in surprise, not understanding what the demure look is all about, because he knew, right from the very beginning when he asked her under Madison bridge how to get to the nearest town, that he was going

112

to get her. María didn't care. César Barbosa took her for drinks, listened to her talk about herself for hours on end, gave her a ride on his motorbike to the corner of her street and on parting said the thing about the heart-stopping arse.

There was no turning back after that.

Chapter 23

A week after he arrived in Madrid, Atticus had moved into the flat on Calle del Alamillo and paid Señora Susana six months' rent upfront; this amount, according to his calculations, was equivalent to less than a week living like a king in the hotel his father had booked for him.

It wasn't that he disliked hotel life. On the contrary, Atticus agreed that there was nothing better in the world than the absolute insouciance that comes from being a hotel guest: the discreet laundry service that asks no questions, the guiltless all-nighters, the permanent availability of the mini-bar and room service, the clean towels, the fresh flowers . . .

But an unyielding conscience, such as afflicts compassionate souls, had begun gnawing at his insides from the moment he crossed the threshold of the *Librarte* office and met the five victims of the magazine's dire economic situation.

If he was to follow his father's advice, he should simply have played the role of an unscrupulous businessman capable of leaving all sentimentalism to one side when it came to defending his own interests. No one but those five women was to blame for *Librarte*'s failure. 'Don't forget that, son, we gave them the opportunity to succeed and they failed to take advantage of it. We gave them the means, we protected, supported and advised them, just as we did with the Germans at *Krafts*, and while they managed to top the sales lists, that lot in Spain have only managed to ruin the business.'

'They have, I'll admit, achieved top marks when it comes to the art of messing up.'

But if, instead of following his father's cold instructions, Atticus let himself be guided by the warm beating of his tin heart, he had no choice but to be sympathetic towards those five women who were about to lose their jobs.

They already had names and faces, and he saw visions of them in the corners of his luxury hotel room, pointing accusatory fingers at him: 'You gave up on me, you abandoned me, it's your fault that I'm living under a bridge, fishing for stinking carp to feed my children, washing clothes in the filthy water of the Manzanares, because you used me while I was useful to you and then threw me in the river.'

At times he was also confronted by the ghost of Karl Marx, despite being completely sure that Marx had never stayed at that hotel, which made him wonder why it really was that he used to see Tolkien's ghost in his room in Oxford. If such visions weren't tied to a physical space, as he had assumed at the time, then he was doomed because James Joyce might appear when he least expected it, furious with him for pretending to have read *Ulysses* from cover to cover when in fact he had only flicked through the Longman reader's guide.

Literary digressions and unfounded fears aside, Atticus Craftsman felt that it was terribly bad taste to go on enjoying the pleasures of that ostentatious hotel while he was causing the girls at the office to suffer. If he did end up having to fire them, it would really take the mickey to be staying in such an oasis of abundance.

That was when it occurred to him that he might rent a studio somewhere near the *Librarte* office – hence his un-fussiness when it came to the imperfections of the flat on Calle del Alamillo, which did, he couldn't deny, have a certain charm to it.

Señora Susana had turned out to be a housewife dedicated to the causes of crochet, dried flowers, housework, stainless steel cutlery and amber-coloured Duralex glasses. Strangely, instead of breaking like any other member of their vitreous family when thrown forcefully against a hard surface, these glasses shattered into thousands of tiny crystals. These looked so like confetti that Atticus had hurled half a dozen on to the kitchen floor and delighted in the spectacle like a small boy.

He hadn't had time to fully admire the floral linings of the drawers, nor the wallpaper that adorned the backs of the wardrobes, nor the stuccoed walls in the hall, nor the collection of porcelain figures in the hall cabinet, because that earth-mover Soleá Abad Heredia had convinced him that they should leave immediately for the Sierra Nevada, in whose foothills, she swore, they would find a treasure that had lain hidden for seventy years, waiting for Atticus Craftsman to unearth it.

'Don't bring heaps of paperwork, *Míster Crasman*,' she had warned him, 'because you're not going to have time to work. My family are pretty intense, you'll see, they won't leave you alone for a minute.'

'Should I bring my overcoat?'

'What do you think, silly? It's boiling in Granada!'

So with his suitcase packed with clothes, his wash-bag,

his pillow, his kettle and plenty of Earl Grey, Atticus decided that he was ready. This time he left behind the small erotic library because, given the way things seemed to be going, it seemed inappropriate to carry such an arsenal of debauchery.

'My cousin Arcángel is going to give us a lift, if that's all right with you, since he's been in Madrid for business and is driving back to Granada with an empty truck tomorrow.' Soleá had suggested this so expectantly that he didn't dare contradict her, despite having planned on hiring a two-seater soft top that would be more in keeping with her curves.

Soleá and Arcángel came to pick Atticus up at eight in the morning that Wednesday. They beeped the truck's horn and blocked the traffic in Calle del Alamillo while they waited for him to come out. The logo on the side of the truck read 'Arcángel Melons, Granada' and inside it smelt like a village fruit shop, not that the Englishman noticed, having never smelt such a thing. Nor had he ever shaken a hand like Soleá's cousin's, with long nails – 'y'know, for playing the guitar' – and hairy fingers.

Arcángel was wearing a black shirt open almost to his navel, and a gold cross the size of an Order of the Garter medal hung from his neck. He was sporting a gold watch, two or three rings, another couple of chains round his neck and pointy shoes. He had skinny legs and wide shoulders, and was about Soleá's age, with a similarly intense gaze and the same manner – at once reserved and outraged, a mixture seemingly only possible in members of their family, who appeared to be both ready to be best friends with anyone and constantly on guard, ever attentive to the slightest insult or lack of respect, ready to flip their lids or come to blows.

117

Atticus reminded himself that he ought to tread carefully if he didn't want to end up in a brawl like the one he had with Soleá the day he met her.

Naturally, the three of them sat in the front of the truck, with Arcángel driving, Atticus by the window and Soleá between them, somewhat squashed between their legs. To the Englishman, such proximity seemed embarrassingly invasive. He wasn't used to having a woman in his personal space. Nor was he used to greeting someone with a pair of noisy kisses, one on each cheek, mouths crossing in the middle, and between kisses, a breath, the smell of flowers. The cousins, meanwhile, would have found it strange to spend the four-hour journey in separate seats. They treated one another with joking familiarity, pinching and slapping, laughing a lot, and sometimes, if there was a lull in the conversation, bursting into song.

'Is that man your father, Arcángel?' Atticus asked, pointing to the photo of an older man, who didn't have many teeth and stared down from a metal frame stuck to the windscreen.

Soleá and her cousin burst out laughing.

'That man is Camarón,' said Arcángel with greater pride than if the photo had actually been of his father. 'There's a CD in the glove box, *niña*,' he told Soleá, 'stick it on.'

Soleá leaned over Atticus's legs to get the CD. Atticus trembled. He was about to lift his hand and stroke her hair, but a weight, heavy as lead, kept his hand firmly pinned to the seat.

She put the radio on, inserted the CD, and the strains of a Spanish guitar cut through the air, followed by the cries of a flamenco singer.

'This is the man in the photo,' said Arcángel.

Then he started singing at the top of his voice, accompanying the singer in his agony. Soleá clapped the rhythm and Arcángel pounded the steering wheel like a drum.

'Don't you sing?' Atticus asked Soleá.

'Badly,' she admitted.

And Atticus, respecting the sudden blush in her cheeks, didn't want to insist.

After a couple of hours, Soleá fell asleep with her head on her cousin's shoulder. They were crossing the Despeñaperros Bridge, the road winding through holm oak woods, when Arcángel suddenly took his eyes off the road and fixed them on Atticus.

'I'm not one to stick my nose in other people's business,' he said, 'but if you touch even a thread of my cousin's clothing,' he threatened, 'I swear to God I'll cut your ears off.'

Atticus swallowed. A tight bend was coming up.

'Please,' he begged, 'keep your eyes on the road, Arcángel. You don't need to worry about me,' he lied with a shaky voice. 'I don't intend to court your cousin.'

'You can court her all you like,' replied Arcángel. 'But if I find out you've touched a centimetre of her skin, listen here: I'll kill you.'

'Understood.'

'You married, *Míster Crasman*?'

'No.'

'Got a girlfriend, *Míster Crasman*?'

'No.'

'Then you can talk to her. That you can do. But no funny business. Is that clear?'

'If I misbehave with Soleá, I'll have you to answer to.'

'Right.'

Once that matter was settled, Arcángel switched his attention back to the road. Camarón continued to sing duets with the truck's owner and Soleá carried on sleeping peacefully and lightly with a smile on her lips.

Chapter 24

At about nine in the evening, having first tried Shakespeare, then Stendhal, then the Brontë sisters, and ending up desperately, but unsuccessfully, seeking refuge in one of Corín Tellado's romantic novels, Berta Quiñones had to admit that some troubles can't be cured with books alone.

This time, she couldn't turn up at Asunción's house and tell her about María's affair. She didn't usually keep secrets from her friend. If it had been any other sort of problem – to do with work, health or loneliness – she would have gone running to pour her heart out to her, but since it was a matter of infidelity it seemed better to keep her worry to herself than spread it to Asunción, who had suffered enough with her own unhappy marriage to start sorting someone else's out. Although they never talked about it, Berta knew that Asunción had to summon enormous courage not to burst out crying every time she remembered her ex-husband and the Iberia air hostess.

In the end, having rejected the option of talking to her best friend, Berta decided to go to Gaby's house to scrounge a cup of tea and some comfort. In Berta's eyes, Gaby and Franklin were the perfect couple. They adored each other.

'Come in, Berta, what a surprise.'

'Is Franklin in?'

'No way. He'll be back really late tonight. He's got a commission for a mural on the entrance to the Naval Museum. You wouldn't believe how good it's looking.'

'All the better, my love, because something bad has happened . . .'

'I can see that. You're pale as a sheet, Berta. Shall I get you a glass of wine?'

The two of them sat on the orange sofa in the living room. The sofa and a blob that looked like squashed fruit – a vinyl on the far wall – were the only touches of colour in the room. Everything else – the shag-pile carpet, the coffee table, the cylindrical standard lamp and the life-size plastic sculpture of a greyhound – was as white as snow.

'Oh, Gaby! This is so horrid that I don't even know how to start telling you about it. I'm sorry to come bursting into your happy life with this.'

'We're all worried, Berta. Atticus Craftsman is probably going to fire us all. We know that. But it's not your fault, these things happen.'

Berta burst out crying.

'That too, what a mess. I swear to you, Gaby, I've been careful, I've never spent more than the magazine can handle. You know yourself the sacrifices we've all made to keep the business going. We haven't allowed ourselves a single luxury, we've been honest, we've tried so hard. And, all the same, it turns out we've done everything wrong. It's horrible. Mr Craftsman spoke to me about debts, ruin, failure in every sense. He says no one reads us, we've got no credibility, no name for ourselves, no prestige. That we're a stain on the Craftsman & Co brand and we're haemorrhaging money.'

Gaby went to get the tissues. The box was white as well.

'I don't get it, Gaby,' Berta confessed. 'It doesn't make any sense.'

'Well, if your conscience is clear, that's the main thing. You'll see it's not such a big deal. It might just be a question of tightening our belts on certain expenses, asking Craftsman to delay his decision and putting our thinking caps on. I can do unpaid overtime, if you like.'

'Thank you, sweetie, you're a gem,' Berta managed to say through her tears. 'The awful thing is I didn't come to talk to you about work, it's something even worse.'

Gaby was taken aback. Her boss didn't usually share her personal problems with her. Their relationship was more like that between a niece and a favourite aunt who never forgets to say happy birthday or send a Christmas present. Berta was a protective, maternal person who you could talk to about your problems, but would never tell anyone about hers.

'Has something happened to Asunción?' Gaby worried, because she knew how close the two women were. If Berta had a personal problem, she would have gone to her best friend first.

'No. Asunción is fine, the poor thing, but I can't ruin her day with this. It's about María.'

'María?'

Berta took a large gulp of her wine to steel herself. Then she launched into the story of how she had caught María in the arms of another man four months ago, on Three Kings morning, to be exact, and how María had later justified her infidelity by saying that she felt trapped in a mundane, unhappy marriage.

'But she promised she would end the affair soon,' Berta said, screwing her face up. 'She swore that the man meant nothing, emotionally speaking, it was only a bit of fun that would last a few days, maybe a month, but afterwards she'd go back to her normal life, with Bernabé and the kids, just like the character from *The Bridges of Madison County*, those were her words, as if her life was a film.'

Gaby said nothing. She squeezed Berta's arm. Sometimes it's better just to listen.

'And today I saw her with the same man again. Four bloody months have gone by, Gaby, and she's still with him.'

'Do you know who he is?'

How strange, thought Berta. No, she didn't know who he was. She had never actually seen his face and it had never occurred to her to ask María his name. She had simply believed what the adulteress said: He's no one, he doesn't have a name, he doesn't have an identity; he's a brief fling, not a real person.

'No.'

'Are you going to talk to her again?'

'Why? So she can lie to me again and tell me I'm seeing things? That what I saw isn't what it looks like and her marriage is back on track?'

'So, what are we going to do?'

'Well, nothing, love, what can we do . . .'

The two of them drank in silence. Women, unlike men, are capable of talking about a problem for hours without trying to find a solution. Not planning the next move, merely talking until their mouths go dry, and their tears stop, and their eyes sting, and the time comes to go home. But they leave with only half the weight of the problem on their shoulders.

'Don't tell anyone,' Berta told Gaby when they said goodbye at the door. 'Let's see what happens. Maybe we'll all be unemployed in a few days anyway, and this mess of María's won't be our business any more.' It was then that Franklin arrived. He was carrying a bunch of orange tulips.

'Where's my princess?' they heard him shout up the stair–well.

Chapter 25

Gaby had never made a mistake in the six years that she had been designing pages for *Librarte*, but for a few days now she had been totally off the ball. Exactly the same few days that had passed since her boss turned up at her house and told her about María's affair.

Asunción had noticed straight away that something had upset the normally level-headed Gaby. Berta had to have words with Gaby several times, sometimes for silly mistakes like forgetting to send the barcode to the printers, rookie errors, and Asunción had caught her off guard, staring at María while she worked away obliviously. A couple of times, María had lifted her head to find Gaby staring at her. 'What?' she had asked. 'Nothing,' Gaby had replied.

On the other hand, Berta, who didn't usually take any notice of what went on outside her office door, now seemed to want to scrutinize everything. She left her door open and craned her neck over her computer, put on her glasses and frowned. Sometimes she cleared her throat, as if trying to warn Gaby that she was watching her, and to tell her not to get distracted, to get back to her work if she didn't want to stay in at playtime. She really did seem like a primary school teacher.

Asunción watched Gaby, Gaby watched María, Berta watched all of them and María watched no one. Some secret or other was hovering over the office and Asunción, astute though she was, came to the wrong conclusion.

The following Monday, after spending the weekend feeling like her heart was melting, she arrived at the office with a small present wrapped in tissue paper.

'Congratulations, Gaby!' she said to her colleague in a shaky voice.

Berta tried to avert disaster by jumping up from her chair with the same agility a real primary school teacher would have demonstrated had she felt the prick of a drawing pin on her bottom. But her effort was in vain. Gaby had taken the gift, was opening it, had already seen the soft ears of the teddy, the first bib, the first dummy. She had already let it fall to the floor – if it had been porcelain it would have broken into a thousand pieces – and had already locked herself in the bathroom to cry. 'But she wasn't even due yet,' said María, who had no idea what was going on, and the damage was already done. Asunción wanted to die of shame.

Chapter 26

According to Sod's law, of all the women of childbearing age in the world, the one who most longs to be a mother will be the one who has most trouble getting pregnant. If there had been one of those University of Wisconsin studies on the level of maternal desire then Gaby would have come out top, scoring much higher than the rest of the women interviewed, including a woman from Maryland who kidnapped a baby with the sole intention of raising it as her own and who would never repent for her actions even if she spent half her life in prison.

The worst thing was that there was no scientific explanation for Gaby's infertility. Apparently, both she and Franklin were fully capable of conceiving numerous healthy babies. At least that's what the exhaustive medical tests to which they had both been subjected in recent years had shown.

Gaby knew the ceiling in her gynaecologist's consulting room like the back of her hand. The doctor, with the good intention of distracting her patients during examinations, had decided to decorate it with photos of the hundreds of babies that she had helped bring into the world. As Gaby lay naked from the waist down with her legs akimbo, waiting anxiously for the results of her latest test, she was scrutinized by Natalia with the chubby cheeks, the twins Rodrigo and Javier, Monica with the sticky-up hair, little round Jorge with his fists clenched, Rosita with the big eyes, red-haired Pedrito and fifty other pudgy little babies whom Gaby had seen so many times that she would instantly recognize them if she saw them in the street. But instead of calming her down, the portfolio of newborns made her feel incredibly, inexpressibly upset. Whenever she lay on the bed, her heart raced, her muscles tensed, her eyes welled up with tears. She preferred to close her eyes and hum a song to distract herself.

'I can't believe you're still scared of examinations,' said the gynaecologist, mistaking all those symptoms for fear of medical instruments.

'I don't mind external ultrasounds,' Gaby confessed, 'but I can't stand the internal ones, Doctor, with that contraption that looks like curling tongs.'

'Open your vagina.'

'How am I supposed to do that?'

'Come now, Gaby, relax, there's no way we can do this if you don't relax.'

And in the end, she always reached the same conclusion:

'Everything's fine. You've got a model uterus, sweetheart. Good enough to put on show, it's in such good shape.'

'Right. What a pity.'

'But it's lovely, really lovely,' said the gynaecologist. 'Your tubes aren't blocked, you don't have endometriosis, your periods are regular, your vaginal mucus—'

'Enough, enough.' Gaby usually cut her off when she couldn't bear to hear any more. 'So, why can't I get pregnant?'

★

129

Franklin Livingstone, on the other hand, would have been perfectly happy without children. For him, nothing compared to the happiness of being with Gaby, but he understood that his wife would never find peace until she had a baby in her arms. He had helped her to paint their future children's room and choose prams, highchairs, dummies and nappies from endless catalogues. He had sat next to her plenty of times while she waited for the negative results of the pregnancy tests she took when her period was more than twenty-four hours late, and had learnt to console her with cups of hot chocolate and spoonfuls of ice cream. And he had managed to convince her that he was every bit as upset as she was, and reassure her that the baby would come in good time, like everyone said.

Out of love for Gaby he had undergone hundreds of medical tests – some of them pretty unpleasant – and had learnt to calculate the days in each cycle that Gaby was fertile, to rush home and love her completely, despite the fact that, sometimes, she forgot to love him back.

'Franklin,' Gaby told him with the utmost urgency one Tuesday at eleven a.m. 'Come home quick, I'm ovulating.'

And he raced home, ran up the stairs two at a time, stripped off in the hallway and found her waiting for him in bed, legs open wide, music on. She asked him to go slowly, to concentrate on the baby, because she had read that conception was a conscious act of willpower, and then she stayed very still, lying on her back for an hour, the way her doctor had recommended, while he got dressed, said goodbye with one last kiss and returned to the trompe l'oeil he had left half-finished in his studio.

Sometimes he let himself think that Gaby had made a mistake marrying him, and this got him down. He hadn't managed to become the well-known artist in whose success she so believed, nor was he the fiery, dreamy lover she had met in Paris, capable of moving mountains, revolutionizing the art world and achieving world fame.

'We'll be like Diego Rivera and Frida Kahlo,' he used to say to her between kisses on the banks of the Seine.

'I hope not,' she replied. 'Frida lost her baby and could never have children. And Diego cheated on her.'

'But they loved each other.'

'I suppose so, in their own way,' she conceded.

'I'll never be unfaithful to you,' Franklin assured her.

'And I'll wax my moustache,' Gaby promised.

Years had gone by: they had loved each other much more deeply than Diego and Frida could ever have dreamed and, all the same, thanks to some cruel twist of fate, they had been unable to conceive a child. No fame, no fortune, no family. In the end, his mother would be proved right: Franklin Livingstone was nothing but a worthless failure. He was no good to anyone, let alone sweet, loving Gaby. Maybe the best thing would be to leave her before it was too late. Open the door of the golden cage, set her free so that she would fly into another man's arms: someone compatible with her genetic code, the acidity of her uterus or whatever it was that was stopping them having children together. If he hadn't left yet it was because deep down Franklin knew that breaking up with Gaby and taking his own life were, essentially, the same terrifying decision.

Chapter 27

One December morning, Moira Craftsman woke up with a start. She had dreamt that a tribe of cannibals had taken her son Atticus prisoner, lowered him into a pot of boiling water and were planning on eating him like a prawn, cooked and pink, while the boy screamed: 'At least toss a few teabags in the stew, you pack of savages!'

As a devoted disciple of Freud, Moira was a compulsive reader of *The Interpretation of Dreams* and was in the habit of asking her friends to let her analyse their dreams, from which she drew the most unexpected conclusions. It was obvious to her that guests at the house in Kent often dreamt of running water, streams and waterfalls because the copper pipes made a tremendous noise when the boiler was on. If it was cold, they tended to dream of polar animals or white objects. If it was hot, they dreamt about aeroplanes not taking off. If they experienced a dizzying sense of speed – scenes that changed constantly, fast thoughts, races, flights, etcetera – she would lay the blame on an empty stomach.

Moira was more cautious when it came to erotic dreams. Desires, fears and inhibitions were all tied up with an individual's private matters, she said, or their sexual history.

'We were making love in front of my stepmother.'

'You lack intimacy.'

'I was sleeping with an elephant.'

'You lack affection.'

'Our dreams expose what is missing from our everyday lives,' she would explain to her rapt audience, 'but they also respond to external stimuli, noises, changes in temperature or recent experiences. For example, following a traumatic experience, or after eating a lot, one is very likely to have nightmares.'

As for the predictive power of dreams, Moira was of the belief that, like all premonitions, only the ones that the dreamer really believed in would come true.

'I dream that I'm falling. The next day there's snow on the ground, and it's icy. I slip. I fall,' she would explain. 'Does that mean that my dream has come true or would I have fallen anyway?'

Moira Craftsman was a sensible woman. But that morning, after dreaming that her son was being cooked alive in a cauldron of tea, she pushed aside all her years of rationality.

'Wake up, Marlow, we're going to Spain!'

It was three weeks until Christmas and they hadn't heard from Atticus since August. However hard Marlow tried to convince her that all was well, that the boy was busy resolving a terribly complicated situation in Madrid and would be home soon enough, Moira suspected that her husband was hiding something from her. Marlow wasn't much of a talker, but the silence to which he had subjected her of late was going beyond a joke. He had even stopped saying good morning to her. He had been getting up in a hurry, jumping in the shower, grumbling something incomprehensible from the bathroom and racing out to the office, without drinking his usual cup of coffee.

He had spent most weekends hunting in Scotland, in the Highlands, as he liked to call those impassable hills upon which roe deer, dogs, pheasants, geese and men all ran amok: some fleeing from others, and others fleeing from their wives and from explanations they didn't want to have to give.

It crossed Moira's mind at one point that Marlow might be having an affair. She soon dismissed such a stupid notion.

No. Any other vice but women. Marlow preferred his club, his brandy, his games of bridge and his hunts. He didn't have the time, or the motivation, to get caught up in an affair at this late stage of the game. Nor did he have any chance to, really. At work Atticus kept an eye on him and elsewhere his friends, mother, wife and the headaches caused by his elder son Holden kept him busy.

But the silence . . .

'Atticus is in danger,' she said that morning, trying to get Marlow to understand. They were still in bed, her hair was a mess and he was in his flannel pyjamas. 'We have to go to Madrid and bring him home as soon as possible.'

'What's got into you, darling?' he managed to stammer, having just woken up from a dream in which he had taken a long run up before jumping and taking off heavily and clumsily, like a goose.

'A mother knows when her child needs help,' Moira said, cutting him off, 'and I can sense that Atticus is in real trouble, Marlow. We have to go and rescue him.'

Marlow sat up against the pillows. He scratched his head. He took his wife's hand.

'I tried to tell you a few days ago, Mo, but you were too tired. You're right, we must go to Spain. There's no other option.'

★

Moira Craftsman immediately sprang into action. She consulted her huge black diary, in which she kept track of all her engagements, and decided there was no way they could go and save Atticus before 15 December. That was ten days away but, unfortunately, back in April she had accepted a dinner invitation from Lord Norfolk for that very Tuesday. What's more, on Thursday they had front-row tickets for the opera, *La Bohème*, bought seven months ago, before they sold out – after all, one has to be prepared. Then, on Sunday, the rector of All Saints College was coming to tea. They couldn't cancel a visit like that at such short notice. It was Monday, only six days until Sunday, if they changed their plans now the rector would crucify them for being so bad-mannered, and he would be entirely justified. And the following Wednesday, Moira had an appointment at the hairdresser's. Religiously, once every two months, she dyed her hair mahogany; otherwise the grey started to show. What's more, cancelling would mean that the hairdresser would have to reorganize her entire schedule and Moira didn't want to be responsible for such chaos.

She also needed to talk to the housekeeper, organize the pantry, pay the suppliers, prepare guest rooms, hire the help for New Year's Eve, sort out the menus, the Christmas tree and the Christmas pudding, and many other things besides.

All told, the earliest they could leave was the fifteenth. And they would have to be back on the twentieth at the very latest because, if not, Christmas would be a complete disaster.

'Marlow and I have to go on an unexpected and urgent trip,' she explained over the phone to Victoria Bestman. 'It's about Atticus. We're worried that something might have happened to him. We haven't heard anything from him since August.'

'Dear God!'

'I'm telling you because I don't think I'll be able to play bridge on the sixteenth. You'll have to find another partner.'

'The sixteenth! That's less than ten days away!'

'I know. It's all happened terribly suddenly, Victoria. I'm awfully sorry, but as I said, it's very urgent. It's about Atticus.'

'Oh, Moira, you poor thing! You must be so worried. I'd come and give you a hug, but as it happens, back in August, I promised I'd help with the fundraising auction for the rectory today . . .'

'I understand, Victoria. An engagement is an engagement. Don't worry. I'll call you when I get back.'

Chapter 28

The journey in Arcángel's truck came to an end shortly before three o'clock. Granada had appeared in two parts; the first was modern and pretty uninteresting, the second, perched on a hill, was embroidered with narrow streets, white houses and stunning views of the Alhambra palace.

To reach El Albaicín they had to negotiate life-threatening hairpin bends and sheer precipices. They arrived at Soleá's family home, got out of the truck and dragged their suitcases to a wooden door in the centre of a stone wall, up which bougainvillea plants clambered.

Atticus had been unable to convince Soleá to stay with him in a charming little hotel that he saw on the way past. She got truly offended, saying she couldn't imagine anything worse than rejecting her mother's and Granny Remedios's hospitality, what an insult, only an Englishman would come up with an idea like that, and Atticus didn't dare contradict her. However, when the two of them were standing at her front door and there was no turning back, Soleá confessed that their visit was going to be a huge surprise for her family.

'What, you didn't tell them we were coming?'

'No, it's better not to tell them anything. More natural.'

Atticus thought about his mother, Moira, and the state she would be in if a guest decided to turn up at her house unannounced. It would throw her entirely, it would drive her up the wall, she would spend months harping on about such a lack of decorum. She would be disorientated, like when you put a twig in the path of an ant and it doesn't know whether to go round it, climb over it or turn around and give up. Bewildered, with nothing firm left to cling to.

But Manuela Heredia, Soleá's mother, turned out to be so unlike Moira Craftsman that Atticus found it very difficult to classify them both as part of the same species: 'mothers'. After hugging and covering her daughter with kisses as if she had been away at war and they had given her up for dead, Manuela set to work on Atticus. Her plump arms wrapped around his neck, her mouth grazed the corners of his lips. It was the closest Atticus had come to rape in his whole life. His own mother would never have smothered him like that, not even when he was a baby.

'Oh, what a joy, what a joy!' Manuela shouted so the whole neighbourhood would know that Soleá was home.

Granny Remedios came to the door, intrigued by all the commotion. She was dressed in black, with some teeth missing and others shining with pure gold, and she repeated and intensified the effusive welcome, adding a few pinches and caresses. She was wearing a white apron speckled with oil and she smelt of flour, onions, and wood smoke.

'What did you say your name was? Tico, was it?' she christened him as soon as she released him from her welcoming hug.

They went through to the courtyard garden and got tangled in the vines and branches of lemon trees, tripped over the potted geraniums, and met a grey cat and a yellow canary, before climbing up tiled steps to a door flanked by two huge old terracotta jars, like a pair of riot police armed to the teeth.

Inside, in the bustling half–light, there were more people: three cousins, two uncles, a drunk, Soleá's sisters, her brother Tomás, Arcángel's mother who had come to borrow some salt and ended up staying for lunch, three or four noisy and quarrelsome children, and another old woman identical to Remedios who was called Dolores. The table was already laid with ceramic plates, and laden with a big pot of food, roast goat, tomatoes with olive oil, potatoes with olive oil; those people even put olive oil on the olives – fat, green, wild olives – and they drank wine with fizzy pop: 'Why would you want water? Water's for toads, or there's Coca-Cola, if you prefer, because you're a gringo, if you'll pardon the expression. But you are really gringo. I hope the salt cod doesn't disagree with your gringo stomach, *míster.*'

And the television was on, turned up loud in one corner of the room, like a painting that no one looks at but which exists and its simply existing is enough. What's a house without a TV? And a sofa. And a narrow staircase leading to a room with an iron bedstead with a wire base, covered with a crocheted blanket – 'my mother made that' – and photos stuck to the walls, a pine window frame, dolls in frilly dresses lined up on the bench, the grandmother's wardrobe, a collection of fans. 'You'll sleep up here, *míster,* get out of here *niño,* go on, or you'll get a clip round the ear, this is *Míster Crasman*'s room.'

'Rest a while, *Míster Crasman,* because tonight there's *jarana.*'

'What's *jarana?*'

★

139

Soleá had stayed downstairs, sitting at the table, where she was laughing more than Atticus had seen any girl laugh in a long time, telling her sisters the latest news from Madrid. Her Madrid was merely an extension of El Albaicín, with the same names and the same faces, because many young people had left Granada and now lived in the outskirts of Madrid.

'But if your mother and your grandmother didn't know we were coming,' Atticus had protested at the door, 'they probably haven't made food for us, and they won't have got a room ready for me. We should find a little hotel instead . . .'

'Look, *Míster Crasman*,' Soleá had replied with her hands on her hips, 'I don't know how you do things in England, but here in Granada we don't put too much thought into laying the table. We bring out the stew, the pot of noodles, the meat or whatever there is, and if there are ten people, then ten, if there are fifteen, then fifteen, and we eat. And there's always enough to go round.'

Atticus made himself a cup of tea with water from the tap, drank it in one gulp, lay on the bed and thought that he would be home very soon. As soon as he managed to persuade Granny Remedios that what she kept hidden in a drawer was a treasure, a find worthy of being declared World Heritage.

He would have to choose his words extremely carefully, he said to himself, and then he fell asleep and dreamt that a tribe of cannibals were lowering him into a pot of boiling water.

A while later, Soleá tiptoed upstairs and pressed her ear against the door behind which Atticus was snoring like a bear. When she felt confident that he was sleeping deeply enough for her to call Berta without him hearing, she dialled the number for *Librarte* and waited.

'Berta?' she said quietly, pressing the mobile to her ear. 'It's Soleá. Just to let you know that so far, everything's going according to plan. We're at my mum's house.'

'Well done, darling!' whispered her boss in response. 'Go on, tell me everything.'

Chapter 29

Following the raid at number 5, Calle del Alamillo, Inspector Manchego began to harbour the uncomfortable suspicion that his accomplice, the locksmith, had pulled the wool right over his eyes. After his quick search that night, another one was arranged in which several officers from the theft department participated, and they confirmed that the flat contained no fingerprints apart from Craftsman's, Señora Susana's and those belonging to Manchego himself. Not a trace of Lucas.

What's more, the inspector had spent a few days trying to get hold of his accomplice on his mobile and the only answer he got was from a robot assuring him that the number he had dialled was not in service.

The pieces of the puzzle had fallen into place of their own accord. Everything fitted.

Firstly: the supposed locksmith didn't have a clue how to open a door silently, which indicated that, in all probability, he wasn't a bloody locksmith.

Secondly: the circumstances in which they had met, casually, in the street, one drunken night, and that scrap of paper with his name and phone number with no other details to link him to an address or a real identity made Manchego think he wasn't even called Lucas, nor would he have any way to find him once he destroyed the SIM card, which he had probably already done.

Thirdly: the guy was clever. He had got Manchego properly tied up, because now he couldn't investigate the case without dropping himself in it for searching without a warrant and using a standard-issue weapon off-duty, as well as making himself look absolutely ridiculous.

When he reached this conclusion, Manchego decided to launch a second line of inquiry, one that would be secret, personal and probably related to the Craftsman case but would never appear in the file. The issue, which the inspector dubbed 'Dossier X', would consist of unravelling Lucas's true identity and discovering what connected him with number 5, Calle del Alamillo. For the moment he wouldn't say anything to Marlow Craftsman about this line of investigation because it was entirely possible that Lucas was involved in something unconnected with the Craftsman case – for example, that the flat, which had been empty for months, was being used as a base to store or deal drugs.

Since he couldn't think of any other way to get new information that would put him on the scent, he decided to arrange a second meeting with Berta Quiñones, the editor of *Librarte*, because she was apparently the only element that linked Mr Craftsman and the Calle del Alamillo flat.

In their first meeting, she had struck him as smarter than she let on. She knew when to keep quiet and spoke with carefully measured words. Such that, at one point during their conversation, the inspector had even suspected that she might have been hiding something.

'So, you have no idea where *Míster Crasman* might be?' he had asked her, his eyes firmly fixed on hers.

Those eyes, as dark as the bottom of a well, like the eyes of a nocturnal bird, and clearly short-sighted, had seemed strangely familiar. They had stuck in his prodigious photographic memory, about which he liked to brag to his friends − 'I never forget a face' − and had been saved on the hard disk of his shrewd detective's brain, where his subconscious had decided to store every face he saw on the off chance he needed it to solve a future case.

On this occasion, Berta was alone when she greeted him at her small office on Calle Mayor, gone eight in the evening.

'I told the girls to go home,' she explained as she served him tea in a porcelain cup. 'They're already worked up enough, what with Mr Craftsman's disappearance and all the questioning. I hope you'll forgive me, Inspector, for saying that your methods are a bit heavy-handed. You've got us all worried, thinking that we're on your list of suspects.'

'For the moment there is no such list, Ms Quiñones.'

'Please, call me Berta.'

'Berta.'

'I assume you've come to tell me about the break-in at Señora Susana's flat?'

'You already know?'

'Of course, Inspector.'

'Call me Manchego.'

'Manchego.'

They took a sip of the Earl Grey that Atticus Craftsman had left behind in the office kitchen. It was very hot, and strong. It proved very comforting for a cold November night.

'Forgive me for saying so, Manchego, but it seems a very odd coincidence that you happened to be passing by at the exact time of the break-in.'

'I see.'

'The thing is, I don't much believe in coincidences, you know?' Berta went on. 'I've always been one of those people who think things happen for a reason. A few years ago I read a book that said just that. For example, it's no coincidence that you've been put on this case, or that we've met, or that we're here drinking tea right now.'

'Oh, really?'

'According to the book, no. Our meeting,' Berta explained, 'is part of a universal plan. It's necessary for both of us that this should be happening. Do you understand? Perhaps I've got an important role to play in your destiny or you in mine.'

Manchego placed his cup back on the saucer and looked up. His eyes met Berta's for a moment. Once again they seemed familiar. Like a long-forgotten dream. Like a lost memory.

'The thing is,' said the inspector, 'you remind me of someone.'

'What nonsense!' Berta replied, blushing. 'What's happened is you've been influenced by my words. It's like Merton's self-fulfilling prophecy. Do you know what I mean?'

'Um, no.'

For the next few minutes, Berta gave a detailed breakdown of Robert K. Merton's work and Manchego listened carefully without interrupting, simply so that he could take a couple of sips of tea. He didn't make much of an effort to understand the theory that Berta was so passionately describing, but he did take in a few words and ideas that seemed intriguing.

'It's an interesting theory,' the inspector said finally. 'And you're a very knowledgeable woman, Berta.'

'Don't kid yourself,' she replied, flattered. 'I'm just a country girl. I come from a small town in the Cameros hills.'

'Me too!' said Manchego in surprise, opening his eyes as wide as dinner plates.

'Ortigosa,' she said.

'Nieva!' he replied.

All of a sudden, the case had taken a 180-degree turn. Berta and Manchego stood up and each saw their surprise reflected in the other. They were about to hug and jump for joy, but they held back. In the end they simply laughed like two teenagers as they looked each other up and down, each trying to see through the image they had in front of them – she, a plumpish mature woman; he, a big stocky man prone to a belly – to a corresponding image from their shared youth. The only thing they could rescue from that time was the same glimmer in the eyes and the same curve of a smile.

'I was sure I knew you from somewhere,' the inspector almost shouted, addressing Berta with the informal 'tú' for the first time without realizing. 'You're the girl from the balcony. Across from the telegraph office. With glasses and plaits. I went around looking for you for months.'

'Looking for me?'

'Yes,' said Manchego. 'That's why your name seemed familiar: Berta Quiñones, I'd almost forgotten it. The theft from the post office in your village was my first case. I'd just graduated from the police academy and they put me on the case because I was from the area. It turned out that you were the most likely witness of the robbery. You were always watching the house.'

'A lot of water has passed under the bridge since then,' said Berta.

'I never found you,' the inspector went on. 'But in the

146

end the case solved itself. With the help of the man who ran the post office, who was, of course, the father of the girl who ran away with her boyfriend and the money – I don't know if you heard about that.'

'I did hear something, yes,' Berta replied. 'But it was five years after I'd left home. I was living in Madrid. Studying Philology. In the end I wouldn't have been much help.'

The tea was getting cold. Manchego lifted the cup to his lips once more, out of habit and to clear his throat, but this time the brew was bitter and disappointing. He screwed up his nose and forced himself to swallow. He coughed.

'Berta . . .' And she was surprised when she heard him say: 'What would you say if I invited you to dinner?'

Chapter 30

The San Miguel market seemed to Berta like the ideal place for a casual dinner. It was the perfect distance away, a short walk from the office, so they wouldn't have to get into the police car that was waiting on the corner with another officer behind the wheel. It would have been awkward to get into the back seat, where you sit when you've been arrested, and explain to Manchego's colleague that instead of taking them to the station he should drop them at a cosy little restaurant for a table for two, candlelight and giggling conversation.

What better place than the old market where you ate standing up, picking at morsels like sparrows, moving from table to table. Some Serrano ham here, some *croquetas de cocido* there, some mussels au gratin here, half a bottle of red wine there.

Berta and Manchego sat down on tall stools in front of a bar covered with tapas, their feet on the brass footrest as if they were ready to do a runner at any moment.

Neither of them ate out much. They both liked the odd drink with friends or a game of cards after work, and then it was home, alone, to their pyjamas and slippers, TV or a book, a toasted sandwich, cold sheets, a pee, the Lord's Prayer, and a touch of insomnia in the middle of the night.

'I solved a mystery once as well,' boasted Berta between laughs. 'It was terrifying. Shall I tell you about it?'

'Go on.'

'Well, I must have been ten or twelve. I was at home alone. It was completely dark out and I was in bed, waiting for my parents to come home so I could stop worrying and go to sleep, when all of a sudden I heard someone at the door. I went to the window but couldn't see anyone, so I went back to bed. But a few seconds later there was another knock. This time I got out of bed and threw myself down on the floor. I crawled to the attic window and stayed very still, waiting for someone to knock again. Then, petrified, I saw the knocker lift on its own and hit the door without anyone touching it.'

'How strange.'

'Of course I thought it was a ghost. What else could it be? It couldn't be the wind because the knocker was made of iron. My heart was in my mouth. I was only young, and I was all alone . . . So I grabbed an old porcelain jug, the kind people used to use for washing, with its dish and everything, and when the knocker lifted I threw it out of the window to see if I could hit the head of the ghost or the invisible man or whatever joker was trying to scare me.'

'You were a very brave girl.'

'Not at all. I was a real coward, I wouldn't even dare run in front of the fire bull at the village fiestas. I used to go up to the club's balcony to watch it from safety and the other kids called me a chicken.'

'Let me guess,' interrupted the inspector, instinctively grabbing her by the arm. 'Say no more. May I solve the case using deduction and logic?'

'Like Sherlock Holmes?'

'Or like Agent Grissom, from *CSI*.'

'Go on, then.'

'Let's see,' Manchego cleared his throat. 'First off, yours was the first house in the village, right?'

'Yes.'

'And there were allotments on the opposite side of the road, if I'm not mistaken.'

'Uh huh.'

'And your parents were out in the square.'

'And I was home alone. Terrified.'

'And you were easily scared.'

'I'll admit to that.'

'And the other kids used to make fun of you.'

'Sometimes.'

'Then, case closed,' said Manchego smugly. 'It only took a minute, miss. The conclusion is as follows: some sneaky little kid had tied a thread to the knocker and was pulling it from where he was hiding in the allotment across the road. Am I right?'

Berta's eyes opened as wide as saucers. She lifted her wine glass and clinked it against the inspector's.

'Congratulations,' she said. 'It took me a while to figure out what was going on. I didn't just throw the jug, I threw a bucket of hot water, a wooden stool and two pairs of shoes. I only realized there was a thread when I threw a blanket and it hung there as if it was on a washing line.'

They laughed like two schoolchildren at break time. They reminisced about growing up in the shadow of the same hills, eating the same wild strawberries and dodging the same cows on the same tracks, spending winters frozen to death, slipping down cobbled streets and taking dips in the same river in summer, fishing for tadpoles in freezing cold ponds and snoozing under the same oak trees, eating fish stew and drinking from a *porrón*, buying warm bread and frothy milk. They had watched the same bus go past and shared the hope of one day climbing aboard and going off to see the world, although the known world extended only as far as Logroño and beyond that there were unimaginable dangers. They had used words from their villages without blushing, words that they themselves had censored in their new lives in Madrid, where they were both considered cultured or clever, but where in fact no one's provincial roots were judged because there was no one in the whole city who hadn't been born in a village they secretly longed for.

When Inspector Manchego got home, after walking Berta back to her flat on the infamous Calle del Alamillo, he realized that tonight, for the first time in ages, he had gone back to being the boy from Nieva de Cameros who wanted to be a policeman more than anything else.

And that he had managed it.

He flashed a satisfied smile at himself in the mirror and promised that the next time they had dinner he would definitely ask Berta about the locksmith Lucas and his possible connection to the Craftsman case. Then he realized that it would be, unofficially, the third date, and he wondered whether he should perhaps start trying to remember how to kiss a woman.

'Hey, Manchego,' Berta had asked him before they said goodbye with a firm handshake and a timid goodnight, 'do you remember what the guy who robbed the post office was called?'

'Rubén something,' he'd replied.

'Almost!' she'd shouted without meaning to. 'And how about you? What's your name?'

'Alonso.'

'Wow! Like Don Quixote!'

Chapter 31

The Pirate definitely knew how to kiss.

You could say that César Barbosa had been born for that. For getting just the right kind of kiss for each woman. Shy, brazen, rude, playful . . . He enjoyed getting the ladies going with this God-given gift of his.

In María's case, the first kiss had been the cautious kind, one that tiptoed up to her mouth, gently stroked her lips and then waited a while for a response before moving in for the kill. His hands were on her waist, ready to descend to her hips and finally to her buttocks. He worked his legs between the seams of her skirt, leant the weight of his shoulders against her body, his stubble scraping against her cheek, before checking that the first battle had been won, that she had closed her eyes and was waiting. Then, yes, it was war, his tongue moved like a wild animal freed from a cage, writhing, clawing, ripping, becoming master of space, time, air and light.

It was a memorable kiss, that first one, against the wall of the San Ginés church, not far from the office. César had left his helmet on the seat of his motorbike: they had been for a spin, as if they were twenty, as if María was even younger and had just finished sixth form for the day, carrying folders and books, her boyfriend picking her up at the gate then saying goodbye outside her house. But they weren't twenty, they were thirty-five, and she had a husband, three children, a home, a shopping list and a heavy conscience.

At first, María swore to herself that her fling with Barbosa wouldn't last more than a weekend: the one weekend of the year she wasn't with Bernabé because he went to Zamora to see his mother. His mother couldn't stand the sight of María because she thought she had trapped her son into marriage, when he had such a promising future ahead of him. Well, Sunday went and Monday came and César Barbosa turned up at the *Librarte* office with a new invoice and a new invitation.

So they started seeing each other in secret, in a quiet little hotel, at lunchtime. Two or three times a week, if not more. And stupidly, stupidly, somehow nine months had gone by since that first cautious kiss.

Gaby was the first one to notice María's swollen lip because she sat directly opposite her, their desks up against one another, and because since her conversation with Berta she hadn't been able to take her eyes off her. She wasn't watching her: she was scrutinizing her. Gaby would *never* cheat on Franklin Livingstone. Not for all the tea in China.

'Asunción, have you seen María's lip?'

Asunción had apologized to Gaby so many times for putting her foot in it with the bib and the dummy that if she went any further it would be public self-flagellation. She had given Gaby flowers, sweets, presents, apologies, hugs, tears . . . Of course, Gaby had accepted Asunción's apology immediately. 'You poor thing,' she had consoled her, 'how were you to know what was going on? We should have told you from the start, it's our fault, don't cry.' Then Gaby and Berta had told Asunción everything, as tactfully as they could: María is cheating on Bernabé, has been for nine months, look how calm she is, and to cap it all she says it's for his own good.

'Her lip?' said Asunción as she appeared at the kitchen door, after Gaby had sent a discreet email and arranged to meet her by the coffee machine.

'Look at her, she looks like Angelina Jolie.'

Asunción had to admit that Gaby was right. Berta hadn't spotted anything. Her head had been in the clouds for the last few days. She was flustered and distracted. The girls put it down to her worrying about the situation with *Librarte*, although they'd noticed that now and again she would suddenly lift her eyes from the computer screen to the window, sigh and smile.

'Well, it is swollen,' replied Asunción. 'Shall we ask what happened?'

'Don't you dare,' said Gaby. 'It must be a bite.'

'From who? Her lover?'

'Who do you think? Bernabé won't have bitten her, will he? You don't start biting someone just like that, after fifteen years of unhappy marriage.'

'Unless it's one of those domestic violence bites.' It was Berta, however, who was first to spot María's black eye, when she opened the office door to find María in floods of tears. There was no way Berta could fail to notice that.

They gave María an ice pack and a glass of water, sat her down in the rocking chair in Berta's office and waited in silence for María to tell them that César Barbosa was, in fact, the most hateful son of a bitch ever to walk the Earth.

'And what am I supposed to say to Bernabé now?' María sobbed into her hands.

'Tell him I hit you!' Asunción volunteered. 'By accident, of course,' she added, immediately regretting her outburst.

The affair had started to turn nasty when María decided to tell the Pirate that Mr Craftsman had come to Spain to close the magazine down and sack them all. This news, which after all didn't really have anything to do with Barbosa, had made him so furious that that same night, on the terrace of the taco place on Calle del Alamillo, he'd slapped María in the face. He had cruelly berated her for not being able to keep that job, or any other. She was stupid, he said, and worthless.

She had agreed with him.

The slap had hurt. But what hurt more was realizing that she had become a burden for Barbosa and fearing she might lose him. What could she offer him? She wasn't a young woman with an irresistible body any more, nor was she a rich, interesting, mature woman who could indulge his fantasies. She was nothing more than a desperate housewife, a shoddy Francesca who hadn't been able to put a stop to the intense relationship and had let it grow until it became an addiction. If César Barbosa left her, María would lose her centre of gravity. If she lost her job as well, that might be the end of her.

Since that first slap, there had been quite a few more times when the Pirate had turned on her like a snake after making love and bitten her. Other times he only threatened her, saying that one day he was going to kill her, and sometimes he starting killing her little by little, hitting her, scratching her, so she felt her soul slipping out through her wounds like air from a punctured balloon.

She said he was right to hit her. She told Barbosa she deserved it and told Bernabé she had signed up for self-defence classes.

But the beating he gave her that afternoon was the worst. They met in their usual hotel, she undressed and he sprang at her, knocking her back against the mattress of that anonymous bed. Then he struggled with his own urgency until he left her defeated between the sheets. Finally, he got dressed, jeans first, belt, pointy boots, and started hitting her with clenched fists. Her back was covered in bruises, her face was a mess, her skin was torn.

'You have to report him immediately,' said Berta. 'I'm going to call Inspector Manchego so he can come and see you before your wounds heal.'

'No, please, no, God, no!' María begged. 'Anything so long as Bernabé doesn't find out.'

'Bernabé doesn't need to know,' Berta replied. 'But that animal has to be locked up.'

'No, Berta, please,' said María, in floods of tears. 'I don't want to turn him in. It's my fault.'

María begged her three colleagues so hard to keep the secret that in the end they had no choice but to bend to her will. If she didn't want to report him, there was nothing they could do about César Barbosa.

'But,' said Berta, 'if that scumbag dares to show his filthy face around here, I'll throw a paperweight right at his head.'

'And I'll throw the scissors,' added Asunción.

María called Bernabé and told him that because Soleá was away she urgently had to go and cover Barcelona's week of culture and wouldn't be back for four days. Bernabé asked if he could drop the kids off at the office after school. She said yes and left with Berta, who had invited her to stay at her place while she recovered.

Chapter 32

And what's eating you?' Asunción asked Gaby as soon as María and Berta had left.

Asunción's ability to pay heed to several bleeding hearts at once was truly remarkable. In the midst of everything that had just happened, as well as concentrating on the mess María was in, she had been watching Gaby out of the corner of her eye and noticing how downcast and unusually silent she was. Although Gaby was naturally curious, she hadn't said a word during the whole conversation. She had stayed to one side, like a UN observer, not asking questions or making any comments, head down and somewhat distracted, letting herself be pulled along and feigning an interest that she didn't really feel.

'What do you mean, what's eating me?' Gaby said with a start.

'Something's up. Don't try and fob me off, I know you.'

Then Gaby crumbled.

Asunción bit her tongue and regretted having stuck her nose in where she wasn't wanted. Each person's life is their own, Asunción, how naïve can you be, you only just finished clearing up the fallout from the pregnancy thing and now you've put your big fat foot in it again.

After an age of tears and apologies, Gaby managed to tell her between sobs that Franklin wanted to go back to Argentina.

'Then go with him, silly,' Asunción replied. 'The timing couldn't be better, love. You're about to lose your job, you're free, you don't have kids to tie you to Madrid. What's stopping you?'

'Franklin's stopping me. He says he wants to go alone.'

'Without you?'

'Yes, without me. In our case, "alone" means without me.'

The bombshell had dropped that very morning before she left for the office. Like every other day of their shared life, Franklin had got up first, turned on the grill to make toast, made coffee, heated milk and gone back to bed to wake Gaby up with a good-morning kiss.

And he had found her crying.

She told him she had dreamt about her baby. They were tears of happiness because she was sure it was a premonition and her body clearly knew that soon, really soon, she was going to get pregnant. After hugging him, still crying, she told him how much she loved him.

'And then, Franklin, just like that, goes and says: "Look, princess, I think the best thing for both of us is if I go back to Argentina."'

'But how can that be the best for both of you!'

'That's what I said, Asunción. What the fuck was he on about?'

Franklin Livingstone knew that his future in Argentina, far away from Gaby, would consist of a cold, lonely street, two or three cardboard boxes, a bottle of cheap booze and a kind of slow, painful living death plagued with memories that would end up merging with his drunken dreams. But he also knew that the time had come to leave Gaby so that she could become a mother.

He cried as well.

'Are you two bloody crazy?' Asunción burst out, emboldened after María's dressing-down. 'I've never met a couple so in love as you and Franklin. You could be peacefully enjoying your love, but instead you spend all your time looking for problems where there aren't any. You want children? Then adopt them, sweetie, the world's full of babies in need of parents who'll love them. Do you think that there's only one way to have a child? No, for goodness' sake, there are all sorts of ways. My Aunt Paca, for example, who's happily single, looked after me and my brothers when our parents died. That was the end of her peace and quiet. And she's been a wonderful second mother to us, even though she never planned to start a family.'

'But I don't want to have just any old babies,' replied Gaby. 'I want to have Franklin's babies.'

'They will be Franklin's, Gaby, as well as yours. They'll have his mannerisms and habits. Even an Argentinian accent, silly.'

Gaby's tears dried up. She got up from the chair, gave Asunción a big kiss and went out in search of Franklin Livingstone, the love of her life.

Asunción turned off all the lights in the office, unplugged the printer and poured the coffee down the sink. Without a shadow of a doubt, the working day was over. It was 10.30 a.m. and there was nothing to do. How quickly children grow up, she sighed, and then remembered that in a couple of days it was her sons' little half-sister's birthday. She should go to El Corte Inglés and buy her a doll like the ones she used to love when she was a girl. 'Tell her it's from her Aunty Asunción, who sends lots of love,' she would say to them as usual, secretly longing for the day when her ex-husband and his new wife would split up, as she was sure would happen sooner or later, so she could take care of the little one on alternate weekends: she knew how incapable her ex-husband would be of looking after a girl.

Chapter 33

One of Soleá's cousins – she called him a 'cousin', although Atticus was starting to suspect that the term was more symbolic than it was representative of actual relationships between clan members – ran a business in the Sacromonte neighbourhood. It was a flamenco show for tourists, staged in one of the whitewashed caves that riddled the hillside. The cave was suitably fitted out with a small dance floor and little wooden tables painted green with flowers.

'My great-grandparents used to live here,' explained Soleá as she showed her boss round the cave. 'They had fifteen children, nine survived and Granny Remedios was the eldest. At the back was the fire, in the middle they had the sleeping mats and there was no water. They carried it up in containers, the ones my mother has either side of the door, on the back of a donkey, from the river, up and down, down and up, all day long. He was called Jenaro.'

'Your great-grandfather?'

'No! The donkey!' Soleá laughed out loud.

She hadn't stopped laughing since they got to Granada. She was like a plant whose roots had tapped into an underground pool and was now blossoming.

'Jenaro lived with them for fifteen years,' she went on. 'All the kids played with him; most of all Granny Remedios, who loved him like a person, you know? And one day Jenaro got too old and was no good for carrying water any more, so my great-grandfather swapped him for a younger donkey. So the story goes, some merchants were passing through with wagons on their way to Madrid and they made a deal: they would trade a donkey for a donkey and some goats and I don't know what else. So, my granny, the poor thing, cried her eyes out for her dear Jenaro and wouldn't have anything to do with the new donkey, which was as black as tar.'

While she talked, Soleá brushed strands of hair away from her face. Atticus walked beside her, over a metre away, in case any of her cousins got suspicious, and tried hard to keep up with Soleá on the steep path. The sun was beginning to set, casting light the colour of pale terracotta, or a Gypsy's skin, over the Alhambra.

'The new donkey was really clever. So clever that it learnt the way to the river without anyone having to show it. My great-grandfather was chuffed to bits for getting such a good deal. And then one afternoon there was a heavy rainstorm, with thunder and lightning and everything, and the donkey was caught in it halfway back from the river.' Here Soleá paused for dramatic emphasis. 'My grandmother spotted him from the top bend in the path and saw that black dye was dripping off the donkey! Old Jenaro was underneath the new donkey! The traders had sold him back to his owner!'

'It was the same donkey?'

'Exactly the same one, *Míster Crasman*, Jenaro himself.'

Soleá paused to draw breath. She pulled her hair into a high bun. She fixed it in place with two hairpins and then carried on up with the wind in her face, her back to the golden Alhambra and Atticus Craftsman breathlessly following her.

'Is that funny?' he asked shyly.

'Of course it's funny. My family have spent fifty years laughing at that story.'

'Can I laugh, even though I'm not from your family?'

Soleá stared him in the eyes. She thought carefully about her answer and finally said:

'Better not.'

Soleá's brother Tomás, her cousin Arcángel and Potaje, who ran the business, were waiting for them at the entrance to the cave, all three with their hands on their hips.

The tourist buses were starting to appear at the end of the road. Atticus hurriedly said hello to the three men and, guided by Soleá, went backstage to where the dancers, who were none other than Soleá's sisters and cousins, had put on their flamenco dresses and clipped carnations into their hair.

Granny Remedios's sister, Dolores, was waiting in her throne-like seat at the back of the stage, and next to her were two empty seats, both with Spanish guitars leaning up against them. She wore her hair in a large bun, with a huge flower, and earrings so big that they looked as if they were about to drop off her ears.

The corner that served as a dressing room was separated from the main area by silk curtains. Atticus and Soleá settled in to watch the show from there, elbow to elbow, sharing a jug of wine with lemon and ice.

About twenty Japanese tourists took their seats in the front rows; behind them, some noisy Americans and, at the back, three or four other couples. In less than ten minutes the room was full to bursting.

'Borrachita is dancing tonight,' Soleá told him. 'Poor

thing, she's always wasted; has been ever since she was a girl.'

A middle-aged woman stumbled into the centre of the stage and clacked some castanets with skill that Atticus admired. Then she began dancing, very gracefully, but Soleá shook her head sadly and started whispering to her cousins.

'She used to be on the street, y'know,' she whispered in Atticus's ear.

Then the younger women came out. The Japanese shouted, 'Ole, ole!' and took photos with their digital cameras.

Aunt Dolores shouted and clapped to cheer them on. They came into the dressing room, changed their dresses, don't look, *míster*, and went out with different flowers, different shoes, different fierce looks.

The show ended a couple of hours later. The tourists left, satisfied, and Atticus got up to go home.

'Where are you going, *Míster Crasman?*' Soleá said in surprise. 'This is when the *jarana* really starts, as soon as the last gringo has left, if you'll pardon the expression.'

It was midnight.

Potaje locked the door and everyone moved the seats to the sides. Arcángel grabbed the guitar and moved into the centre. He played.

This time Atticus felt a strange magic spreading through his body and taking hold of him. Potaje struck the *cajón* and toothless Aunt Dolores chanted a spell: a youthful spirit thrust her forward into the space. She danced.

The girls let their hair down and formed a group in the middle of the stage, surrounding the old woman. They all moved their hands like glow worms as they danced. You could feel the blood beating round their bodies from their heads to their toes, while a group of guys led by Tomás feasted on them with their eyes, their hands, their mouths.

165

Atticus couldn't take his eyes off those writhing waists and the legs that sometimes escaped from the frills of their skirts. Ankles, sweat, heaving chests, smooth hair cascading down backs. Clapping hands, stamping heels, the grandmother's keening song, the beat of the guitar. Little by little, the cave filled with other men and women, other guitars and other echoes, until the air became hard to breathe.

After what felt like an eternity under some kind of hypnosis, Atticus realized that Soleá wasn't by his side. He sought her with his gaze and found her in a dark corner of the cave. A young man was closing in on her, and she was letting him. He put a strong arm round her waist, she flung her head back. He leant in to say something in her ear, she laughed, lifted her hand to his mouth, blew him a kiss.

And Atticus Craftsman, bewitched by the dark arts of the cave's music, felt the urge to kill that man with his bare hands.

He went outside. He breathed in the fragrant air of the Sacromonte hillside. The heady scent of jasmine turned his stomach. Then he saw the sun rising on the other side of the hill. Dawn had caught him unawares. He didn't know the way back to Soleá's house, so he lay down to sleep by the side of the road, next to a yellow rubbish bin, like a true drunk, muttering curses on all the women on Earth.

When he woke up, he discovered Granny Remedios's toothless smile a few centimetres from his face.

'Good morning, *míster*,' she said with a naturalness that didn't square with it being four in the afternoon. 'Your stew's getting cold.'

Atticus suppressed the urge to vomit. He got up as best he could and recognized the room, his room, with its collection of fans and dolls in flamenco dresses. The rest of the family were spread about the house. The table was

166

laid, the kids were squealing in the courtyard, the girls were chatting by the window, Tomás was snoozing on a sofa and Soleá was smiling at him out of the shadows. He imagined her sharing her bed with one of those exotic-looking men, making love to him with a passion only comparable to that shown onstage by her cousins, those three felines.

'I'm pleased to see you, *Míster Crasman*,' she said jokingly. 'It looks like you survived your first night in Granada.'

'Good morning, Soleá,' he replied.

'My brother Tomás brought you back,' she explained. 'He found you lying in the street and talking English. Bravo!'

'What was I saying?'

'No one knows. I'm the only one here who speaks any English and I was already in bed.'

Atticus started daydreaming about seeing her asleep.

'I'm so ashamed . . .' he began, but Soleá put her hand over his mouth.

'Shush,' she said. 'Don't beat yourself up because you had fun. Y'know what we say here? No one can take away last night's dancing!'

They sat at the table a long while after lunch, digesting slowly. When evening came, Soleá took Atticus out for a walk, leading him as if he was a pet dog, guided by the wind in her hair, through the old streets of El Albaicín. She told him stories about her family, gradually sharing more. When they got to the San Miguel viewpoint, she stopped by his side, facing the Alhambra, and took a deep breath.

'So,' she said, 'it's time to think about the plan.'

'What plan?' Atticus had lost all notion of time and space.

'*Míster Crasman*, what plan do you think? The plan to convince my granny to let us see the poems!'

'Oh, yes! That plan.'

Atticus hadn't thought about any kind of strategy. The

matter seemed simple: he would present his credentials to the old lady and make her an offer she couldn't refuse. He had imagined that his visit to Granada would consist of sitting down for a couple of hours of formal negotiation, shaking hands and then beating a polite but hasty retreat.

However, things had changed radically since he had arrived at Soleá's house. The spirit of *el duende*, the mysterious imp everyone talked about, had seized control of his will to such a degree that he was starting to doubt his true intentions. In the time he had spent there, he had felt like he was being dragged from one scene to another, unable to intervene in the main plot, and, in some way, he had come to the conclusion that the real treasure wasn't the Lorca poems, it was the blood that ran through those people's veins.

It was 30 May, and Atticus Craftsman, standing in front of the Alhambra palace, understood that up to that moment he had only been sampling flavours with the tip of his tongue and now he wanted to eat the whole dish. Mop the sauce up with bread, lick his fingers, clean the plate.

'The first thing,' he said, 'will be to buy myself a Spanish guitar.'

Chapter 34

Berta didn't have a guest room at her tiny flat on Calle del Alamillo, so María had to make do with sleeping on the sofa, although she was wrapped in the finest linen sheets and covered with a mohair blanket that her boss had bought especially for the occasion, out of maternal instinct, at a homeware shop they came across on the walk home.

Despite having eaten the bowl of hot soup and the potato tortilla that Berta made for her while she had a hot bath, with aromatic candles and relaxing oil, María was still trembling with cold. Her teeth chattered and her joints ached. She bundled herself up in the blanket even more and hugged the pillow as if it was a life jacket and she was on the point of drowning at the bottom of a freezing cold lake.

Berta sat on the sofa beside her. So far, neither of them had wanted to start the conversation they both knew was inevitable. It had all been kind words and good intentions, a mug of warm milk, cotton pyjamas, a bit of classical music and a few tears of thanks and shame.

'So, César Barbosa,' Berta finally said, to break the ice and get a bit of warmth flowing.

María could do nothing but nod, her hands clutching the mug of milk and her eyes fixed on the carpet.

'What a scoundrel,' Berta went on. 'I had him sussed the day he walked into the office with that stubble and that dirty jacket, the tattoo, the tough-guy look and the motorcycle helmet. I really don't know what you see in men like him when it's clear as day that they have no good intentions.'

'Because you're clever, Berta,' María turned on her, 'and that's why you've been single your whole life.'

'Better alone than in bad company,' Berta replied, somewhat put out. 'I hope you'll call the whole thing off now.'

'It's not that easy,' replied María nervously. 'Things are a lot more complicated than they seem. I've tried to break up with César loads of times and he's got violent. He says there's no way he's going to let a stupid woman like me leave him.'

'Sure, because he's the kind of guy who thinks he's better than you, right?'

María burst out crying.

'Oh, Berta! What have I got myself into?'

'I hate to say it, but I told you so, María,' said Berta. 'I don't want to be cruel, but remember what I said to you? That you were risking your family and your happiness. You should've listened to me.'

Exhausted by her fear and pain, María slowly began to drop off into a deep sleep; she felt as if the pillow was suffocating her, but she didn't have the strength to lift her head and breathe. Berta watched her sleep for a while, then before long she too began to nod off. It had been an intense day.

When Berta got up from the sofa to turn off the living room lights, she saw that María had gone to sleep clutching her mobile. She was gripping it with superhuman strength, as if it held the key to her survival. Gently, trying not to wake her, Berta uncurled each of María's fingers from the device, one by one, until she was able to extract it. Then, when she was just about to turn it off and leave it on the table, she noticed that the little red 'new message' light was flashing.

She peered at the phone and saw the name César Barbosa light up intermittently. Then, feeling no pang of conscience, she decided to read the latest abusive and threatening text: 'I know you're at your boss's place. If you grass me up I'll kill you both.'

The phone dropped to the floor. María let out a weak moan. Berta felt the room spin around her, as if she was on a merry-go-round at the fair, and the lights, the music, the laughter and the shouts of children were making her nauseous. She was defenceless, trapped in a tiny flat on Calle del Alamillo, with nothing to protect her but an old lock and an old door and a few old neighbours.

She picked the phone back up and read the last phrase again: 'If you grass me up I'll kill you both.' She went out to the balcony. She scanned the street from one corner to the other, looking for the sinister figure of César Barbosa, his leather jacket, his pointy shoes, and his metal belt buckle, but the night was calm and silent. It was too silent.

She crouched down. For no particular reason. She simply crouched down.

She crawled on all fours to the table where she kept her house phone. She lifted the receiver. She dialled the number that she had memorized, absurdly, as if she was the girl eating sunflower seeds in the square, who sees the short-trousered boy, the one who stares at her, bumps into her all over the village, throws pebbles at her window and dreams about her, who repeats her name in the echoing gully and then writes it in white chalk on the wall by the allotment.

'Manchego?'

'Berta?'

'Help, come quick!'

Chapter 35

Inspector Manchego was on a winning streak: he had been dealt three aces, and the pot, a pile of five-euro notes, came to over two hundred and fifty euros. Macita looked like he might have two pairs, Josi had just said 'I'm out' and Carretero was bluffing, not very well because when he was lying he always got a nervous tic in his nostrils and Manchego, who had known him since they were kids, couldn't fail to notice the flapping of those enormous blowholes. So they were either neck and neck or Carretero was done for – as he well knew from the days when they used to play *mus* together at the village club.

Manchego was already rubbing his hands together and mentally savouring some tasty dish from the restaurant he had promised to take Berta to when his mobile rang in his trouser pocket.

'Christ on a bike, don't you dare pick up,' spat Macita; the poor sod thought the money was his.

Manchego looked at him with a mixture of disdain and ferocity as he took the mobile out of his pocket quicker than John Wayne drawing his pistol in *Stagecoach* and waved it in front of Macita's eyes.

'For fuck's sake, this isn't the phone in a grocery shop, Macita,' he said. 'It's crucial for my work. It's the line that can separate life and death, catch a killer, avert tragedy. And you're telling me not to pick up, Mr Small-timer? Stick to what you know. However many times you write *gourmet* on the tacky sign outside your shop, you're still selling tins of tuna. Don't pick up, don't pick up,' he added mockingly, imitating his friend's nasal voice. 'And what if it's to do with drugs, or a gunfight, or an armed robbery?'

He answered.

'Berta?' he stammered.

'What a prick!' exclaimed Macita.

The truth is, Manchego found it easier to hide three aces than keep his cool when he had a new love interest. His friends had noticed something stirring the inspector's complex emotions the first time he turned up late for their game of poker with some excuse about work piling up, his face flushed, a stupid smile on his lips and an absent look. He had confused a pair of queens with a pair of jacks, left his portion of garlic prawns half-eaten and hadn't been on the ball all night.

'Mancheguito,' Míguel said to him teasingly, 'you've fallen in love again, say no more.'

'Who? Me?'

The inspector was one to fall in love easily. And he wasn't picky. Nor was he very realistic. The guys had accompanied him on many drunken nights when his hopes had been dashed; together they had damned all the women on Earth to the fiery pits of hell because of their treacherous ways, sworn they would never fall into their traps again. And even though all of them, except Manchego, were married, they had all broken their promises in the most shameful ways. The inspector's last conquest had turned out to be a con

174

artist who stole his wallet on their first date. Her name was Piluca and the guys suspected that she used to be a man; her hairy hands, her shaven moustache and her Adam's apple were all dead giveaways in their books.

There had been no way of verifying their suspicions, however, because that particular ill-fated love story ended before it had even started, in the local restaurant where Manchego lost his money, his wallet and his dignity.

Since then, Manchego had attempted to remain celibate in thought, word and deed, partly to protect his emotional integrity and partly because so far he hadn't come across a new candidate for breaking his heart.

But Berta Quiñones, the mild-mannered editor of *Librarte* magazine, whom the inspector had described as middle-aged, plump and short-sighted, seemed, for some strange reason, to have found her way inside Manchego's head. He maintained that his interest in Berta was purely professional – he had kept his friends in the loop about the Craftsman case – but the guys knew him well and were in no doubt that the way Manchego trembled every time his mobile rang owed to a different kind of interest, most likely the amorous kind. What they didn't understand was what their friend could see in a woman like that; she was so different from the girls he usually went for, who all seemed to be straight out of American TV series. He had always liked them tall, blonde and voluptuous, a bit dumb, a bit easy, with absurd names like Babi or Mimí, poor helpless things in need of a brave police inspector who would risk his life to save their handbags.

Set the bar lower, they told him, or you'll end up lonelier than Gary Cooper in *High Noon*. You'll end up old before your time, you'll develop all sorts of strange habits and in the end you'll die, like we all do. What they didn't realize was that the bar, in all senses but the physical, was already set so low that it would hit the floor if it went any lower.

No woman had ever really loved Manchego. He was at the disadvantage of having been born with a naturally fabulous body, well out of the league of mere mortals like plain old Berta, and so far he had known nothing but physical attraction and emotional turmoil. He was still relatively handsome – he was a big man with wide shoulders, large hands and athletic legs – but grey hairs had begun to lay siege to the part of his head that hadn't already succumbed to baldness; his standard–issue belt sported two new holes made by the local cobbler; and sometimes he got breathless if he exerted himself more than usual. The good thing was that he had arrived at the point at which the unequal pairing of a bookworm and a hunk was starting to reach a natural balance, giving way to the credible image of two members of the same species stumbling along side by side.

The guys, who, just as they looked at themselves in the mirror and refused to see the ravages of time on their own skin and hair, could only see the old Manchego, a dashing chap, hence dismissed the whole Berta thing as nonsense. They listened to their friend talk about the unremarkable, fifty–something ex–librarian and couldn't accept that they themselves were pushing sixty. Manchego's surrender to a love that was more emotional than physical felt like a collective defeat that they weren't prepared to accept.

'Come on, Manchego,' they said, 'it's one thing to lower the bar, but you're a fool to scrap it altogether.'

But that night at the *fonda* – that's what they called the bar, as if they were still back in the village – they could see traces of love in their friend's half–closed eyes, his twitchy hands, his constant swallowing and the curse that he couldn't help but mutter when he hung up and slapped his phone down on the table.

'I'll kill him,' he said. 'I swear to God, I'll kill him.'

'Who are you going to kill? Watch what you say, because if you actually end up killing someone you'll get us all done as accomplices,' said Josi, his best student.

'Some guy who's out there threatening defenceless women, the son of a bitch.'

Inspector Manchego, in all his glory, heaved the hundred kilos of his monumental body out of his chair, lifted his hand to his waist, checked that his gun was in place, put on his Gore-Tex jacket and left, almost without saying goodbye.

'Wait, Manchego, we're coming with you!' shouted Macita, acting as spokesman for the rest of the guys who stood up simultaneously, knocking a few chairs over, left their cards and the money on the table, followed him out into the street and squeezed into the car. Five greying men, five prominent bellies, five youthful lads from Nieva de Cameros, all ready to beat the shit out of the outsider who dares come to the village fiestas to dick around, get off with the girls and disrespect the grandmothers – but who runs off with his tail between his legs after the first punch, shits himself when he's faced with the lads from the village, Macita, Josi, Míguel, Carretero and Manchego. Like the old days, on a cold night with the car windows steaming up and their blood boiling.

Chapter 36

Berta's nativity scene was set up in a prominent corner of the living room, between the potted ficus tree and a portrait of her parents. She had covered a small folding table with a red velvet cloth and arranged the stable, the empty crib, Mary and Joseph, the Three Kings (Melchior in his red cape), the donkey and the ox, a bit of moss, a starry background, two cork mountains capped with floury snow, and the baby Jesus hidden in a music box that, when you opened it, played 'Silent Night'.

She was weeping like a helpless lamb and made a gesture to say: 'Don't make a sound, Manchego, poor María has finally fallen asleep on the sofa, don't wake her.' All of this, along with the nativity scene, took the inspector right back to childhood memories of icy streets and sharing hot wine in the square, singing 'Christ the saviour is born', socks hanging from the chimney, new shoes, a ball and a Scalextric set.

The guys had stopped the car in a no parking zone at the top of Calle del Alamillo. Macita and Josi had stayed there, with the lights off and their collars turned up, one smoking a cigarette and the other biting his nails. Míguel and Carretero had gone with Manchego to the door of Berta's building and then carried on without him to the end of the street, where at that moment they were both standing and keeping watch, beating off the cold as best they could, on the lookout for anyone prowling about who might fit the description of 'some tough-looking guy', which was all the information they had about Barbosa's appearance. Inspector Manchego had gone up the poorly lit staircase to the third floor, left-hand flat and bumped right into the Sacred Heart pendant and the hand-shaped knocker, identical to the knocker at his house in Nieva. There was also a bell, but, given the circumstances, he decided to knock quietly and wait for Berta, who was in a real state, to open the door after checking through the spyhole that it was him.

She invited him in, offered him a coffee and asked him to take a seat next to the window. From there they could keep an eye on what was going on in the street without being seen, just like from the attic window in the first house in the village, the one opposite the telegraph office.

'If he decides to show up tonight, I swear to you he'll end up sleeping in a cell,' Manchego assured Berta between sips of sweet, black coffee.

'What a swine! What a total swine!' she repeated, shaking her head, unable to believe that anyone so cruel as César Barbosa could exist.

'So, María,' said Manchego, nodding in her direction, 'was seeing this guy behind her husband's back.'

Berta nodded sorrowfully.

'Since when?' asked the inspector.

'As far as I know, for about the last year,' she replied. 'But it started turning nasty in May, when he found out that María was about to be made redundant. That's when the swine began threatening her and hitting her.'

179

'Because she was going to lose her job?'

'He said she was stupid, incapable of keeping a job as simple as hers, that she was a worthless shit, that kind of thing.'

'What does he do?'

'He's a photographer. Freelance. One of the ones we sometimes get to do jobs for the magazine. That's how they met. Rue the day.' Berta clenched her fists angrily, as though she felt somehow responsible.

'I'll see if we have a file on him as soon as I get to the station tomorrow. These offenders tend to be reoffenders,' said Manchego, trying to play it cool. 'We can use the text message as evidence. But first we have to convince María to report him.'

'I don't see how we'll get her to do that,' Berta replied. 'She's scared to death about what'll happen if Bernabé finds out. Think about it: she's married, she's got three kids. She's convinced that something will happen to her kids if she talks, because this Barbosa is a real monster, or Bernabé will kick her out.'

'That's what's so frustrating. Christ on a bike, women like María refuse to come forward and the abuse just escalates.' Manchego scratched his neck.

'How long might he get?' Berta asked.

'For threats, anything from six months to three years.'

'And physical abuse?'

'Two to five years.'

'So, if we did manage to get him put in prison, even being optimistic, he'd be out in a couple of years.' Berta looked him right in the eyes. 'And María wouldn't have a family.'

'I understand,' Manchego replied.

All of a sudden, and for the first time in her life, Berta felt the shared intimacy of hot coffee and hushed conversation, and once more, she was the little girl with plaits and glasses hiding behind the lace curtains of a lonely window. Despite the painful circumstances, it was a strangely pleasant sensation that tingled its way across her skin, stilled her trembling hands, calmed her upset stomach and banished the cold that had settled in her body.

Inspector Manchego's presence in her living room felt remarkably like a tree under which Berta might shelter in a storm: big, firm, and strong. A beech, or an oak, like the ones that cover the hills around Cameros.

Berta had told Manchego to put his mobile on vibrate mode so as not to wake María unless it was strictly necessary. Its mechanical sound startled them sometime after half one in the morning.

'Manchego,' said Macita, 'a rough-looking guy's just gone past. We followed him at a distance so he wouldn't suspect anything. Have a look out of the window and call Carretero if we need to take action.'

The inspector sprang up. He startled Berta and made the coffee cup wobble on its saucer. María opened her eyes before they woke her, as if some kind of survival instinct alerted her to the danger as she slept.

'What's going on?' she managed to say, somewhat shaken.

But Berta and Manchego didn't answer. They were both scrutinizing the dark street from the window, waiting for the figure of Barbosa to suddenly appear out of the mist. Which is exactly what happened next. Under the streetlamp on the opposite side of the road they saw a bulky form that gradually took the shape of a person – one with two-day-old stubble, a swaying seafarer's gait, a tattoo, no doubt, under his leather jacket, and a lit cigarette.

'Barbosa!' said Berta, shocked, when she recognized him.

'The locksmith!' exclaimed Manchego at the same time,

still incapable of understanding what a few minutes later, when his head was level enough to think it through, was clear as day: that César Barbosa and Lucas the fake locksmith were one and the same delinquent.

Manchego opened the window, took out his gun, aimed at the streetlamp and roared 'Stop!' without calculating the opportunities for escape that were open to the Pirate, who was twenty years younger than him and his guys. He tore off like a hare, swerving Macita and Josi, who by chance found themselves in front of him, and disappeared in the opposite direction down the street, the same street that was home to Berta, Señora Susana and her tenant Atticus Craftsman, whereabouts unknown since the end of May.

The situation was either the result of a cosmic coincidence of supernatural dimensions or there was a logical explanation. The seven people present were about to discover just how the pieces of the puzzle fitted together, as they sat in Berta's living room, their hearts racing, and talked non-stop through the night.

Chapter 37

We had two choices, to diversify or specialize, and in the end we decided to specialize, because I've always done really well with melons but had no luck with oranges. That's life, what can you do?'

Arcángel liked to talk. This was becoming clear to Atticus, particularly in contrast to his own reserved nature. Like father like son. 'You talk, I'll listen and, in return, you teach me to play the guitar,' were the terms Atticus proposed and which Soleá's cousin gladly accepted because, like he said, until the melons ripened for the next load to Madrid he didn't have much to do, apart from playing in Dolores's cave. Dolores, Atticus had learnt, was Potaje's mother, and Potaje had turned out to be Soleá's uncle and not her cousin.

Arcángel was the grandson of Consuelos, another of Remedios's sisters, and because he was the eldest of Manuela's nephews it had fallen to him to take charge of the fruit business when Soleá's father, Pedro Abad, died. Tomás had told his mother and sisters that he would rather make a living from music because horticulture clipped his wings and withered his soul. Manuela, a young widow with four single daughters, knew that she was better off selling the land and the trucks to someone in the family so that, at the very least, the name of the business wouldn't change. Arcángel, however, paid no heed to this wish, the result being a thorny issue that was best avoided, *míster*, why dig up old bones.

Aunt Consuelos had healing powers. Soleá's great-grandmother used to say that her labour pains and afterpains had vanished the moment Consuelos came into the world; her body relaxed completely and her own heartbeats synchronized with the baby's. It was true. It was an inexplicable phenomenon: anyone who came close to Aunt Consuelos (close being less than fifteen centimetres away from her chest) noticed that their own pulse slowed down – the woman had a pulse rate like a lizard at rest – and that all their worries and stresses gradually disappeared.

For a few years she had been well known in Granada as 'the pain lady', a title she hated because she said it referred to the problem and not the solution. Her own name, Consuelos, which means 'comfort' and was given to her by her mother precisely because of her gift, would have done the job perfectly well. In the end, though, that's what people are like, what can you do? When she turned seventy she closed the small clinic she had set up on Camino del Monte, scared she would die in the middle of a session and take the patient with her. But now she was over eighty and saw her life unfurl before her like that of an ancient ficus. She had begun to lose her fear of death and was pondering the idea of opening up shop again for the time she had left. Because people with a gift like Aunt Consuelos's might never die, they could go on living for ever, in slow motion, like Ravel's *Bolero*, do you know the one? The one you can play all day, that starts where it ends and vice versa. Shall I play a bit for you, *míster*?

Arcángel, with his messy hair and his long nails, taught guitar to Atticus in the courtyard at Soleá's house, at any time between eleven in the morning and two in the afternoon, according to what was on the menu that day. The classes were structured around mealtimes because Atticus had developed an unhealthy appetite for the stews that Granny Remedios cooked on her open fire, the smell of which wafted out into the courtyard. As soon as the oil started to heat up and the onion began to brown, Atticus lost interest in guitar chords and became obsessed with the blessed cooking pot. At that point, Arcángel knew it was better to leave the class for the next day. He would get up out of his seat and say: 'You're quite the musician, *míster*,' giving him a pat on the back. Then Atticus would go into the house, following the smell of frying onions and say hello to Granny Remedios, who would reply: 'Well, here you are again, Tico, *niño*,' handing him a sharp knife so he could help chop the vegetables.

Sometimes the broad beans needed shelling so they would sit opposite one another at a small table and pass the time discussing serious matters. She liked his way of speaking, with that funny accent of his, and would ask him things about his home, his family, the countryside near where he lived, and would listen in amazement, sometimes in dismay, like when she found out that he had spent his childhood at boarding school, or when Atticus said in passing that he couldn't remember his father hugging him a single time in all his life.

'Do you believe in God, Tico?'

'I think this life is all we've got, and we should be thankful for it.'

'Thankful?' Granny Remedios had the ability to flip the meaning of anything she didn't agree with to align it with her own beliefs. 'So then of course you believe in God, Tico, *niño*, think about it, who are you thanking?'

'Life.'

'You can't thank life for life; it would be like saying good-night to the night itself. A right mess, whichever way you look at it.'

'Then I must believe in God.'

'Right. Hey, Tico, you want to marry my Soleá, don't you?'

'I've never thought about getting married, Granny.' Atticus had learnt to give ambiguous answers as a way to combat Remedios's conversational manoeuvres.

'I didn't ask if you want to get married in general, like you might ask a person if they want to have some fun or want to travel, Tico, *niño*. I asked you if you want to marry my Soleá.'

'There's a lot of Soleá to Soleá.'

'Listen, Tico.' The old woman was losing her patience. 'Do you know what *pelar la pava* means?'

'No.'

'Well, *pelar la pava* is the same as chatting and shelling beans, but with the granddaughter instead of the grand-mother, do you see?'

Two months had passed since he had arrived in Granada; July was almost at an end and August was hot on its heels. Soleá got more beautiful every day, every afternoon they went out for a walk, but she still called him *Míster Crasman* and politely addressed him as *usted*, and every day Atticus fought against the animal instinct to devour her before the moon was up.

Atticus was getting mixed messages from Soleá. On the one hand, she treated him with astounding familiarity, joking with him, scolding him and confiding in him exactly as she did with her cousins, but she definitely wouldn't let him respond in the same way. The day he dared to give her bottom a friendly pinch, which was something all the men in the house seemed to do to all the women, without exception, including the grandmothers, and were usually just pushed away with a laugh, Atticus got a resounding smack. Soleá slapped both his cheeks and stood waiting for his reaction, coldly observing his hangdog look, his apologies in English, his blundering attempts to regain balance and his plea that she shouldn't say anything to Tomás, I beg you, he'll kill me. This last bit was the only thing that softened her stony heart.

On the other hand, he also found it difficult to guess what she felt and work out what she really wanted from him. If she caught him looking at another girl, Soleá would get in a huff, storm off in the middle of the street, and spend a couple of days not talking to him. But if she felt that he was watching her too much, if she felt that he was following her like a shadow through the parched streets or if they met in a corridor and he held her gaze, then she made it clear that his presence bothered her. She would suggest that he went out for a bit of air, it feels a bit oppressive in here, *Míster Crasman*, and shoo him away like a bothersome beggar.

Then Atticus would hug his guitar, walk away from the Heredias' house, wander up and down the streets, and sit down on any old corner to practise his new, solitary passion. Sometimes tourists would leave coins in his hat as they watched him tear at the strings of his wooden lover.

Then there was the question of accommodation. Soleá was still flat-out refusing to let Atticus take a room in a hotel, but he felt that if he was to stay any longer, which looked likely, he wanted to contribute in some way to supporting the family. He suggested it to Manuela, the mother, and she

187

got horribly offended. He asked Tomás, Soleá's brother, and he stopped speaking to him. In the end, Soleá asked him earnestly to stop embarrassing her family with the envelope of notes he kept flashing around. He was unable to make her understand that he hadn't wanted to boast, quite the opposite, Soleá, I can't believe you could think such an awful thing of me. Eventually he decided that the only way to shake off the terrible feeling that he was scrounging his meals was to buy a tourist ticket every night to the show at the cave, watch the performance and leave a tip.

'You fancy one of the girls, don't you?' Soleá said to him one evening with her eyes half-closed.

'I do?'

'Otherwise why d'you come to the cave every single night?'

'To see you, Soleá,' he replied.

'Stop messing with me, *Míster Crasman*, I know what you're like.'

Granny Remedios had picked up on this state of tension and disillusion – if nothing else, old age brings wisdom – and she thought the gringo could do with a little nudge to help him win Soleá over. The old woman knew Soleá was ready to be won over, you could see it from the way she came down in the morning all done up and asking for him, where's *Míster Crasman*, is he up yet . . . So she lay in wait until the opportunity arose to intervene in her grand-daughter's fate.

In the first week of August, Atticus received a call from England. His father wanted to know how he was getting on. Atticus had no choice but to lie. He made something up about studying the business and assured him that he would have good news soon. Then he asked if his father knew of anywhere in Spain that sold Twinings Earl Grey, his favourite kind of tea, because otherwise he was going to have to order some from England, which would be complicated. His father promised to find out, and they hung up.

Because this conversation took place in the courtyard, Manuela, Remedios and the girls had no choice but to listen through the kitchen window and ask Soleá to translate what the *míster* was saying to his father.

'He's not talking about us,' Soleá explained. 'It seems he's run out of tea and wants to buy more.'

'Tell him there's a woman who lives on the way up to Antequera who makes herbal teas!' her grandmother suddenly exclaimed.

'But, Granny Remedios,' said Soleá in surprise, 'they sell the kind of tea he wants in all the supermarkets.'

'You tell him,' the old woman replied, 'then I'll explain how to get there. Tico!' she shouted out of the window. 'Come over here, I'll tell you where you can get some lovely tea!'

Two days later, on precisely the tenth of August at eight in the evening, Atticus Craftsman went on the strangest adventure of his life, driving Arcángel's truck with Soleá fanning herself at his side, the picture of Camarón staring at them from the windscreen while his voice strained to be heard over the noise of the motor. Before they set off, Atticus took out his mobile, called home, waited for the tone, and when he heard the answering machine kick in he decided to leave a message so that his father wouldn't waste time with an exhaustive investigation of Spanish tea distributors: 'Leave it to me, Dad. I've got it all under control.'

Chapter 38

Señá Candela had discovered the calming effects of valerian, the hallucinogenic properties of jimson weed, the digestive qualities of camomile, and the therapeutic benefits of quinine long before herbalist's shops, artichoke tablets and Schweppes tonic came into fashion. The only thing that took her by surprise was the appearance of Coca-Cola – so similar to the sarsaparilla root beer they had always drunk and yet so successful. She had spent many years investigating the therapeutic properties of wild herbs, but she would never have imagined that such benefits could be reaped from selling them wholesale. She only ever asked for a donation in return for her masterly formulas, and the queue that formed outside her house stretched around the block. Her husband, Agustín, kept an eye on the hotchpotch line of people, some in pain, others heartbroken. Unlike his wife, he did take advantage of the clients, who he arranged not in the order of their arrival – which would have been the fair way to do it – but according to the tip he pocketed, so that the rich always went before the poor. Señá Candela turned a blind eye, because she didn't want Agustín to leave her at this late stage of the game – she was well over eighty –

but in return she dedicated much less time and energy to the first in the queue than the last.

'Give Agustín fifty euros and tell him to put you at the back,' Granny Remedios told Soleá, knowing that plenty of people had already worked out about the difference in treatment and did their best to stay at the back of the line.

As a result, it was a strange sort of queue that formed. At the front were the rich outsiders, who were oblivious to the mad logic whereby the more you gave, the worse off you were. Then came the poor from the village and then those from elsewhere. Then the rich from the village and, finally, the few who were able to precisely calculate their place in the queue relative to the size of the bribe they gave.

Agustín pocketed the fifty euros that Soleá gave him and then put the three or four clients who arrived later in front of them, despite their protests.

'I don't get it,' said Atticus.

'Because you're English, *Míster Crasman*, and you lot have a different way of queuing.'

The house was identical to all the others, whitewashed, with iron grilles in front of the two windows that faced the street. The door was open, but to get inside you had to pass through a beaded curtain that tinkled musically. The interior smelt like boiled vegetables.

'What's cooking, Señá Candela?' Soleá asked as the old woman kissed her affectionately.

'Cabbage for dinner,' she replied jokingly before looking Atticus up and down. 'So you're Soleá, our Remedios's granddaughter,' she added, 'and this is the Englishman.'

'*Míster Crasman*,' said Soleá before Atticus had time to open his mouth.

Atticus held out his hand to shake the old woman's but she took the opportunity to flip his over.

'My Lord, what luck!' she exclaimed. 'Your luck line goes right from one side to the other. Your love line is another matter,' she added and then, pointing to a seat, 'sit down.'

They both silently obeyed the order, like a pair of infantry soldiers.

Atticus had brought one of his last teabags with him. He took it out of his pocket and showed it to the old woman.

'I would like to buy a large quantity of this tea,' he said.

'Give that here,' she replied.

She ripped the sachet open, let the contents fall into the palm of her hand, tried it with the tip of her tongue and said:

'Twinings Earl Grey.'

'Remarkable!' exclaimed Atticus.

'It says so on the label, *míster*,' the old woman pointed out. 'I'll go and see if I've got any in the store.'

Señá Candela got up and left the living room, leaving behind her a strange smell, like that of a wheat field at dawn.

'Is she a witch?' asked Atticus in a hushed tone.

'She's more like an old-fashioned psychiatrist, the kind who doesn't have a certificate on the wall but cures people all the same,' replied Soleá, amused. 'She's an old friend of my granny's, godmother to my uncle Manolo, the one who owns Manolo's Bar. She knew we were coming because my granny phoned her.'

Atticus looked around. The living room was welcoming, shady and cool. The only furniture to be seen was the small round table they were sitting at, an old spice rack with lots of drawers and three or four framed photos from Easter celebrations featuring la Virgen de la Macarena and el Cristo de la Legión. On the table stood a kettle, several cups, a set of scales and a locked metal box where Señá Candela kept the money.

Atticus and Soleá remained in silence until the old woman came back carrying a heavy packet.

'You're in luck,' she told Atticus. 'I've got two kilos.'

That packet could have contained tea or animal feed: there was nothing to guarantee where it had come from or the state it was in.

'Try some,' she said, dropping a pinch into the strainer she had placed on top of one of the cups and pouring hot water over it. 'You too, girl,' she added, pouring a cup for Soleá as well.

Her expectant look meant they couldn't refuse the offer. They both drank the black tea with a certain amount of apprehension and then, to Soleá's surprise, Atticus shouted:

'It's perfect! Bona fide Twinings Earl Grey!'

And at once he placed a hundred-euro note on the table in payment for such a delicacy. Then he took Soleá by the hand – she felt his rough skin on her fingers – bade goodbye to Señá Candela and, with the packet under his arm, went out into the street where Agustín was waiting for them to leave so he could shut the door and call it quits for the day.

'How far are we from the sea?' asked Atticus when he was back behind the wheel of the truck.

'About an hour's drive, *Míster Crasman*,' Soleá replied.

'Then we can still get there in time to see the sunset,' said Atticus with a smile.

Chapter 39

The beach was no more than a little crescent-shaped patch of sand sandwiched between a reef and an old ruined fort. They sat as if at the theatre. Their screen was the horizon, the scene was the sun disappearing in the distance: an orange spot sinking into the black ocean. The only audience was Soleá, covered in goose bumps, and Atticus at her side, barefoot, his trousers rolled up to his shins, white skin, open shirt, closed eyes.

He moved his hand towards Soleá's arm – what could there have been in Señá Candela's tea? – and then upwards, slowly stroking her skin with his pale fingers, up to her shoulder, up to her neck, up to her hairline on the dark side of the moon. He wound his fingers in her hair, drew spirals in the air.

When Soleá felt Atticus's hands creeping up her, she was tempted to stop him. But when she saw that his eyes were closed, she suddenly felt sorry for him and let him carry on in silence, blindly – if only to see what happened, where his hand would go next. Down her back, to her waist, then over her hip to the hollow of her belly button. Then his hand opened and came to rest warmly on her stomach.

Then came his mouth — what could there have been in Candela's tea? She felt him bite her lips. His tongue tasted hers, and Soleá opened up completely — *what* could there have been in Candela's tea? — just as a watermelon splits open when hit, incapable of concealing its red, juicy, sweet fruit inside that hard, dull shell any longer.

Atticus was very experienced. Soleá was not. She hadn't yet understood what her hair was for, or why her breasts were the shape of cupped hands, or how her mysteries fitted into the paths that he was moving along. Now you have to throw your head back and I kiss your neck, now to one side and I bite you gently on the earlobe, and now you let me help you lie back on the sand, that's it, slowly, so you don't break into a thousand pieces and disappear into the ground beneath us.

Atticus drew his lips away from Soleá's mouth to confess that he had wanted her since the very moment he fell under the spell of her blue eyes, that when he was at her side the heat suffocated him, that he couldn't look at her without his soul aching, and that she was so evasive, flighty and mysterious that he didn't have a clue what she felt. He got the impression that Soleá felt something for him too but, even so, she was trying to avoid him, as if she was scared of him. What am I to you, Soleá? A heartless fiend ready to throw you and your friends out on the street in order to save my father's business some money? Is that how you see me, Soleá? Or is it just that you don't like me, you don't like my clumsy hands, my awful accent, the way I am with you, laying everything bare? Because if there's something about me you don't like, Soleá, whatever it is, I can change it. I'll learn to play the guitar, I'll eat ham and pretend it's delicious, I'll share my secrets with your whole family, I'll live in a cave if that's what you want, or get drunk on wine with fizzy pop, or watch a bullfight without looking disgusted (it'll be fine, I'll just think of something else), I'll grow old in Granada, sit on a bench, watch the cars go by, anything, so long as you, Soleá, want to be by my side and have a cup of tea with me.

She sat up. She lifted a hand to her mouth. She wiped her red lips. She looked at him. Her blue eyes had become as black as olives, Candela's herbal tea was sloshing round her belly and Atticus's hand was still resting on her stomach.

'Look, *Míster Crasman*,' she said. 'Why should I lie to you any more. I tricked you into coming here, with that story about the Lorca poems, so you wouldn't close the magazine. That's all.

'I call Berta every night, I tell her what's happened during the day, I tell her you haven't asked about the poems, in fact you seem to have forgotten about them, and Berta breathes a sigh of relief, and she tells the others that, at least for now, they can carry on with their lives. She thanks me and says: "Thank you, Soleá, for the sacrifice you, your mother and your grandmother are making," and I reply that it's not such a big deal, you're a good man and I feel bad for lying to you. But you see, *Míster Crasman*, I'm twenty-five years old, I've got my life ahead of me and I can find another job or move back home, but Berta and Asunción, the poor things, what are they going to do at their age, or María, with three kids and a useless husband, or Gaby, who's married to the kind of painter who never sells a painting, however much she tries to convince herself otherwise? The four of them barely scrape by with what they earn at the magazine.

'It was my idea. It's not that the poems don't exist, they do. But it wasn't Lorca who wrote them, *Míster Crasman*, it was my Granny Remedios, an uneducated woman. And she keeps them in the attic with her sewing machine and old bits of junk, because they're worthless, they're scribbles, that's all. You can go now, I've told you the secret, you can close the magazine quite happily and go back to England and forget about me and all of this. I'm so sorry that you got your hopes up about me; you don't deserve to have it broken to you like this. I didn't mean to hurt you, *Míster Crasman*, that's the absolute truth. The only truth among all these lies.'

Then she got up, shook the sand from her dress and slowly walked the short distance to Arcángel's truck, started it up, and vanished.

Atticus was frozen still. Cold ran down his spine. Bare feet, open shirt and a broken heart.

Darkness fell on him and he didn't want to push it away. The only sensible thing he did that sleepless night was to take his mobile, his last link to the rest of humanity, out of the back pocket of his trousers and hurl it into the waves with all his rower's strength, to be lost in the depths of the sea.

Chapter 40

The fifteenth of December was a cold, cloudy Friday, the kind of day you wish was a Saturday so you could spend all morning in bed. Asunción arrived at the office at nine o'clock sharp, carrying a flask of hot chocolate and two paper cones of *churros*. She hung her coat on the hook behind the door and sat down to wait for Gaby to arrive and join her in getting drunk on sugar and grease, her drugs of choice at such an early hour, on such a grim day and with such a painful, empty stomach.

She thought Gaby would probably be a while yet. She and Livingstone had made up the day before and, according to what Gaby had said over the phone, they were going to take things easy from now on. She no longer had the same urgency to become a mother, thanks to Franklin's cuddles and his confession that he had never really wanted to go back to Argentina, he only said so because they were having such trouble conceiving a baby. He had sobbed as he admitted this, and Gaby thought she had never seen a more helpless child than her husband. Now nothing could upset her. Not even the problems at *Librarte* or the unremitting arrival of her period every twenty-eight days. She said she felt as calm as can be, and couldn't stop grinning like a Cheshire cat.

A couple of hours earlier, when it was still dark, the phone had rung on Asunción's bedside table, waking her up and giving her the fright of her life, followed by terrible news, which caused her to burst into floods of tears. Berta had brought her up to speed with the tale of César Barbosa's serial abuses, in which María had turned out to be the unwilling accomplice, and the rest of them the innocent victims. The inevitable result was the demise of the magazine. Now, while she waited for Gaby to say goodbye to Franklin at the door, Asunción tried to find the words to break the bad news to her in the nicest way possible.

She didn't have time to rehearse her speech. Gaby arrived at nine thirty, humming, bounding up the stairs two by two; she unbuttoned her red coat before starting to search the labyrinthine depths of her bag for her office keys, took off her orange scarf, her blue hat, her green gloves. She shed her colourful woollen skin. She opened the door, came in, was shocked to find Asunción waiting for her with breakfast laid out on the photocopier, calculated that there were over a dozen *churros* each and understood that something bad was up.

'Come on, Gaby, have some of these, come into the warm, have a seat here,' said Asunción, pointing to the rocking chair that she had dragged in from Berta's office and which now took up most of the free space between the desks and the bookshelf.

'This can't be to celebrate me and Franklin making up. Something's happened, right?'

'Yes, love, it has. Something awful.' Asunción couldn't stop the tears welling up in her eyes again. She downed her hot chocolate and left the empty cup on her mouse mat.

199

Gaby did as she was told. She sat down and clung for dear life to the arms of the rocking chair, as if it were a raft in the middle of the ocean.

'Do you remember César Barbosa?'

'The Pirate.'

'The very same. Well, it turns out that he and María have been seeing each other for about a year now.'

'Bloody hell, so María's lover is Barbosa!'

'Look, Gaby, I couldn't name a bigger son of a bitch than Barbosa if you paid me. It turns out that last January, by mistake, he got paid twice for an invoice and María called him to ask for the money back. So he, the crafty thing, realized that María was the only one who'd noticed the double payment. He invited her out to dinner a couple of times, seduced her – you know, with that stubble, the tattoo, the motorbike and the bad-guy look – and bit by bit he got her to tell him how the *Librarte* accounts worked. María explained that Berta signed the invoices and gave them to her, she made a copy for our records and sent the original to England, so they could pay out from the central office. I don't know if you knew that that's the way it's always been: *Librarte* only has a tiny amount in the bank and everything else, our wages and all that, is paid for from London.'

'Yes, I knew that.'

'So, the Pirate, by the looks of it, had an idea: he told María to forge Berta's signature and send off an invoice for a non-existent piece of work, to see if they'd pay it. The next month, like clockwork, the money arrived from England. María had sent the invoice direct to London and, of course, she hadn't kept a copy or left any trace of it in Madrid.'

'Because it was fake.'

'Right. Then, when they saw the trick had worked, they did the same again, this time with a larger amount.

And so, all year, María and Barbosa have been splitting the money, which has gone into different accounts in different banks.'

'I don't believe it! That's why the magazine was haemorrhaging money! And poor Berta slaving away, unable to understand why we were going under when she'd been so careful with all the expenses!'

'Berta's a wreck. She hasn't stopped crying. Put yourself in her shoes: everything she's done for María, how much she's cared for and protected her, and now she discovers this.'

'Poor Berta.'

'But that's not the worst of it. Do you remember María's black eyes and bruises? And we thought that the disgusting chauvinist pig was abusing her? Well no, love, it wasn't just domestic violence, he was threatening her, trying to get her to keep her mouth shut. Because when *Míster Crasman* showed up in Madrid, María wanted to tell Berta what they'd done. She wanted to confess everything, beg forgiveness, pay the money back. She was ready to sell the little house and piece of land that her father left her in a village near Valencia to account for the losses, but she realized that the amount was huge, it'd got out of hand and something of that scale counted as serious crime. She was afraid she'd end up in prison and, what's more, would end up separated from Bernabé without custody of the kids, her life in ruins.'

'And she was scared.'

'She told Barbosa that *Míster Crasman* had taken the account books home to study them in detail. The whole thing was going to come out as soon as he looked at the books and saw the fake invoices, the payments to Barbosa, the accounts in different names, the fake businesses they used to receive payments, etcetera.'

201

'So the Pirate broke into the flat!'

'So it seems: he found out which police officer was in charge of tracking down Mr Craftsman – who, as you know, is still in Granada, under Soleá's watchful eye – because he was scared that once the police got involved, the case would be solved immediately. He figured there was no time to lose so he won Inspector Manchego over, told him he was a locksmith and that he could help him get into the flat on Calle del Alamillo; that way he managed to kill two birds with one stone.'

'Get into the house, steal the account books and slip out through the door without fear of Manchego arresting him.'

'Because at that moment they were accomplices. If the inspector arrested him, he'd look like a corrupt officer and, what's more, a real idiot.'

'Right.'

'He said his name was Lucas and then covered all the tracks that might connect him to the Craftsman case. Manchego thought that the so-called Lucas, surely a drug addict, had gone to burgle the Alamillo flat and, of course, he'd had the wool pulled right over his eyes. He suspected it wasn't the first time Barbosa had done something like that, probably other officers had fallen into the same trap and kept quiet so as not to look like idiots. But he never imagined that the locksmith was really after the accounts.'

'So César Barbosa managed to steal the books and threatened María and beat her up so she wouldn't talk.'

'Things were getting ugly. María's life was at risk. Sooner or later, César Barbosa would've made a fatal decision so as not to end up in prison.'

'He almost killed her yesterday.'

'Exactly. He wasn't far off. María hid out at Berta's house, fell asleep on the sofa and, while she was sleeping, got a message from Barbosa saying she'd better keep her mouth shut or he'd kill them both.'

'Oh my God! What did Berta do?'

'She called Inspector Manchego. Then, apparently, he came with four friends and they spent the night on guard, waiting for Barbosa to show up.'

'And did he?'

'Did he show up? At three in the morning, ready to kill them both, for sure, but when he saw that the police were there, he ran off.'

'And he's still on the loose?' They were interrupted by someone banging on the office door. It made Asunción and Gaby jump out of their skins. They hugged one another like two terrified schoolgirls, thinking it was César Barbosa, crazed and out of control, come to take them hostage, threaten to kill them, gag them and hold them at gunpoint, until the police promised immunity and a plane ticket to some secluded Caribbean island.

Whoever it was banged on the door again.

'Who is it?' Asunción managed to stammer.

'Open the door!' they heard someone on the other side say in perfect English. 'This is Marlow Craftsman.'

'*Míster Crasman*?'

Asunción and Gaby looked at each other in astonishment. They pulled themselves together as best they could and hurried to open the door to the man who owned not only that office but *Librarte* magazine itself and the entire Craftsman publishing house. Mr Marlow Craftsman, whom they had only ever seen in photos, had arrived, unannounced, at the worst moment in the history of the magazine.

Asunción was trembling as she opened the door.

On the photocopier was a crocheted blanket, and on the blanket sat a flask of hot chocolate, sugary *churros* and two cups. The computers were all switched off, the phones were unplugged, only two of the five staff had turned up to work, Gaby's chair was still rocking, it was almost ten o'clock on a Friday and that man was not only very important, he was also English.

'Welcome to *Librarte*,' was all Asunción could think to say when she saw the disbelief on the boss's face.

Just then, they heard voices on the stairs. The voices of three small children. And coughs.

From behind Craftsman appeared the flushed faces of María's three children, who all had fevers – Bernabé had left them at the door, they could find their way from there – and, without a word, they came into the office and launched themselves at the *churros* and chocolate.

'Want you breakfast, *Míster Crasman*?' asked Asunción in her rusty English.

Chapter 41

Moira Craftsman couldn't make up her mind whether or not to unpack the suitcase that she had crammed with items she considered strictly necessary for the rescue mission. Everything fitted so perfectly inside the Louis Vuitton case that she was afraid she wouldn't manage to get it all back in once she unpacked and spread her belongings out on the bed at the Ritz. She was a sensible woman. She decided to wait and see what Marlow said once he had spoken to Inspector Manchego again and interrogated each of the *Librarte* employees. If they were going to stay a while in Madrid, then it would be better to tidy her things away in the chest of drawers; arranged, as usual, according to colour. If, on the other hand, this garlic-scented city wasn't to be their final destination – how right Victoria Beckham had been, it smelt of garlic and onions, of fried squid and other unidentifiable fatty substances – and they were to continue along the winding roads into deepest, darkest Spain, then she should leave everything as it was: shoes in their covers, hats in their boxes and underwear neatly folded inside the Liberty bags she had kept so carefully for years.

So she put the closed suitcases in a corner and went down

to the dining room for breakfast. She sat at a round table next to a window that looked out on to the garden. The bare branches of chestnut trees greeted her. The night had been cold and damp and Spain's famous sun was startling in its absence.

It had been her idea to stay at the Ritz, of course. Marlow wouldn't have minded where he stayed; he was immune to strange smells and noises in the night. Moira, on the other hand, only trusted well-known hotels, the kind that look as if they've come off a production line. The Mandarin Oriental, for example, with its silk-lined corridors, its exotic fruits and its unmistakable scent, was exactly the same in London or New York or Bangkok. What a shame that Spain's only Mandarin Oriental was in Barcelona – although it was no surprise, because that city was much more cosmopolitan, if she was to judge by the Woody Allen film she had seen with her film club, in which a reckless foreigner got mixed up with a crazy Spanish couple.

In Madrid they had to make do with the Ritz, with its air of aristocratic nostalgia, its grand piano and its chandeliers, its uniformed porters, its maids in caps and aprons, and eggs Benedict for breakfast. As Moira well knew, it's better to play it safe than take a gamble with local food. Would madam like to try *migas*? It's a typical Spanish dish, with bread fried in garlic and olive oil accompanied by rashers of bacon . . . No, thank you, bring me a cup of tea and some eggs Benedict, please, and a copy of *The Times*, if you'd be so kind.

The dining room slowly emptied of businessmen and filled with newlywed couples, rich tourists and lone guests like her. She had the morning ahead of her and nothing better to do than dwell on her reason for being there: her poor Atticus, missing in combat in a hostile land, surrounded by savages capable of eating garlicky bacon for breakfast, swallowed up by the heart of darkness, like Kurtz who ended up cutting off heads and leaving them out to dry.

She thought about the premonitory nature of her husband's name. After living a peaceful life for sixty years, the time had come for Marlow to undertake the mission he had been destined for since the beginning: he would have to go into the jungle and save his son from the clutches of the natives who were about to devour him in a cauldron full of Twinings Earl Grey.

As for her, she felt just like Mary Livingstone, the ideal partner for an explorer. She kept her feet on the ground, acting as his guide and compass, because she understood that the greatest danger on a mission like this, far away from civilization, was losing one's own identity and ending up adopting the barbarous customs of the natives: renouncing good manners, scruples and social differences, giving oneself over to the pleasures of the flesh, letting oneself be swept up in their magic rituals and forgetting, for example, to always ask for bottled water and absolutely no ice. With the pressure of such a responsibility resting on her shoulders, Moira came over quite weak. She went back to her room, slumped fully dressed on to the bed, and placed a cold, damp flannel on her forehead. She decided she would stay in that position until she received instructions from Marlow about whether to unpack or not. The uncertainty was killing her: should she hang her shirts in the wardrobe or fold them neatly in the top drawer?

Chapter 42

A t first light the next day, Carretero, Macita, Míguel and Josi set off for their jobs in the suburbs and Berta's house was finally left in silence. María, exhausted from crying and the weight of her conscience, got into the only bed in the house, took a Valium, and swore to herself that tomorrow she would grab the bull by the horns, turn Barbosa in and make her shameful confession to the rest of her workmates.

With María so deeply asleep, Berta called Asunción to bring her up to speed on everything. 'Tell Gaby as soon as she gets to the office,' she said, not expecting that Mr Craftsman himself would turn up in Madrid that very day, denying them the time they needed to invent a story that would be more palatable than that of theft, adultery and his son's secret journey to Granada in search of Lorca's poems.

Berta had no time to think of something that would justify her betrayal of Manchego's trust, either. So far, the inspector had believed every word of her version: 'While they're still paying our salaries, we'd rather not delve too deeply into where Mr Craftsman might be; he's a grown

man after all, and free to do what he wants with his life.'
But sooner or later the time would come to tell him the
truth. And it would hurt.

Perhaps they could find a way to make Manchego understand that they hadn't acted out of spite and hadn't had the
least intention of harming anyone, that Soleá's plan wasn't
dangerous, Atticus was fit and well in Granada and all that
remained was to put Barbosa behind bars, make him pay
back the money he had stolen and refill *Librarte*'s coffers.
After that they would call Marlow Craftsman to explain
the real reasons behind the economic damage, bring Atticus
back to Madrid and plead with him to trust them and give
them a second chance – well, not María, she would have
to find another job, unfortunately, one in which she didn't
have access to anyone's bank account – 'But have pity on the
four of us, *Mister Crasman*, can't you see it wasn't our fault,
we were victims of the theft just like you.'

It was difficult to predict how Manchego would take the
news of Berta's deception. He might get angry, or he might
start sobbing hopelessly. 'I trusted you,' he would tell her
with tears in his eyes, 'I even thought I felt something for
you, Berta, despite your frumpy figure and your swotty
ideas, at this late stage of life I was ready to believe I'd found
my soulmate.' It would be heart-wrenching.

Berta's mind went blank when she tried to think of
an alibi that wasn't an even bigger lie. Because one thing
was clear: the day they spoke for the first time, that cold
November morning in the office, when Manchego asked if
she knew where Atticus Craftsman was, she had said no. A
resounding 'no', unsoftened by any nuance or excuse. And
to make things worse, over a month had gone by since that
first interrogation and, although she received regular updates
from Soleá about every step Atticus Craftsman took around

209

the Sacromonte hillsides, she had never told Manchego the truth.

Berta knew, for example, that Atticus Craftsman had stayed at Soleá's house from his arrival until 10 August, the day when Soleá tearfully admitted that his visit to Granada was part of a shady plan dreamt up by the *Librarte* girls with the sole aim of drawing out their anxious wait until they were made redundant. She also knew that that revelation had been like a stab in the back for poor *Míster Crasman* who, it seemed, had got his hopes up about Soleá and had gone as far as to kiss her on a beach, at sunset. She knew that after that disappointment, Atticus drifted for several days like a soul in limbo through the streets of El Albaicín with only his guitar for company, sleeping rough, drinking too much, getting into plenty of trouble and finally finding accommodation in a cave run by Soleá's cousin, where on certain nights he stood in for one of the musicians – to the delight of the tourists, whose understanding of flamenco music left a lot to be desired.

As for Soleá, she had called a couple of days after the incident on the beach with the fear of death circling. That's what she told Berta: that death was circling her house, Granny Remedios was gravely ill, the whole family had moved into the house, they had brought the bed down to the living room and put it near the fire, you understand, don't you, Berta? In such circumstances there was no way she could go back to Madrid, what with all seventeen members of the family sleeping, eating and living there, she had to look after them, they had left their homes in Antequera, their businesses, their commitments, so they could say goodbye to Remedios properly.

'It's not like all seventeen of them are at the foot of the bed all the time,' Soleá explained, 'the family come and go, but there are always ten or twelve of them, a dozen mouths to feed and my granny, who's very old, says she can see Christ, as if he was walking towards the other side and leading her behind him.'

'Has the doctor been to see her?'

'Yes. But he can't find anything serious. He says it's an illness affecting her spirit more than her body, but it could kill her all the same.'

The problem was that, after four months in bed, Remedios was still firmly in this world, not budging, and the *Librarte* team was suffering as a result of Soleá's absence.

'I can work from home, Berta, if you'll let me. I can cover the cultural life of Andalusia. I can do "on this day in . . ." lists, articles, profiles, whatever you want, but don't make me go back to Madrid, I couldn't bear for my granny to die without me by her side.'

'And what about Mr Craftsman?'

'*Míster Crasman* visits every morning. He brings flowers for Granny Remedios, or sweets, things like that. But I always try not to bump into him; it breaks my heart to think how badly I've treated him. I peek down the stairs and if I see he's in the living room, I hide. One day I even jumped out of the window so I wouldn't have to say hello to him. Do you get what I'm saying, Berta? It would be better if he went back to Madrid, or England so I could forget about him because, as it stands, seeing him every day, hearing him talk to my granny, singing things to her, playing the guitar, with that accent of his, which cracks me up – an Englishman singing flamenco! – and that walk of his, he looks like he's about to fall over all the time, well, I think it's sweet, Berta, what can I say, I think I'm warming to him.'

Given how things were, Berta thought the time had perhaps come to share this information with Manchego. As

211

awkward as things might turn out, the right thing to do was collaborate with the investigation and allow the inspector to solve the case. Otherwise it would be an obstruction of justice, not to mention a horrible betrayal of trust, which could have nasty consequences for the future of her friendship with the man who was slowly stealing her heart.

But Manchego, sitting across from her at the kitchen table, couldn't tear his gaze away from her tired eyes. He was looking at her with a mixture of tenderness and affection that seemed out of place in a large man like him. What's more, he had been moving his hand across the table until it met Berta's, and had placed it on top of hers, warm and protective, and now he was stroking her trembling hand, with the obvious intention of squeezing it tight, lifting it to his lips and kissing it. And then maybe, taking advantage of María's deep sleep in the other room, Manchego would get up without saying a word, stand behind Berta, wrap his arms around her, stroke her hair, kneel at her side, bring his manly lips close to hers, their mouths would brush together, their souls would meet and then . . .

The phone rang, breaking the spell. Berta realized that the inspector's hand was in the same place that it had been all along. Just a few centimetres from his coffee cup. Motionless.

She jumped when she heard the phone, got up, and answered: 'Who is it?'

She heard Asunción's anxious voice on the other end of the line.

'Berta, please, come quick! *Mister Crasman* Senior, the boss himself, has turned up without warning. Gaby and I are in the office trying to talk to him in English, but you know I haven't spoken it since school and Gaby only knows French. On top of that, María's kids are here, all with sore throats, and this man, who really is incredibly English, can't believe his eyes. He's turning red, Berta, all up his neck and behind his ears. Please come quickly before he passes out.'

Chapter 43

Asunción hadn't been lying: half an hour after her call for help, the tension inside the *Librarte* office had become unbearable. Manchego had insisted on going with Berta – 'You don't want me to stay here, alone, with María, I'll only be accused of something later.' He had left his partner watching the door to Berta's building and got into a taxi with her, excited by the prospect of telling Mr Craftsman that the investigation was going well and he had new information and leads that would probably guide them to Atticus sooner or later. But when they reached the office and came face to face with the Englishman's anger, Manchego elected to remain silent, at least until Berta, in her flawless English, had managed to calm the Shakespearian tempest that had been unleashed in the office and was threatening to destroy everything. The kids were playing on Berta's computer behind the closed door of the small office. In the main office, Berta, Asunción, Gaby and Manchego were all holding their breath while Marlow Craftsman repeatedly slammed his fist down on the table.

'Now,' roared Mr Craftsman, 'either you tell me where my son is at once or I will ensure that the whole weight of the Commonwealth falls on you, and let me remind you that Great Britain has an impenitent parliament, an implacable queen, unconditional allies and an incorruptible police force. And nightmarish prisons! There is one particular one on the Isle of Wight from which no one has ever escaped alive. And, it so happens that it's a women's prison, would you believe it, for female delinquents, kidnappers, thieves and rapists.'

'He's in Granada!' said Asunción suddenly. All heads turned towards her.

Asunción was pale and sweating. She had blurted out her confession at the same time as letting out an almighty sigh. The tension had done her in – that much was clear. For years her body had been like a pressure cooker, always on the point of exploding. Every now and again she had to open the safety valve, like a submarine releasing ballast or a hot-air balloon dropping sandbags. Now she was visibly deflating. Her body went first, followed by her head. She fell to the floor and lay half-buried by the office supplies she took with her as she descended.

Her colleagues rushed to help her: they laid her on her back with her legs up, they fanned her, gently slapped her face and gave her mouth-to-mouth resuscitation, asked for water, splashed her, shouted for help, we're losing her, it might be a heart attack, if she dies it's your fault, *Mister Crasman*, you're a potential murderer of helpless women like poor Asunción, you tyrant, scumbag, cold-hearted monster.

But Asunción came round in a couple of minutes. And she was glowing because, as she told them later, she had been at the gates of heaven, she had seen the tunnel, she had gone towards the light.

Marlow Craftsman was relieved, however hard he tried to maintain his unruffled appearance. He waited for a few

215

minutes to pass, for the fan, the glass of water, the valerian and the cool breeze from the open window to do their job, and then, in a much more sympathetic tone, he dared to ask:

'Did you say, Miss Asunción, that my son is in Granada?'

'Yes, *Míster Crasman*. He's in Granada. Safe and sound.'

Manchego fixed his eagle eyes on Berta's short-sighted ones. She lowered her gaze and he understood that what Asunción had said was true. That all this time his supposed missing person had been in a known location, at least known to those five witches from *Librarte*. He imagined a hole dug in the chalk hillside and the prisoner bound and gagged behind bars, eating only what they brought him, pissing in a bucket, slowly going crazy.

'Where are you holding him?' Manchego shouted at the top of his voice. 'Confess, damn it!'

Gaby, Berta and Asunción opened their eyes as wide as dinner plates.

'Are you accusing us of kidnapping?' said Berta in disbelief.

'Of kidnapping, obstruction of justice, theft, capital flight, fraud, everything.'

It was Berta's turn to get angry.

'Well, if that's what you think of me, you worthless cop, I don't care if you know the whole truth, however much it hurts. You idiot, you stupid yokel!'

Marlow Craftsman thumped the table once more, daring to interrupt what to all intents and purposes, and to his amazement, looked like a lovers' tiff.

'Tell me once and for all where my son is!'

Berta sat down, defeated. She spoke slowly, in an English that was comprehensible even to Manchego. She punctuated her speech with gestures, sighs, tears and tissues. She explained about the fake Lorca poems, Atticus's stay with the Heredia family, Soleá's cousin's cave, the Spanish guitar. She said that Atticus had been free at all times: free to return to Madrid and close down the magazine, free to throw them all out on the street, free to go home to England, and if he hadn't done so yet, you'll have to ask him yourself, Mr Craftsman, I can't guess what's keeping him in Granada, other than perhaps an unrequited love that's got him wandering like a lost soul, begging on street corners. A cruel, pitiless, unrequited love, the kind that burns you on the inside, the kind that comes with disillusion, disappointment – the worst kind. And as she said the last bit she was looking at Manchego, in the hope that he would read between the lines and understand what she wanted to say to him, and would be capable of forgiving her.

But Manchego had been absent from the office for some time. Not physically – his big, ungainly body was still there, leaning against the wall, with one hand covering his eyes like a blindfold – but in spirit. His soul had escaped the physical being that housed it through some mystic crevice and was hovering over the scene instead. The inspector had a true out-of-body experience as he observed his own desolation from above. It was so embarrassing to watch: a couple of tears rolling down his cheeks, Berta begging his forgiveness, Craftsman speechless, Asunción about to faint for the second time and Gaby fanning her as if her life depended on it.

Manchego's soul flew out through the open window. It looked down on the roofs of Madrid's historic centre, the Royal Palace, the cupola of the Almuneda cathedral and the Moorish gardens.

It was a grey, cold, sad day. He wished it was Saturday so he could spend all day curled up in bed.

Chapter 44

If there's one thing that luxury hotels and state-funded hospitals have in common, it's the possibility that someone determined to get their job done, no matter what, might burst in when you least expect it: checking blood pressure, temperature or antibiotics, stocking the minibar, changing the bedclothes or cleaning the bathroom are seemingly tasks to be carried out regardless of the patient's need for rest or the guest's state of undress.

'Excuse me, madam, I've come to change the towels,' said a maid, standing in the middle of Moira's room, ignoring the fact that she was sprawled out on the bed with a cold compress on her forehead. 'Or would you rather I came back later?'

'Who are you? What are you doing in my room? Where am I?' Moira replied in English.

She had woken up horribly disorientated after dreaming that her rose bushes, instead of tea roses, were flowering with red carnations.

'I think I'll come back later,' the maid decided, spinning round and fleeing. 'It's just that you didn't put the "do not disturb" sign on the door . . .' At that moment, the phone rang.

'Mrs Craftsman? It's the concierge. I wanted to check if everything is all right. If you're happy with your room.'

'Yes. It's fine. Thank you.'

Someone knocked on the door.

'Minibar service, shall I bring you some ice?'

'I don't want ice!'

'Your chauffeur is waiting for you.'

'My chauffeur?'

The maid came back in.

'Now that you're awake, I'd better change the towels, if that's all right, while my colleague brings the ice.'

'Laundry service,' said another voice. 'I'll leave your clean shoes on the sofa. Have a nice day.'

'I have a message for you, Mrs Craftsman,' she heard the concierge say before the receiver fell heavily and cut off the call.

'Get out of here, all of you!' she shouted, managing to make herself heard over the racket.

Moira took such an attack on her privacy as a sign from on high that she couldn't spend all day waiting for Marlow. Knowing him, he would probably come back empty handed. Marlow had never been very pushy. On the contrary, he was an excessively careful man who had only dared ask her to marry him when she threatened to end their relationship if he didn't propose. She bought the ring, she organized the wedding, she brought the children up and she, in consultation with her black diary, decided what her husband fancied doing at any given moment.

'Moira, dear, do I fancy going to watch the Wimbledon final on Sunday with Charles Bestman?' he might ask her, covering the mouthpiece of the phone in their Kent home.

'No, darling, you fancy staying here to have tea with your mother who's coming down from London.'

'Thank you for the kind offer, Charles, but I don't fancy it this time.'

And that would be that.

It was time that she stepped in to investigate Atticus's mysterious disappearance herself, thought Moira, and with renewed strength she jumped up from the bed, got dressed in the first clothes she pulled out of the suitcase, which happened to be a tweed suit and a felt hat, and went out into the cold Madrid street. Just as the concierge had informed her, there was a uniformed chauffeur waiting for her outside the door.

'Very pleased to meet you, Mrs Craftsman,' said the chauffeur in perfect English. 'Would you like me to take you to Calle Serrano, El Corte Inglés, the Museo del Prado or anywhere else in particular?'

Moira consulted her black notebook.

'Take me to number 5, Calle del Alamillo,' she replied, sounding very serious.

A few minutes later, having swapped Madrid's wide modern avenues for the narrow streets of its centre, Moira's heart sank to the pit of her stomach. She couldn't believe that her son had had to survive among those old houses and narrow pavements. Calle del Alamillo was tiny, and the green-painted, plywood door to number 5 felt to her like the entrance to hell, and the stench in the hallway – a kind of cooked fart and burnt-on grease – was surely worse than the smell of brimstone.

She struggled up two flights of stairs and rang the bell of the right-hand flat without the least hope of anyone opening the door. Her plan was to ring the bell a couple of times and then try her luck with the neighbours' flats, to ask after Atticus, try to get information about the people he knew, his habits and anything that might shed light on where he could be.

To her surprise, the door to the left-hand flat immediately opened behind her.

'Can I help you?' asked an old woman wearing a sky blue woollen dressing gown and slippers.

Seeing Moira's stupefied expression, Señora Susana felt obliged to give some kind of explanation.

'I'm Señora Susana, the neighbour. I have a bell connected to that flat, you see. The police installed it for me after what happened a few weeks ago, I almost died of shock, some guy came in to burgle the flat and he pushed me down the stairs, dear Lord, I nearly didn't live to tell the tale. If you're looking for *Mister Crasman*, madam, then I have to inform you that unfortunately we haven't seen him for six months, we think he might've been kidnapped, it's awful, either that or he's dead, or something, because it's just so strange, there's been no sign of him, and he was such a nice, polite young man. He left his coat and everything. And here I am, wanting to rent the flat out again, but what happens? I tell people about the kidnapping and the theft, and no one dares stay.' Señora Susana paused for a moment and frowned. 'You aren't here, by any chance, to ask about the flat? It really is a great little place, with all mod cons, clean as anything, furnished and tastefully decorated—'

'*No comprendo*,' replied Moira in her awful accent.

'You don't understand me?' replied Susana. 'Come on, come in, we'll have a coffee and I'll explain it to you slowly and then, if you want, I'll unlock the flat and we can have a look. You're going to love it, I've got it done up so nicely.'

Susana pushed Moira Craftsman into her flat and made her sit down on the sofa in the living room. While she boiled water and heated milk, her cat rubbed itself against the terrified Englishwoman's leg. Moira had assumed that in Spain everyone would speak perfect English, perhaps slightly contaminated with an American accent from watching Hollywood films, but comprehensible none the less, and she had assumed that cultural differences wouldn't be a serious impediment to understanding the locals.

How wrong she was.

The old woman was still talking at the top of her voice from the kitchen, even louder now that she knew her guest was foreign, and Moira still couldn't understand a word.

A few minutes later she returned with the coffee on a little tray covered by a crocheted cloth and sat in front of Moira, not once stopping to draw breath.

'It's eighty square metres: a spacious bedroom, gas cooker, bathroom and living room with a colour TV. The maintenance costs are low, each person takes their own rubbish out, because we haven't had a caretaker for years, since what happened with poor Angelines, who was eighty years old and as fresh as a daisy but social services took her to a home because they said she shouldn't be working at her age, and she lasted two weeks. We didn't even have time to go and see her at the home, to take her sweets or anything. She died of a broken heart, you know?'

Moira was trying to interject and ask if the woman knew where her son was, but every time she drew breath to say his name her host had already started her next sentence. She seemed to have the ability to talk without pausing for breath, inhaling and exhaling without breaking her flow.

At long last, after more than ten minutes of unintelligible speech, Señora Susana got up, took Moira by the arm as if they were old friends, and led her to see the flat that was up for rent.

Moira's eyes filled with tears when she saw where Atticus had spent his last days. The flat smelt stale and damp, it was cold and the shadow of the building opposite meant that hardly any light filtered in through the windows.

'Why are you crying? Are those tears of joy? I did tell you how lovely it was.'

Moira shook off the housewife and decided to explore that miserable flat on her own. The living room was clean and empty, the kitchen was abandoned, the bathroom was closed and the bedroom was in semi-darkness. She managed to heave the blind up.

'The lad only spent three nights here. He didn't have time to enjoy it,' Señora Susana was saying as she followed Moira around the house. 'The police were the worst, they covered everything in white dust looking for fingerprints and went through all the drawers. But, as you can see, it's all spick and span again now.'

Moira opened the wardrobe. To her surprise, hanging there was the Burberry coat she had given Atticus the previous Christmas. She hurriedly unhooked it, grabbed it with both hands and brought it up to her face. She buried her nose in it, breathed in its scent, kissed it, put it on over her tweed jacket and wiped her tears on the sleeve.

'What are you doing?' Susana exclaimed. 'Put that coat back where you found it at once, madam!'

Moira ignored the old woman's protests. She put her hands in the pockets of the coat and pulled out a piece of paper folded twice, with a strange message written on it in pencil: 'Arcángel Melons, Granada, 8 a.m.' This had to be a lead. She recognized the word Granada, and was amazed that the police had searched the flat and forgotten to check the pockets. She got ready to hurry off and tell Marlow about her find – but she hadn't counted on Señora Susana's wrinkled little figure blocking her way as she tried to escape and her shrill voice alerting all her neighbours: 'Get the thief! Get the thief!' After the first break-in, the residents of the building had prepared themselves – 'They won't catch us off guard again!' – by installing an automatic lock on the main door, and making sure there were buckets of water, tomatoes and rotten eggs at the ready: they planned to hurl these from the stairs at whichever good-for-nothing delinquent came in to ransack the place.

Moira found herself trapped, rained on by repulsive projectiles, while seven toothless faces watched her being pelted from the landings, and as much as she shouted, 'Stop, stop! Help, help!' her torment didn't come to an end until the chauffeur, wondering why the Englishwoman was taking so long, rapped on the door with his tough knuckles and was able to explain the situation in Spanish to the panicked neighbours.

'Take me back to the hotel,' Moira managed to beg him, her hair sticky and the coat covered in rubbish.

Then she turned on her mobile and called her husband.

'Darling, I think I know where Atticus is.'

'In Granada,' replied Marlow. 'I left a message with the concierge, dear. Didn't he give it to you?'

Moira slumped into the seat of the car, took a handkerchief out of her pocket and began to sob.

Chapter 45

'Mrs Craftsman still doesn't understand why we need to bring María to Granada with us,' said Berta in the terse tone she had been using with Manchego since the previous day.

'Fuck Mrs Craftsman – don't translate that, Berta, I'm just letting off steam,' said Manchego. 'This woman is going to make me throw myself out of the car, mark my words, unless I throw her out first.'

'As I've explained several times already, Mrs Craftsman, the inspector thinks we need María with us in Granada for two reasons,' said Berta in English. 'Firstly, to protect her from Barbosa, and secondly, to lure Barbosa in so as to arrest him.'

'And why not arrest him in Madrid?'

'Mrs Craftsman wants to know why you can't arrest him in Madrid.'

'Christ on a bloody bike!'

'Because, Mrs Craftsman,' Berta replied patiently, 'if we don't catch him red-handed we won't be able to pin anything on him. The only evidence we have against him is María's statement. She is, how should I put this, a "protected witness", I don't know if you follow me.'

'Bait,' said Moira, suddenly grasping what Berta meant and sneaking a glance at María in the rear-view mirror.

Marlow Craftsman had hired a black eight-seater Mercedes with tinted windows for the journey to Granada, and had engaged a smartly dressed driver to make sure he and the motley bunch, with whom fate had decreed he would spend the day, got there safely. Under different circumstances he never would have made a journey of over four hours in such company. He would have thrown himself off the white cliffs of Dover before voluntarily spending a car journey with the likes of them.

Manchego sat in the passenger seat, next to the driver, and to make matters worse he was dressed in civvies. At least in uniform he commanded a certain respect, but wearing corduroy trousers, a knitted tank top and an old jacket, he looked like a Suffolk sheep farmer. Behind him sat the Craftsmans, one either side of the centre seat – his briefcase and her handbag acting as a barricade in the middle – and María and Berta were squashed into the back, huddled up to one another like two little girls afraid of the dark.

The plan was to get to Granada as soon as possible, walk the last bit up to Soleá's house, wait for her at the door, go with her up to Dolores's cave, knock, ask for Atticus, wake him up from his deep sleep, give him the fright of his life, tell him everything that had happened, get him into the car, on to the plane, on to the train, and take him home to Kent and ensure that little by little, with the help of plenty of tea and good sense, he slowly detoxed from all that unrequited love, cheap wine, cured ham and tinned tuna, forgot those wasted months and got back to being a well-bred, responsible young man, heir to Craftsman & Co, his mother's pride and joy, his father's hope, Bestman's success story, the company's

226

future. A promising young man, yes siree, worthy of his ancestors, faultless, proper and respectable. And English. Above all, English.

The previous day, Marlow Craftsman himself had, without a second thought, sacked Asunción, Gaby, Berta and María and closed the *Librarte* office with a slam that rang out like a gunshot. They didn't get their redundancy cheques and weren't brave enough to ask for them. The girls, all distraught, saved what they could from the carnage: they shared out a few books, kept the coffee cups as souvenirs, along with the crocheted cloths, Berta's rocking chair, the potted roses and other personal items that they packed into miserable cardboard boxes.

Asunción was in charge of switching off the fuse box and disconnecting the gas. She did the job with tears in her eyes. Gaby wiped the memory from each of the computers and turned them all off – someone would come soon to collect them and send them back to England. María organized the shoe boxes full of receipts and the useless, deceitful records, so that they could be included in the indictment for the fraud investigation.

Berta couldn't bear to watch the eviction. All she could manage was to take María's kids away as soon as possible before their mother arrived. She went out with one of the twins in her arms, the other hanging off her hand and little Lucía jumping down the stairs ahead of them, singing a nostalgic ballad that told the story of some shepherds going to the hills and who didn't know when they would be home again.

Berta walked with her head down, tearful and forlorn.

Manchego was about to run out after her and say to hell with it all, but good sense got the better of him in the end and he simply stood in silence, in a corner, for the two hours it took the girls to clear the office. Together with his client, Marlow Craftsman, he oversaw the process, and impassively carried out his duty as a police officer.

Then he escorted the gentleman to his hotel, the Ritz, and bade him farewell until early the next day, when, following the plan they had made, they would set off for Granada in a rental car with Berta, so she could translate, and María, so she could act as bait.

'Precisely, Mrs Craftsman,' repeated Berta for the ump-teenth time, 'María is the bait, and she has to come with us to lure Barbosa in so we can catch him red-handed, do you see? She's the only one who can testify against the thief and we can assume that he'll try to find her so he can shut her up.'

'Shut her up?' said Moira, wide-eyed.

'Do her harm, yes,' said Berta. 'Threaten her, beat her up or even kill her.'

'So you're putting us all in danger,' remarked the English-woman, 'by bringing the bait to Granada in this car. Bravo, very clever.'

Marlow Craftsman turned round in his seat. There was some logic to what Moira was saying. Having María in the car with them was a risk he hadn't taken into account. He glanced nervously in the rear-view mirror. The motorway was busy.

'César rides a Harley Davidson,' María informed them, aware of Craftsman's sudden anxiety. 'He's easy to spot. He usually wears a leather jacket with an orange logo and boots with pointed metal toes. You have no idea how much a kick from those boots hurts. It feels as if all your ribs are going to get smashed to pieces.'

'Son of a bitch,' muttered Manchego.

Berta hugged María even tighter. Moira opened the

window, stuck her head out and inhaled the cold December air. For some strange reason, she felt overwhelmingly hot instead of cold. The eggs Benedict were churning in her stomach, making her feel almightily sick.

'I don't feel at all well,' she managed to say before her mouth filled with vomit.

Because the back window was also open, the stream of sick flew directly on to María and consequently on to Berta, who was holding her like an overprotective mother.

They had to pull the car over on to the hard shoulder in the middle of nowhere, where there was nothing but sheep grazing and a windmill on top of a distant hill, and while an embarrassed Moira apologized in English, opened her bag, took out a silk handkerchief, a bottle of mineral water, a couple of clean shirts – 'don't look, please, gentlemen, cover your eyes, we're going to get changed in this ditch' – a Harley Davidson passed unseen behind the car, as quick as lightning, ridden by a delinquent called Barbosa, heading for Granada, where he planned to round off his criminal activity by grabbing María by the hair and taking her with him to a Caribbean island where no one would ever find them. He had already bought the tickets. He had a bag full of cash. 'Say goodbye to your children,' he was going to tell her, 'because you're not going to see them again. Either that or I kill you. Your decision.' And she would surely make the right decision: she would run away with him, despite knowing that from that moment on she would become her executioner's property, the object of his beatings, a slave to his desires. A thing, an animal.

It had been easy to follow María: all he had had to do was scare the life out of Señora Susana on the dark landing outside her flat on Calle del Alamillo. She immediately confessed that Berta had left her keys with her and asked

229

that she please water the plants because, apparently, she had to go to Granada for a few days, Señora Susana didn't know who with, Berta didn't say that, and she would be back before too long.

'Manchego,' Berta had warned the inspector in the car, after speaking on the phone to a terrified Susana who stumblingly told her what had happened. 'Barbosa's on his way.'

'Right,' he had replied without looking at her.

Chapter 46

Berta called Soleá that evening and told her every last detail of what had happened in the past few hours. María had confessed, Barbosa was the biggest son of a bitch in the history of the world, *Míster Crasman* himself had sacked everyone, they had closed the office – 'Asunción's got your things, don't worry, they're in safe hands' – and, most importantly, she was going to leave for Granada first thing the next day with María, Manchego and the Craftsmans to try to rescue Atticus and take him back to England.

The mixed emotions swirling around Soleá's soul inexplicably condensed into a single feeling: that of a broken heart. Just as a doctor touches different parts of their patient's ailing body and says: 'Does this hurt?' until they find the source of infection, Soleá ran through all her current sources of anxiety – María's betrayal, the loss of her job, her uncertain future – and, to her surprise, she found that the epicentre, where it really burned, pulsated, writhed, screamed and died, was located precisely in the tiny corner of her heart that belonged to Atticus Craftsman. She noticed how the rest of her worries paled in comparison to the unbearable idea of living without Atticus.

She hardly slept that night, bathed in sweat, tossing and turning on the mattress she had chosen solely because he had slept there, sometimes getting up to look out of the window, straining to hear the distant sound of his guitar, his foreign accent, his childlike laughter, recalling the kiss, the beach, the colour of the sea, the smell, the taste, the colour, the softness, the hand spread out on her stomach, the heat.

She got up when it was still dark, sticky with sweat, and went down for breakfast.

Granny Remedios, who never slept, was awake and waiting for her, propped up on the cushions of her deathbed. However, in contrast to the lamentable state she had been in recently – her moans and cries of 'Take me, Virgen del Carmen, take me, Jesus, oh, the pain!', her faints and other torments such that Soleá had begged the Lord to take her grandmother so she wouldn't suffer any more, so she might rest in peace – Granny Remedios looked fit as a fiddle and was grinning from ear to ear.

'Come 'ere, Soleá,' she said under her breath so as not to wake the children, grandchildren, nephews and nieces who were spread around her bed, awaiting her death, taking it in turns to stay by her side at night.

The fire was lit. The whole house was sleeping silently.

'My girl, you look like a lost soul,' she whispered to her granddaughter, who flopped down next to her. 'You're shaking, your feet are freezing and you're all hunched over. Have you finally realized?'

'Realized what, Granny Remedios?'

'What do you think, Soleá? That you're in love with Tico and have been since the day you met him, since you brought him here, since you two first laughed together, since you both drank our Candela's tea, since you jumped out of the

232

window so you wouldn't bump into him. *Niña*, if that's not love, then God knows what is.'

Soleá lowered her eyes. The white sheet looked pink in the glow from the fire; her grandmother's hands were lined with deep paths; her eyes were two mirrors that had seen so much; her words were truths that cut like knives.

'But I didn't . . .'

'Of course you didn't know. Sometimes, the person in love is the last one to realize. But Tico, he knew it from the first moment. He wouldn't have followed you to Granada if he hadn't known, he wouldn't have spent days in this house, shelling beans, he wouldn't have learnt to play the guitar, he wouldn't have walked back from the beach – he walked three days and nights, that's what he told me – just to be at your side. He knows it, Soleá, but he's English, sweetheart, and he doesn't understand that we do things differently here. He doesn't understand that you can turn up one night at your girlfriend's father's house, take her away and give her a child – that's what your grandfather did to me – and rip your shirt open, and beat your chest, and fight savagely for her if they won't let you marry her because you're only a cattle trader and you don't have a fortune, and take her back to your village, quick as lightning, to the hills, love her furiously, tenderly, passionately. Tico's cut from a different cloth. He acts like he doesn't want to get his clothes dirty, Soleá, but in actual fact he's desperate to eat you up. I can see it in his eyes every time you come downstairs and walk straight past him. It's as if his body lights up when he sees you and switches off again when you leave.'

Soleá felt that rain of burning truth cascade over her and remained silent, while her eyes focused on counting the wrinkles on her grandmother's hand. She knew that

Remedios, who was an expert when it came to human emotions, was absolutely right.

'So what do I do now? How can I tell him I'm in love with him when I've treated him so badly?'

'You don't have to tell him anything, girl. Just keep quiet, let him come to you and be ready for him. No one likes to feel as if they've been trapped. You leave it to me. Tell him I'm dying and he has to come and see me because I won't live through another night.'

'Oh, Granny Remedios, don't scare me!'

'But I'm only pretending, Soleá, my girl, you silly thing. Haven't you worked out that I've been in this bed for four months, healthy as a horse, waiting to see if you'll make up your mind to go for Tico?'

Soleá couldn't believe what she was hearing. Remedios was smiling beatifically, as if it was absolutely fine to give them all the fright of their lives by telling them she was dying. The cousins had come from Antequera, they were sleeping piled on top of one another, afraid to leave her bed-side in case the Lord suddenly came for her in the night.

Remedios slipped out from between the sheets, small and wrinkled as she was, her hair all messed up, her nightie threadbare from lying in bed for so long. She said: 'What a relief, Soleá, I was going to catch something bad cooped up in there. Your mother is such an awful cook! What a relief that I can take over the kitchen again, my Manuela was going to starve us all to death!'

Some of the cousins who were sleeping in the living room stirred. The fire crackled in the hearth and Granny Remedios did some yoga stretches.

'Don't look at me like that, close your mouth before the flies get in,' she told her granddaughter. 'Go and find Tico and tell him I'm dying, go on. Tell him I've got something

234

important to say to him before I cop it. A big fat secret that I don't want to take to my grave.'

After her stretches, Granny Remedios went back to her hollow in the mattress, pulled the sheets up to her nose, put on her invalid's face, shouted: 'Virgen del Carmen, take me soon!' A distant cousin finally woke up from her deep sleep, approached the deathbed, touched the old woman's forehead, thought to herself that she didn't have a fever, and asked if she wanted anything for breakfast.

'*Migas* with bacon and a fried egg,' replied Remedios, who might have been dying but certainly hadn't lost her appetite.

Chapter 47

The only prayers Soleá knew by heart were the Lord's Prayer and Hail Mary. She made the rest up to suit the occasion: 'Virgen del Carmen, patron saint of sailors, save me from this shipwreck,' or: 'Sacred Heart of Jesus, have a heart,' prayers that were hardly liturgical but truly sincere, because she wasn't the kind of person who only thinks of Saint Barbara in a thunderstorm, no, Soleá thanked God every day for the good things in her life: her mother, her grandmother, her siblings, the fifty members of her extended family, her colleagues at *Librarte*, her work, her flat in Madrid and even the spicy potatoes they made in the bar on the corner. And to this list she now added Atticus Craftsman's green eyes when he stared at her back.

She carried on up the steep little street to Dolores's cave, praying under her breath all the way, oblivious to the fine rain, like angels' tears, that was falling and making her hair wet and frizzy, soaking the hem of her long skirt and her ankles. She asked the Virgin Mary – because you're a woman and you'll understand better than the others – to help her find her way out of the impasse of her love for Atticus Craftsman, that pale, clumsy Englishman who wasn't at all religious, which the poor thing couldn't help, because, you see, Virgin Mary, he was born into a family of agnostic Protestants, although Granny Remedios had managed to pretty much convince him that heaven existed when she told him it was like having tea with Soleá for all eternity.

Up until that moment Soleá had done everything she could to avoid opening the doors to her heart. They were shut fast, surrounded by crocodile-infested water, defended by an army of prejudices and customs that would be tough to dismantle now that she had fed them so fervently. And yet, with every step she took through the rain, a tower or a battlement fell, the drawbridge was lowered, offering him a way to get into the castle, the heart of darkness, where she was waiting for him, asleep, or rather unconscious, unaware that only his kiss could save her, only his love could redeem her, only his company could be her heaven.

The cave was firmly closed. Atticus Craftsman was sleeping beside the only window, next to the door. Soleá knocked once, twice, three times, waited, and knocked again.

At last she heard the sound of scraping metal – oh, he was so clumsy! – and then the lock clicked, the door opened and a warm darkness seeped out, carrying with it the smell of the tourists' cigarettes, spilt wine, the spoils of the night before.

'Soleá,' said Atticus, surprised, his hair messed up, wearing only his vest and Ralph Lauren boxers.

'Granny Remedios is dying,' she blurted out. 'She's asked for you, she wants you to go there, she's got a secret she wants to tell you before she dies.'

Atticus Craftsman's reaction to that news was far from the cold response Soleá had expected; all of a sudden, he hugged her as if she was a life raft, crying inconsolably like a child, his tears soaking her hair. She was the granddaughter, the one who should have been in pieces, but instead she remained calm, stunned to find the man she secretly loved in her arms, unsure what to do or say in the face of such an outpouring.

'Your hands are freezing, *míster*,' she managed to whisper. 'Put something on or you'll catch cold.'

But because he carried on hugging her like a big brown bear and she didn't really know what to do with her arms, which were hanging down by her sides, she decided to hug him back, but more in the way you hug a small boy than a boyfriend: with a touch of compassion and pity. Softly, to see if he would calm down so the two of them could set off down to the Heredias' house, where Remedios was waiting for them in perfect health, anxious to cast the spell that she planned to use to sort out her granddaughter's messy love life.

In fact, there was no need for the grandmother, or anyone else for that matter, to intervene in this story of deception and disillusion. All they needed was for Soleá, there at the top of the hill, under the lintel of the cave door, to confess to Atticus Craftsman that she was crazy about him, despite being terrified by his English education, his addiction to Twinings Earl Grey, his vegetarianism, his slight limp that was a constant reminder of that fateful day on the Thames, his fierce father and his uptight mother, his aristocratic, antiquated and cold Englishness, and his freezing cold fingers which that day at the beach had crawled over her back, her waist and her belly button before coming to rest on the curve of her stomach.

'Come on, *Míster Crasman*, Granny Remedios is dying to see you.'

Atticus dried his face on the blond hairs of his forearm.

He sniffed, ducked his head and went into the cave. A couple of minutes later he emerged wearing a black shirt, black trousers and a black belt, carrying a black umbrella which he used to protect Soleá from the rain that was still falling on her wet hair.

If it wasn't for his wheat-coloured hair and the white skin of his neck and hands, anyone would have taken him for a true Gypsy. Because that was what Atticus Craftsman was becoming: he was becoming Tico from Dolores's cave, the guy who played the guitar with all his heart and sang the saddest *soleás* in all of El Albaicín.

And so, slowly but surely, under the December rain, the two of them made their way to the Heredias' house and went into the living room where the family were keeping watch over Remedios night and day so she wouldn't be alone when God came for her.

'Granny,' said Atticus.

'Tico, my boy,' she replied from her deathbed. 'Come close to me, here. And the rest of you, get out,' she ordered, echoing the words of Lola Flores: 'If you love me, get out.'

The grandchildren, nephews and nieces went off to eat bread rolls drizzled with olive oil and drink coffee. They left Remedios, Atticus and Soleá alone, telling each other old secrets.

'Tell me, Tico,' began Remedios, 'let's see, why did you come to Granada?'

Atticus squirmed in his seat.

'I came to buy some poems,' he confessed. 'Because I thought you were different, Granny, I thought you had some unpublished papers belonging to Federico García Lorca hidden in the attic and you were too ashamed to let anyone see them.'

'Ashamed of what, Tico?'

Now it was Soleá's turn to squirm in her seat. She clearly remembered the morning at *Librarte* when she almost beat Atticus Craftsman to death for having insinuated that her grandfather might have been homosexual.

'That people might have thought your husband was . . .'

'That Lorca's thing was catching?' asked the old woman, her voice full of irony. 'That they were lovers? But my boy, he gave me a child before we were even married and three more after the wedding . . . How could my husband have been gay, eh?'

'With difficulty,' he admitted.

At no point did Atticus switch his gaze from Remedios's friendly face to her granddaughter's vexed expression. Soleá was praying the earth would swallow her up.

'The thing is,' Remedios went on, 'we needed a reason to bring you to Granada. That's why we spun that yarn about the poems. Then we fell in love with you and didn't want you to leave. So we kept stringing you along.'

Soleá felt as if she was suffocating. Apparently, her grandmother had just declared her love on her behalf. She had said '*we* fell in love with you' and nodded towards Soleá as she said it.

'But this time I was the one who lied to you,' Remedios confessed. 'Because I was scared that my Soleá would go back to Madrid and you'd go back to England, and the two of you would go your separate ways. So I got into bed and told everyone I was dying.'

'You're not dying, Granny?'

'No way, *niño*! I'm in better shape than you are.'

She couldn't help letting out a little laugh as she said this last bit. Atticus leapt forward to kiss her wrinkled hands.

'But you scared me to death, Remedios! I believed every word!'

'I'm truly sorry, poppet,' she replied, flattered. 'I didn't know you cared about me so much.'

Salty streaks left by the tears he had shed were still visible on the Englishman's face, and his hands were still as cold as blocks of ice.

'But I can see that you really do care,' she went on. 'And I think you're the right person to trust with my secret. The part about me having a secret is true, and I don't want to take it to the grave with me.'

'Granny,' Soleá protested from the foot of the bed. 'Don't keep tricking *Míster Crasman*. We've pulled enough wool over his eyes already.'

'Shut up and listen, you!' said Remedios. 'This secret concerns you too, the colour of your eyes and the tone of your skin.'

Soleá looked fearfully at Atticus and he returned a look full of curiosity. Soleá's eyes were two blue beacons; her skin was the colour of sand, and although she was tanned she was much fairer than her sisters and neighbours.

'You see, Soleá, you take after your great-grandfather. That's why you're so blonde.'

'Blonde' wasn't exactly the word that Atticus would have used to describe the woman who had him under her spell. He would have said exotic, mestizo, mixed race. Dark hair and blue eyes, with tanned skin that looked peachy at times. But, it was true, compared to other women around her it was possible to describe her as blonde. A different kind of blonde to the Scandinavian variety, of course, a Sierra Nevada blonde, which is something else entirely.

'Because you see, Tico, my boy,' said Remedios from among the bedclothes, 'it turns out that my mother, when she married my father, was pregnant by another man. Only my father knew that. He'd loved her since he was a boy and

241

cried when she went to serve in a big house in Granada because he thought the masters of the house would steal her. "Don't go, Macarena, don't go, if you go I'll lose you," he said, but she went. She was a real handful, that Macarena, no one was going to tell her what to do. She went, she worked, and one day a friend of her employer's son arrived, a young English guy who can't have been much older than twenty and was already messed up because he'd fought in some war or other, and was traumatized by what he'd seen. He used to scream at night and wake up bathed in sweat and tears. And my Macarena, God rest her soul, well, she let him convince her to sleep beside him, because he was scared, he said, of the ghosts of all those dead soldiers. So she slept with him and cured him of his demons and then, when she found out she was pregnant, she didn't tell anyone, only my father. She went back to Camino del Monte, had her white wedding, went to live in Dolores's cave, which before that was called Macarena's cave, and my father gave her fourteen children, fifteen in total.'

'So, Granny,' said Soleá, 'are you saying that my great-grandfather was English?'

'Yes. English. But not English from England, English from America. And he became really famous, that great-grandfather of yours.'

'Famous?'

'Well, that's the whole point, you see,' she went on. 'Why would I be telling you all this if he hadn't got so famous. No one else knows about it, and until I met Tico I was ready to take the story to the grave with me.'

Atticus sat in stunned silence. From the date, from the man's description and the location, he was sure he knew who Remedios was referring to.

'You already know who I'm talking about,' she guessed.

'Hemingway.'

'The very same.'

Just then, someone knocked at the door. Manuela, who was in the kitchen, rushed through the living room to answer it. She mumbled a good morning to the three of them, then turned the handle to let in whoever it was had come to pay their respects to the dying woman.

When she came back she was as white as a ghost.

'Soleá, your boss, Berta, is at the door, and your friend María, with an English couple and a man who looks sort of like a police officer. Have you done something wrong, love?'

Chapter 48

Fate chose the worst possible moment for Soleá Abad Heredia to meet Moira Craftsman, her future mother-in-law, for the first time. Maybe that's why it was so hard to break the arctic ice that lay between them for years, despite poor Atticus's efforts to bring the two very different women together. From the moment they met, the hatchet was out and was only buried the blessed day that the twins Tom and Huckleberry came into the world; one fair, one dark. Their maternal grandmother inexplicably nicknamed them Zipi and Zape, which seriously disconcerted the Craftsmans, who had never heard of that Ibañez chap and had no interest in broadening their knowledge of Spanish humour or its great masters. 'My grandsons,' said Marlow, 'will bear the names of protagonists from great novels, following a Craftsman family tradition that has existed since time immemorial, not some vulgar comic-strip character.' 'By Jove!' added Atticus, provoking an outburst of laughter from Manuela, Remedios, Consuelos and the seventeen cousins who had gone to visit the hospital in Granada to keep Soleá company while she was in labour.

The day they met, Soleá's hair was wet, her skirt was

covered in mud, her eyes were full of tears, and she was sitting at the foot of an old, toothless, dishevelled, dying woman's bed, and the old woman was inexplicably clutching Atticus's hands.

Of course, because the only light in the room was a dim glow from the fire, it was too dark for Moira to see that the young Gypsy with long blond hair was in fact her missing son. It was Atticus who recognized his parents, despite how awful his mother looked: pale, having just thrown up, and wrapped in a dirty coat that was too big for her.

'Mother! Father!' he exclaimed, jumping up from his seat next to the bed.

'Atticus?'

Moira Craftsman fainted. She froze on the spot, started trembling and then keeled over so the full length of her slim body slammed on to the floor, and she hit her nose on the terracotta tiles.

'Tell Consuelos to get down here!' shouted Remedios from her bed, remembering her younger sister's therapeutic powers and forgetting, meanwhile, that the Andalusian regional council had recently opened a state-of-the-art medical centre only three or four blocks from the house, where they dealt with all sorts of emergencies.

Consuelos came running down from where she had been sleeping in one of the rooms upstairs and hurled herself to the floor, wrapping her arms and legs around Moira as if she was saving her from drowning and had to swim her to shore.

Marlow Craftsman couldn't believe his eyes when he saw the old woman's unconventional approach, much less the behaviour of his son who, instead of prising the woman away from his mother's body, was trying to hold everyone else back so they wouldn't intervene in the rescue.

The madness was over in next to no time: as soon as Moira's heartbeat had matched the rhythm of Consuelos's, Manuela brought a damp cloth from the kitchen and cleaned the blood from the nose of her daughter's future mother-in-law, and then between them all they settled her into the bed recently vacated by Remedios who, to the great surprise of her daughter and sister, had jumped up and was now standing to one side in her crumpled nightie.

Consuelos had to lie next to Moira, because every time the Englishwoman opened her eyes she fitted and fainted again. Soleá moved to one side, protected by her mother and grandmother; Atticus and Marlow stationed themselves at the head of the bed; and Berta, María and Inspector Manchego stood at the foot. They all remained deep in silence until the seventeen cousins came back from Manolo's Bar.

In the semi-darkness it was easy to confuse one person with another: the unwell woman with Remedios, the Englishmen with priests, the strangers with distant relatives.

'Oh, oh, my dear Remedios has left us!' cried one of the aunts from Antequera at the top of her voice.

'Oh, my dear, sweet Remedios!' shouted six or seven cousins in unison.

Marlow Craftsman, with the sole intention of setting them to rights, took a step forward and tried to explain that the woman wasn't their Remedios, it was his Moira from Kent, and that she wasn't dead, she had simply fainted.

Because none of them understood what he was saying, and before Berta had time to translate, there was a growing murmur of voices complaining about the church, the clergy, and the habit they had of coming into someone's house as if it was their own, get away from my aunt, you sour-faced old git, I want to give her a last kiss.

246

The lack of respect towards his father implied by the words 'sour-faced old git' unleashed in Atticus the same rage that had ripped through Soleá that day in the *Librarte* office when he called her dead grandfather gay. Marlow, in shock, watched the transformation of his son into a wild beast: Atticus's body grew rigid, his fists clenched, his eyes closed to a squint, his voice became hoarse, he turned the air blue.

'I shit on *all* your ancestors!' shouted Atticus. 'Every last one of them! Tico from Dolores's cave won't stand for anyone insulting his father, by Jove!'

Atticus, with his shirt open to his navel, launched himself at the cousin from Antequera, pushed his chest at his and both of them rolled on the terracotta floor, to the astonishment of everyone around.

Suddenly they heard a gunshot and plaster dust rained down on the terrified Marlow. All eyes turned to the corner where a big man dressed like a sheep farmer had just fired at the ceiling with a gun that was straight out of a gangster movie.

'Are you crazy?' Soleá exclaimed. 'The kids are sleeping upstairs, and that bullet could go through the ceiling and kill one of them!'

These wise words were enough to make most of the rabble rush noisily upstairs. They were led by Manuela, shouting like a madwoman, with Remedios bringing up the rear in her nightie and between them the Heredia cousins, aunts and uncles, Berta, María and Consuelos, who had managed to jump out of bed as soon as the silence was broken.

Upstairs it was all shouts and screams; they counted the children and found that the number of kids sleeping peacefully was the same number as had been put to bed the night before. All safe and sound, thank God. They stomped back down, thirty of them in total, children and adults, Gypsies and *payos*, friends and strangers, and all surrounded Moira Craftsman's bed, some of them shocked to find an English-woman in Remedios's place.

'Would you look at that, I'm cured!' shouted Remedios from halfway down the stairs. 'Everyone can go home and Manuela will let you all know about the wedding.'

'Who's getting married, Granny?' asked one of Soleá's sisters in amazement.

'Who do you think? Your sister and Tico, for God's sake.'

Moira Craftsman, who had managed to stay conscious for a couple of minutes, fainted heavily again. And she hadn't even understood what Remedios had said. It was enough for her to see the huge smile on Atticus's face and the blush on Soleá's to understand that the dark-skinned woman with witch's eyes, wide lips, toasted skin and curly hair was – unless Freud stepped in – in all likelihood the mother of her future grandchildren.

This time she had fallen so deeply unconscious that they decided to rush her to the health centre that the Andalusian regional council had opened three streets from the house, to see if modern medicine was capable of reviving her.

Chapter 49

Granada had never shone so much as on that sunny after-noon after the rain: the orange trees were a glistening green, the geraniums were overflowing like whole forests and a fresh dusting of snow lay on the mountain peaks like icing sugar on cakes.

Atticus and Soleá went up to the San Miguel lookout point from where they could see the Alhambra, Granada's second sun, waking up, stretching, shaking itself out and glowing.

As they gazed at that magical scene, Soleá learnt that Atticus had the warmest heart in all of England. His hands were still freezing, the poor thing, but the blood that rushed around his body was boiling hot. Everything about him was scalding hot: his kisses, the passion of his words, his downy blond skin and his eyes, if he opened them, or if not, his eyelids.

If it was a single kiss, it was the longest in history. If there were several kisses, Soleá didn't know where one ended and another began; they were all like water from the same stream. Kisses that destroyed bridges, waterlogged crops, swept livestock away and flooded houses. Mud up to knee level, the dog on the roof, rescue helicopters and fallen trees.

Atticus received Soleá's kiss like a hard-won trophy; the prize for his efforts, the boat race, at long last the cup for Oxford, after seven years of disappointment, the taste of glory. While he nibbled her lips he revisited one by one the scenes from his erotic library, which he had left behind in the flat on Calle del Alamillo, what an oversight, in the hope of putting them into practice as soon as this no-nonsense woman let him unbutton her shirt and rip off her skirt, something he thought might be tricky, because Soleá, while they were kissing, had already slapped him when she felt his hand trying to make tracks for her cleavage.

'Why not?' he had pleaded with her, his face red and stinging.

'Because I don't want you to,' she had replied.

So as not to drag out any longer the agony of wanting to touch her and not being able to, Atticus asked her to marry him, as soon as possible, that very day, or tomorrow, at the cathedral, in a little chapel, out in the countryside, just the two of them or with the fifty cousins from Antequera. He didn't have a ring, so he gave her the gold crucifix that hung from his neck, so the Gypsy Christ could bless their union. He pulled it off over his head, placed it on Soleá's chest and the heat it held made a mark, like a tattoo, in the shape of a cross, that he had to kiss better. More kisses.

He did it by the book, Soleá later told her mother and grandmother; on one knee, the classic formula, first in Spanish – '¿Te quieres casar conmigo?' – then in English – 'Will you marry me?' – because it had always been his dream to ask the hand of the woman of his dreams in the language of Shakespeare. And Soleá said 'sí' and then 'yes,' and then, finally, she let him kiss one of her breasts, the right one, not because she wanted him to, but because the cross had burnt her.

Chapter 50

Moira Craftsman soon came round from her 'emotionally triggered panic attack' as it was diagnosed by a doctor who had to check three times that the electronic cuff wasn't broken because each time it gave a blood pressure reading of one sixty over one hundred. On Atticus's insistence the doctor prescribed two cups of Twinings Earl Grey Tea, conceding that: 'It can't do her any harm, she is English, after all.'

At around seven in the evening, the Craftsmans, Berta, María and Inspector Manchego were finally able to settle into their charming little hotel, a pretty house with a courtyard and flowers. They were all exhausted from the journey, the emotion and the hospital visit.

Why Moira didn't notice the cross that hung from Soleá's neck is a mystery that will never be solved. She didn't say a word on the matter; it was enough for her to feel the icy cold of her son's hands to know that something serious was going on, and to fear the worst. She ordered a soup, a French omelette and a cup of tea; she complained because the soup had bits of chickpeas floating on the surface and the omelette was less like a soufflé and more like the sole of a shoe. She cried for a while, and around nine o'clock she fell fast asleep. Marlow read until the words started to blur in front of his eyes. Then he turned off the bedside light and fell into a deep, snoring, whistling sleep.

Inspector Manchego sat with his ear pressed against the door and took all of this in. After all, it was his job to protect these people round the clock and deliver them safely back to Scotland Yard along with their son, Atticus, the missing person, you'll never believe where he turned up, in perfect health, and all thanks to the investigative prowess of Inspector Manchego, who should be made superintendent and given a medal for bravery.

Berta, meanwhile, after ensuring that the Valium, blessed Valium, had finally done its work against María's stubborn insomnia, went out into the courtyard for some air and came across the sturdy backside of Inspector Manchego, who had his ear against the Craftsmans' door, his back tense, his gun at his waist.

She hesitated, unsure whether or not to sneak back to her room and avoid another confrontation with him. She still hadn't managed to forgive him for all the unfair accusations he had hurled at her and the people she most cared about. Kidnapping, obstruction of justice, theft, capital flight, fraud . . . Manchego had deeply offended her, she felt like she had been seriously let down and, however much he had apologized afterwards – 'Forgive me, Berta, you know I didn't really mean it, I said that in the heat of the moment, I love you, do you hear, I love you, there you go, three words I've never said to any woman' – the fact that he had embarrassed her so much still tipped the balance more towards resentment than compassion.

However, the trip to Granada, the persistent morning

rain, and Manchego's look of a helpless little boy who has put his foot in it but later feels bad and grovels for forgiveness . . . all three softened her heart like a boiled potato.

'Fancy a cigarette?' she said to his back.

Manchego spun round, moving his hand to his gun.

'My God, Berta, you gave me the fright of my life!' he protested. 'Don't do that. It's dangerous to scare an officer when he's on duty. I'm armed and I'm jumpy.'

'OK,' she replied. 'I can see you're jumpy, so a cigarette and a bit of a rest will do you good.' Then she added: 'Are they sleeping?'

'Like two bloody great angels.'

'María's finally managed to get to sleep as well.'

'So it's just us two still awake. Have you noticed how empty the hotel is?'

He was right. It was the 18th of December, a Monday, and they had the hotel to themselves, with its Andalusian courtyard, its wooden balconies and its geraniums.

'People are saving for Christmas.'

'Must be.'

Thinking of Christmas made Berta's heart sink. She would normally decorate the *Librarte* office. She would buy a Christmas tree, cover it in baubles, buy poinsettias to put on the desks, spread a velvet cloth over the photocopier and place the nativity scene on top of that and put a bottle of cider in the fridge, to celebrate with her colleagues on the morning of the 24th. 'Here's to my good friends, God bless you, I hope the Three Kings bring you lots of presents, and may next year be the best one yet.'

But this year was a mess: the office had just been closed down, they were all out of work, María had turned out to be a liar, a thief and a traitor. True, she had been forced into it, beaten and threatened by a heartless man, but she was a crook none the less. It was her fault that the magazine and the girls' lives were ruined.

'What have you got planned for Christmas?' Manchego asked her.

'Other than taking some biscuits to María in prison, not much,' she replied, feeling resigned to sadness.

'Right,' sighed Manchego.

'And you?'

'I was thinking of going to Nieva. Do you know, it's three years since I've spent Christmas with my family.'

'How come?'

'Well, Berta, the truth is,' Manchego replied, 'every time I go home they ask me if I've been promoted, if I've got a girlfriend, if I've solved any important cases, and I get the impression they're disappointed every time.'

'This year's different, though.'

'Work-wise, yes,' he replied. 'Girlfriend-wise, no.'

Berta felt heat rising through her whole body. Like when she was a girl and drank hot wine in the village square and her ears would start throbbing, her legs would start wobbling and her eyes would fill with tears.

Manchego hadn't lit the cigarette. He was holding it between two fingers that were trembling as much as Berta's legs. He suddenly fell silent. Their eyes spoke for them, the feelings of hurt giving way to something else. Somewhere along the way, these two had shed their pride, their singletons' peculiarities, their love of solitude, and they met midway between hope and fear.

'Maybe we can do something about the girlfriend thing,' said Berta, drawing a bit closer to Manchego.

He dropped the cigarette into the courtyard and threw his Suffolk sheep farmer's arms around her. She felt like she was hugging an oak tree, a beech with yellow autumn leaves, and she breathed in the smell of damp earth, wild mushrooms, farm animals and wood smoke.

The kiss tasted of nuts and chestnuts, hot wine, an open fire. Manchego and Berta, as different and as inseparable as two sides of a coin, remembered at that moment the sound of the San Martín church bells on a wedding day and how the echo rumbled and rang down the cliff until it hit the stream where they used to paddle as children. And the taste of stew, the whole village invited, finally our Berta is getting married, so grown up, how lovely, with a great guy, look how handsome he is, he looks like George Clooney, but taller. And the sound of fireworks, with a big finale, someone on the bridge sending rockets into the starry sky. That's what the kiss was like.

Chapter 51

The hotel, before it was a hotel, had been the palatial house of a once-wealthy family. It was full of odd corners, corridors and staircases, and the emergency stairs were made of mahogany and led down into a coach house with a coffered ceiling.

César Barbosa snuck in through the back door, silently crossed the garage and poked his head out into the darkness of the courtyard. Everything was quiet except for a couple of voices, a man's and a woman's, whispering sweet nothings on the first floor.

He tiptoed around the edge of the courtyard, and as he passed under the spot where the voices were coming from a cigarette dropped on his head. Then he heard the unmistakable sound of kissing, like soap bubbles bursting, and seized the opportunity to slip through the shadows unnoticed, sticking close to the walls, to go up to the door of the room where María was sleeping, to open it with a homemade lock pick and to give her the fright of her life.

María had fallen into a deep, Valium-induced sleep, and this complicated the attack somewhat. Barbosa shook her, slapped her, splashed her with water from the glass on her bedside table, lifted her sleeping body, put her under a cold shower, hit her with a wet towel and finally managed to reinstate the anxiety that the drugs had helped her overcome.

'Get dressed, slag, we're going,' he said under his breath.

'Where are we going?'

'To the Caribbean, can you fucking believe it . . .'

Just like he had seen in detective movies, Barbosa knotted the ends of the sheets together, and tied this improvised rope to the balcony. It was no more than four or five metres down to the side street where he had parked his Harley Davidson, so the end of the sheet dropped into a puddle on the ground.

'Get down there!' he ordered María. 'And if you do anything stupid, you're dead.'

María obeyed. She waited for him at the end of the rope, got on to the back of her lover's motorbike without a word of complaint, clung tightly to his leather jacket and let herself be whisked off towards the unknown like a feather in the wind, having lost all her willpower the day she was first unfaithful to Bernabé.

Perhaps she was aware that she would never see her children again, or the man she once swore to love in sickness and in health, in good times and in bad, for as long as she lived. And perhaps she could remember the good things from the marriage that had been built on hope, strengthened by the arrival of beautiful children, sustained by the everyday happiness of drinking hot chocolate and spending Sunday afternoons out in the country, and nourished by dreams of saving little by little, bathing at some beach down south, travelling, seeing her children graduate from distinguished universities and finding Bernabé, after all those years, as exciting as when they first kissed.

The brutal sound of the motorbike's engine starting up was multiplied a hundredfold by the damp walls of the narrow streets, producing a hellish noise that made Marlow and Moira Craftsman stir in their beds and shook Manchego and Berta out of the ecstasy of their embrace, catapulting them back to reality. As soon as they heard the roar of the motor and the sudden acceleration they ran straight to María's room, knowing they wouldn't find her there.

When he saw the open window and the dangling sheet, Manchego didn't think twice: he grabbed the improvised rope, jumped down into the street, drew his gun and pointed it at the disappearing shape of the motorbike.

'Don't shoot!' shrieked Berta, who was leaning over the balcony. 'You might hit María!'

'Christ on a bike!' shouted Manchego, defeated.

The inspector felt for his mobile and found it in his trouser pocket. He made one call: to his colleagues in the Granada police force, to whom he described the circumstances of the kidnapping and the two people involved.

Berta took out her mobile as well. With trembling fingers, she called Soleá.

'Soleá, do something, Barbosa has taken María away on his bike!'

'Where did they go?'

'Along the street behind the hotel, the one that goes up-hill.'

Soleá hung up without another word. She had arrived home moments earlier after spending the best afternoon of her life wrapped in Atticus's arms. He had left her on the other side of the wrought-iron gate, as though it required a monumental effort to leave her, if only for a few hours, until morning came and he could knock on the door again, say good morning and invite himself in for breakfast, see her still groggy with sleep and verify that it was true, that Soleá existed and she was his.

'Arcángel?'

'How's it going, Soleá?'

In all probability, Soleá's explanation was poor at best. But three or four reasonably coherent words were enough for Arcángel to understand that he needed to chase a Harley Davidson up Camino del Monte and beat the shit out of the guy riding it, the son of a bitch who had kidnapped his cousin's friend, because none of the Heredias, the Amayas, or any of the El Albaicín cousins – 'cousins' in the broadest sense of the word, as used by that family – were going to put up with that.

So, in less than two minutes over two hundred ruthless men were ready to tear Barbosa to pieces. Some in cars, some on foot, others on motorbikes or bundled into trucks, surrounded Sacromonte, cut off the nearby streets, the periphery of the old town, the new exits on to the motorway, and at some unknown point they merged with the police force and the civil guard. They were all disconcerted to find themselves fighting on the same side for once in their lives, a multicoloured army of uniforms, official vehicles, Seat Lagunas, black shirts, standard–issue guns and handmade penknives, the city stormed by the good guys to catch the bad guy Barbosa who Manchego and Soleá both despised in equal measure.

César Barbosa couldn't believe what he was seeing. Wherever he tried to escape, his path was blocked. Six or seven armed men lay in wait for him on each corner, with light glinting off their knives, gold teeth, crosses and police badges. That night there was one thing all those men could agree on: doing away with him.

In desperation, he stopped the motorbike in a wide street. He grabbed María by the hair. He shouted:

'I'll kill her! Let me out of here or I swear I'll kill her

right now!' He held a penknife in his hand up against María's neck.

'Everyone stay where you are!' ordered a police chief who took charge at that moment. 'We need a negotiator!'

But from among the crowd came another, louder and more authoritative voice.

'There's nothing to fucking negotiate!' bellowed Manchego as he jumped the barrier and ran into the street where Barbosa was threatening to cut the terrified María's throat.

Manchego slammed into Barbosa and the impact took out María, the Harley Davidson, a full rubbish bin and a poster advertising a flamenco recital. The two men rolled on the floor, fighting like gladiators, they bled, bit and hit, they thrashed one another, and the rest of the spectators looked on, stupefied, for some reason not splitting up the fight, until Berta screamed to make herself heard over the uproar:

'Somebody help him, for fuck's sake!'

That's what she said. 'For fuck's sake.' It was the first time in her life that Berta Quiñones had used a swear word, probably the only one she knew, because the other possibility – 'Somebody help him, please' – wasn't going to have the same effect under the circumstances. It was a highly conscious, planned and efficient use of a swear word that Manchego would revisit with his friends, in stitches, at every party. Especially when he described the tone of her voice and the purple tinge to her contorted face.

'It's not funny,' she would complain.

And Manchego would wrap his arms around her to quieten her with kisses.

Berta's scream managed to break the spell that had paralysed everyone present and bring them back to life. More than twenty burly men, some police and some Heredia cousins, were needed to finally contain Barbosa and free

María. But the difficult part was deciding what to do with the prisoner, whether he should be dealt with according to civil law or Gypsy law. The civil guard won, of course, but in exchange and by way of thanks for their help in detaining Barbosa, they gave Tomás, the family representative, a life-size image of the Virgen del Pilar to symbolize friendship and collaboration between the two sides.

That night, the only ones who slept like logs, thanks to one of Señá Candela's special herbal blends, were Marlow and Moira Craftsman. And they didn't just get a wonderful night's sleep but, for some strange reason, during the night the fire of their lacklustre relationship was rekindled and they both developed wolfish appetites – what could there have been in Candela's tea? – and when they awoke the next morning they made passionate love, like two wild animals, with teeth and nails, grunts and scratches, a pitched battle that drained their strength until lunchtime.

The rest of the inhabitants of Sacromonte congregated in the early hours at Dolores's cave to celebrate the capture of Barbosa with drinks and music that thundered like a tropical storm on the new city of Granada. That night, over a thousand complaints went unheard at the central police station by order of the provincial chief of the civil guard, who, alongside about ten of his colleagues, took part in the midnight celebration.

They sang and danced until their hands hurt from clapping and their feet from stamping, their nails from playing guitar and their hands from beating *cajones*, because, as Dolores reminded them all at the top of her voice, they had plenty to celebrate. Barbosa was going to spend a long time behind bars and, what was more, Soleá had met the love of her life, Tico from Dolores's cave, a Gypsy at heart, with Gypsy customs already deep inside him: no one was going to shake Tico's new home, his new identity, his new family out of him.

'What can I get you, Tico?' asked his future mother-in-law cheekily.

'I'll have ham!' he replied, adding: 'By Jove!'

Chapter 52

That morning, after his unexpected dose of unbridled passion, Marlow Craftsman was breakfasting on bread rolls with olive oil, tomato and ham in the tiled courtyard of the charming little hotel when Atticus arrived in last night's clothes, having not slept a wink, with raw fingertips, a throat like sandpaper and messy hair. Atticus asked for a glass of tap water and sat down opposite his father at the table for two.

They had always got on well. Perhaps in contrast to his brother Holden, the rebel, who had never bent to paternal authority and always did what he liked, Marlow and Atticus knew one another so well that a glance was enough to understand what the other was thinking at any moment.

'Business is business,' said Marlow. 'We're not an NGO.'

'But, Father—'

'We've already lost a lot of money with *Librarte*.'

'We wouldn't have lost so much if we hadn't been robbed,' protested Atticus. 'Give us a loan,' he pleaded, as if he too was part of the disaster.

'With what guarantees, Atticus?' replied Marlow. '*Librarte* has no readers, no advertisers, no name for itself, nothing.'

'But it will have. You'll see.'

Marlow shook his head and swallowed half a bread roll. Oil ran down from the corners of his mouth. After sitting in silence for a few seconds, Atticus had an idea. While his father devoured his breakfast, he drew up a plan in his head that would help save the magazine and its staff from ruin. He would lead the project himself if necessary. *Librarte* would relaunch, would be reborn from its ashes, like a phoenix, thanks to Remedios Heredia, her granddaughter Soleá and Hemingway himself.

'OK,' he spoke up. 'You want guarantees? I'll give you guarantees!'

Then he pushed his chair back and got up from the table, grabbed his father by the arm, dragged him out of the hotel, driven by hot-blooded fury, led him through the narrow streets and stopped in front of the door to the Heredias' house.

He knocked loudly. They waited.

The family were spread out among various houses in Sacromonte. Some had found places to sleep on sofas or mats, in hammocks or shared beds, others were still in Dolores's cave, passed out on the floor, and others were sleeping soundly in the backs of their trucks. The only person who was awake at noon that day was Remedios, wearing her housecoat and an apron spotted with tomato, her grey hair up in a bun, her face clean, her movements brisk from all that yoga and a smile showing off her gold teeth, ready to face a day of salt cod and potatoes, a collective hangover and the retelling of old stories.

She wasn't ready, however, for the surprise of being confronted by Marlow's blank face and Atticus's excitement: as soon as he saw her, Atticus threw himself into her arms and covered her with noisy kisses.

'Granny Remedios, go and wake Soleá up, this is important.'

Remedios shot off, convinced that those two upright Englishmen had come to ask her granddaughter's hand in marriage, and because Soleá's father wasn't alive to give his blessing, she would have to call Manuela and Tomás as well so they could be witnesses to what was about to happen.

'Soleá! Soleá, Manuela, Tomás, come down to the courtyard, all of you!'

'What's going on, Granny?' various rasping voices said from the windows.

'Tico has come to formally propose!'

Atticus heard Remedios and was terrified. He hadn't intended to publicly declare his love for Soleá: that wasn't the motive for his visit that morning. In reality – which now seemed treacherous – it had occurred to him, faced with his father's refusal to cover the costs of *Librarte*, to tell him the story about Hemingway.

Atticus thought he had found the solution to the magazine's problems in the family secret, which they could shout to the four winds, spread across the five continents, to bring renown to *Librarte*. 'We found Hemingway's unknown and illegitimate daughter,' the headline would say. 'Remedios, an old woman who lives in her Andalusian house in Granada's El Albaicín district, surrounded by her large family, many of them grandchildren or great-grandchildren of the famous North American writer.'

There was an enormous difference between that plan and the glorious prospect of getting down on one knee in front of Soleá and declaring his love to her, with his father and the entire Heredia family as witnesses. But when he saw the shocked Soleá with her tangled hair and shining eyes, and behind her all the other members of the clan, he was left in no doubt that Remedios was right: there was no other reason for that visit than to ensure he would be by Soleá's side for ever.

Atticus unbuttoned his shirt. He dropped one knee on to the floor, bowed his head, took Soleá's hand in his and said in Spanish with a London accent:

'Soleá, I came to your house with my father as my witness. Will you marry me?'

'That's not how it's done, Tico,' she said. 'Your dad has to ask my brother.'

Tomás came out from behind a group of cousins, with his arms open wide and a smile across his face. Since Marlow Craftsman was unable to speak a single word of Spanish, it was unanimously decided that they should skip the formalities. Marlow received the hug with a smile, not really understanding what it was all about.

Then Soleá's sisters and cousins started dancing around the couple clapping and singing a folk song that went: *'Ali ali ay! Ali ali ay! Ali, ali, alay, he's taken her away!'*

Arcángel, noticing how pale Marlow looked, went up behind him and whispered in his ear in rudimentary English, 'My cousin woman, your son man,' so that he could at least participate in the general merriment with some idea of what was going on.

Marlow sat down on a step next to a very old earthenware jar, wide-eyed. He took a silk handkerchief out of his pocket to wipe away the sweat that covered his forehead, and started racking his brain for ways to tell Moira without the shock killing her.

Just then, Granny Remedios sat down beside him.

Chapter 53

'Look, *Míster Crasman*,' said Remedios, despite knowing perfectly well that Marlow couldn't understand her, 'my Soleá hasn't got any kind of dowry. The only thing that all the girls have between them is this house and the little we have left from when Arcángel bought the land from Manuela. But it upsets me to give her away like this, without a penny to her name, and I've come up with an idea. You're an editor, you like books, and authors, and all that stuff, right? Well, come upstairs with me because I'm going to show you something.'

Remedios took Marlow's hand and tugged hard until she got him to stand up. Then she pulled and pushed him inside, crossing the living room, up the three flights of narrow stairs to the attic door, which she opened with one of the keys that hung round her neck in a bundle which included ten or so medallions bearing images of the Virgin Mary.

The roof sloped and light entered through a small window at floor level. There were bits of furniture, lamps, books and cobwebs. It was obvious that someone went up there a lot but never did any cleaning. Remedios bent to unlock a velvet-lined wooden chest with another key that hung around her neck.

By this stage, Marlow didn't know what to think. The sound of shouting, clapping, stamping feet and singing was drifting through the walls from the courtyard, and there he was with this solemn old woman, who was turning the key to what looked like a coffin. It could just as easily contain treasure as the body of some unburied relative. A mummy, complete with hair, teeth and scraps of clothing.

The lock gave, the lid opened with a piercing squeal and Remedios moved aside so that Marlow could see the contents of her best-kept secret.

'These things belonged to my father, Ernest Hemingway,' she said. 'My mother kept them to remember him by. She didn't steal them,' she clarified, 'he gave them to her to wash and then, when she went to give them back, he said he didn't want to see them again and told her to burn them. But she didn't burn them, because she was in love with him. And then, when she found out she was pregnant and left the house, she brought them here, put them in this box and didn't tell anyone.'

Marlow knelt down next to Remedios. Two big fat tears were rolling down her cheeks. With great ceremony, the old woman showed him a First World War soldier's jacket, which bore the name 'Ernest Hemingway' sewn on to the lapel. Seeing the disbelief on Craftsman's face, Remedios found the two English words she was looking for:

'My father,' she said.

Then she removed the rest of the uniform from the chest: trousers, socks, boots and a rusty pistol. Finally, she held out a very old leather-bound notebook that was full of the famous writer's famous handwriting.

Marlow turned the pages one by one: there were over a hundred.

Taken aback, he understood that what he held in his hands was no less than Hemingway's personal, secret and unpublished diary, with notes, drawings, thoughts, verse, stories and love poems. On the last page he discovered the key to the mystery in a drawing showing a woman's name piercing a heart: Macarena.

'My mother,' said Remedios.

At the bottom of the chest there was a small black-and-white photo of a very pretty and very young woman who had doe eyes, dark hair and Gypsy blood. She was dressed in a long skirt, a black shawl and a white apron, and she was coquettishly lifting the hem of her skirt above her ankle. He took it, thought Marlow, Hemingway took it himself when he was in Granada for the first time. He mentioned her in countless stories and we never knew who he was thinking about when he described Spain with female characteristics.

'My mother told me when I was old enough to understand, after my father had died, the poor thing, because she thought I'd see him differently if I knew that I wasn't his daughter and my father was another man, Hemingway, whom I'd never seen in all my life. She said that she had really loved him, because it was the kind of first love that you don't forget however many years go by, and a lot of the time, without me noticing, she used to try and find things in me that looked like him. The square chin, the fierce look. Not much more. In the end, my Soleá inherited most of it, to the great surprise of her father, Pedro Abad, who couldn't understand where the girl's blue eyes came from when everyone on both sides of the family was so dark. So I had to tell him too, and Manuela. I said to Manuela: "My girl, your grandfather wasn't your grandfather, this guy Hemingway was, but you must swear you won't tell anyone." Then one day, my Soleá was shut in the attic as punishment, and she opened the chest and found all this. She didn't understand anything. She asked me, "Whose is the uniform, Granny?" and I said, "It was your grandfather's." "Who wrote the poetry, Granny?" And I said, "I did." And because she was only little and couldn't read or write yet, she believed me.'

Marlow didn't understand a word of what Remedios was saying. What he did understand was that he had discovered a treasure which would generate immense interest, an incalculable fortune and unknowable consequences.

The story of Hemingway and Macarena's affair needed to be told. Someone would have to do the research, analyse the writer's words one by one, together with the context and situation in which they were written, the effects of that passionate love story on Hemingway's later work and his indomitable spirit. They would have to revisit his entire oeuvre in the light of the new information and, of course, the diary would have to be published, with footnotes and contributions from biographers and scholars. They would have to arrange for the diary to be exhibited at an important museum, to present Remedios in society as the illegitimate daughter of one of the greats of universal literature, along with the whole family, including Arcángel, Potaje, Aunt Consuelos and the seventeen cousins from Antequera. They would have to track down the family in Granada that the author stayed with and the house where Remedios was conceived. There was so much to do that they would probably need a whole team of researchers to work on it for months or even years.

The team would have to be made up of Spaniards, of course, given the fact that the Heredia family's skills in English left a lot to be desired. They would have to be completely trustworthy, capable of keeping a secret of this size completely under their hats, competent, with knowledge of literature, discreet and personally committed to the Craftsman publishing house to the point of feeling that its successes and failures were their own.

People like Berta Quiñones, Asunción Contreras, Gabriela Fernández and Soleá Abad Heredia. The *Librarte* girls.

And, of course, a solid man from Craftsman & Co to lead the project. A young man with a promising future and the desire to prove his worth. Someone who couldn't sit around waiting for Bestman to retire before he carved out a future for himself in the publishing world: his son Atticus, of course, whom Marlow mentally designated that very moment as head of Craftsman & Co's new secret and special operations team.

Who knew the soul of the Heredia family better than him, who else knew how to caress it more tenderly? Who was capable of touching Remedios's heart? Who, as it happened, was going to be the father of Hemingway's great-great-grandchildren?

'Well, this is my Soleá's dowry,' said Remedios. 'You can do what you like with it all. Take it to England if you like.'

Marlow wished he could have told the old woman that the value of this literary land exceeded all his expectations. All the money in the world couldn't repay her, but he would ensure she received regular royalty cheques for the intellectual rights. She would be rich and famous, the memory of her mother would be extolled and the name Heredia would go down in history, forever linked to Hemingway.

But, instead of words that would've been totally incomprehensible to the old woman, he decided to use the universal language of shared tears.

Marlow Craftsman and Remedios Heredia drew each other close, in a hug capable of going beyond borders, formalities, cultures, distances, explanations and conventions. That's how Atticus and Soleá found them after searching for them all over the house: inexplicably clinging to one another on the attic floor.

Chapter 54

When Moira Craftsman managed to compose herself after the excesses of lovemaking and restore some dignity to her immaculate appearance, she remembered that she had dreamt about Atticus again that night. This time it wasn't a cauldron of boiling water, it was a stretcher made of sticks bound together with twine that the natives were using to drag her son out of the jungle while he, sickly, feverish, wide-eyed and dripping with sweat, was shouting: 'Love, love!'

Her powers of analysis and her compulsive reading of Freud's *The Interpretation of Dreams* led her to the only possible conclusion: that instead of spending that Christmas at home in Kent, Atticus would stay in the heart of Spanish darkness, adopted by the exotic tribe of the Heredia cousins, their rustic drums, unfamiliar Christmas songs, processions and vigils. He wouldn't eat roast beef and Christmas pudding, he would eat stew and marzipan. He wouldn't spend the morning listening to the Berlin Philharmonic's concert, he would spend it sleeping off the excesses of the night before, and he wouldn't get a new Burberry coat as a present, he would get all the albums Camarón de la Isla ever recorded.

She switched on her phone and dialled a number. She waited.

'Holden, darling?'

'Mum?'

'I'm ringing because I've finally found out what your brother will be doing for Christmas. I'm so sorry it's taken this long,' she said. 'We can put your parents-in-law in Atticus's room after all.'

'You've found him?'

'Yes.'

'Is he all right?'

'Absolutely,' she managed to say with a shaky voice.

And she hung up quickly, so Holden couldn't ask her any more awkward questions.

In the end, they did all have very different Christmases that year: Marlow and Moira Craftsman returned to England on an Iberia flight, and for the first time in their lives they tried Galician octopus with peppers, a dish that the rest of the (Spanish) passengers devoured enthusiastically but which they chewed cautiously before spitting back out into their serviettes.

Manchego invited Berta to Nieva de Cameros and introduced her to his parents as his official girlfriend, which they couldn't believe. Either Berta had some hidden charms or their son's sudden love for a rather plain fifty-something woman was the result of witchcraft. It was best not to think what those hidden charms might be. It was best not to think about what kind of witch might be responsible.

Asunción took charge of returning the office to its former glory. At least the computers were still there, the photocopier still worked and they still had time to pay the rent. The only thing that needed to change was the sign on the door. It wouldn't be the *Librarte* office any more, it was now the headquarters of H&H: the coded acronym united the surnames Hemingway and Heredia, and under Atticus Craftsman's leadership the new organization would study the literary find of the century. Atticus and Soleá would do the fieldwork in Granada and then Berta, Asunción and Gaby would document and edit everything in Madrid.

After a jury in Granada found him guilty of kidnap, absconding, intent to kill and a whole load of other crimes, Barbosa was taken into custody, condemned to ten years' imprisonment and sent to the El Puerto penal colony, the furthest possible from María, on Inspector Manchego's recommendation, since she was a key witness in the case and implicated therein, as demonstrated by the knife wound on her right shoulder.

María returned to Madrid in quite a state: her nerves were shot and her soul destroyed. She stood in front of Bernabé with her head hanging, feeling sorry and ashamed. She told him that for about a year she had been stealing money from *Librarte*. That at first it had just been small amounts, but that those amounts got steadily larger, which explained the expensive bags and the fur coats, and the gifts for the kids, the trendy trainers and the plasma TV. That she hadn't sold the land in Valencia like she had told him – not that it mattered now, because in all likelihood the judge would order all her assets to be seized, so the little bit of land practically belonged to the bank already, as well as the money she would have to save over the next few years to repay *Librarte*. She also told him that she would probably be sentenced to between three and six months in Yeserías prison, and that she would rather the kids didn't see her in there. She asked him to tell them she was off travelling, a kind of half lie because she did have to travel to get from her house to Yeserías, and that she loved them, and missed them a lot.

She also told Bernabé about Barbosa, but presented him as a partner in crime rather than a lover. She explained that it had been the Pirate's idea, after she mistakenly paid him twice for the same invoice, and everything started from there, they split everything down the middle, like Bonnie and Clyde, but without the sex. Definitely no sex. She explained as well that at one point she had got scared because she wanted to stop stealing but he made her carry on, threatening to harm the kids if she grassed him up, so she had no choice but to carry on doing wrong without benefiting from the thefts. By the end he was keeping everything. All she had left was her fear.

And that was true. It was almost entirely true.

Strangely, the flame of María and Bernabé's lost love was rekindled in prison. For some mysterious reason, on the three or four times they were allowed to be alone in the small cell in Yeserías, their passion was so devastating that it smashed through concrete walls and behind them lay a white sandy beach, a perfectly tranquil sea, a full moon and a starry sky.

So when, at the beginning of May, her four-and-a-half-month sentence complete, María breathed her first lungful of freedom and found Berta, Asunción, Soleá and Gaby waiting for her outside with their arms full of flowers, hugs and forgiveness, the first thing she did was tell them about her unexpected pregnancy, a child conceived behind bars, oh well, we'll tell everyone it was on a beach down south.

'We'll have to go together to buy maternity dresses for

Berta's wedding,' said Gaby suddenly and to everyone's surprise.

'You too, honey?'

'Yes! Me too, María, just like you! Due in December.'

They hugged long and hard, jumping and laughing hysterically. There was no pretty garden to sit in and tell each other the details, so the five members of the *Librarte* team sat down in the shade of a maple tree in the first green space they came across, at the junction of two roads.

'It was a few months ago, right, Asunción? Franklin told me that he wanted to go back to Argentina. He said he thought it would be best for both of us,' said Gaby. 'He even bought a ticket.'

'But, sweetie,' said Berta in shock, 'there's no couple in the world more in love than you two. What had got into him?'

'I had,' said Gaby. 'I wouldn't stop going on about having children, I didn't talk about anything else. I made him read books about pregnancy, take vitamins, make love in the weirdest positions, have heaps of tests. I was so obsessed with having a baby that I couldn't see what was in front of my eyes. Poor Franklin started thinking that we could never have kids.'

'So he thought that you could get on with it if he left,' said María.

'That's when I spoke to Asunción,' said Gaby, nodding towards her friend, 'and she gave me the key to everything. I went home, found him crying, I threw him on to the bed—'

'OK, OK,' interrupted Berta somewhat violently, 'we don't need all the details, we can imagine the rest.'

'I'm not imagining anything!' said Soleá. 'Come on, I want details!'

'Well,' Gaby went on, 'I kissed, bit and scratched him all over, and I convinced him that there's nothing in all the world that can make me happier than being with him. And at that moment I realized I was telling the truth. Our marriage is already the loveliest family in the world, with or without kids. So I stopped obsessing about pregnancy. I completely forgot about the whole thing and when I went to see the gynaecologist last week, she said I was two months pregnant.'

'There's nothing like a bit of distraction for getting pregnant,' said María. 'As soon as I get distracted, pow!'

Chapter 55

The dresses were made to fit their different-sized bellies; María's was twice the size of Gaby's because she was expecting her fourth baby while her friend was having her first, but they were the same cherry red to match the bride's bouquet.

Berta chose to wear a white suit, because she thought that at her age and size it was silly to stuff herself into one of those long silk and organdie dresses or shove a tiara and a lace veil on her head like a princess. She wore white flowers in her hair. On her finger was the engagement ring that Manchego had given her when they got back from Granada; round her neck, the pearl necklace that her four best friends had given her; in her hands, a bunch of wild peonies.

The service was held early so it wouldn't clash with the solemn mass for Carmen, patron saint of Ortigosa de Cameros, which made most people in the village happy. They didn't want to miss the wedding. Their little Berta, the girl with plaits and glasses, was now a radiant bride.

The groom arrived from Nieva in a car full to bursting with his parents, still looking astounded, and the witnesses, Macita, Josi, Carretero and Míguel, all wearing incredible suits, the same colour as the morning coat that Prince Charles wore to Prince Felipe's wedding, the day that half of Spain learnt you should wear grey to daytime ceremonies.

Manchego, meanwhile, had been determined to wear the National Police Corps full dress uniform – peaked cap, blue jacket with gold buttons, tie and white gloves – despite his mother's objection that it looked horribly plain without medals or the sabre she had begged him to borrow for the occasion. Many of his police colleagues were also in uniform, which scared a lot of the little kids and old folks from the village, the only groups who still feared authority, but the single and married women loved it. They succumbed to the undeniable attraction of a man in uniform, better still a police or army uniform, with the corresponding connotations of power and authority that last until the morning after a night of lovemaking when the man wakes up naked and defenceless, his uniform crumpled at the end of the bed, and the girl asks what happened to turn her handsome prince into a hairy frog in a matter of hours.

Macita stopped the car at the entrance to San Martín church, at exactly 11 a.m. on a warm 16 July, in front of the small group that had formed in the portico. Manchego was pushed out, followed by his cortège of parents and witnesses, and strode into the church to the sound of applause, on the arm of his mother who was squeezed into a sky blue suit with lace edging, holding an antique fan and wearing little heels.

Under her gold canopy and surrounded by irises, the Virgen del Carmen held the Christ child in her arms and awaited the procession. The first rows of the church were already filled with guests and nosy parkers, the women and girls in typical dress with cloth skirts, embroidered shawls, silver brooches and their hair scraped up into buns on top of their heads, while the men wore neckerchiefs, berets, sashes around their waists and waistcoats. Carmen's day was important, and everyone had to open trunks, air out shawls, check that there were no marks from the previous year, backstitch sleeves, starch shirts, sew buttons on firmly, try on skirts – oh, look how you've grown, my girl – let down hems, find ways of doing up the little bows or polishing espadrilles.

Berta arrived fifteen carefully calculated minutes late so as to look neither too keen nor too laid back. Bernabé drove her in his Rodius, from which he had previously removed the three kids' car seats, sweet wrappers and sand from the park. He stopped in front of the church and waited patiently for his eleven passengers to alight: the bride, María and her three children, Asunción, Gaby and Soleá, Asunción's two sons and Atticus Craftsman, looking like a dandy with his light-coloured jacket, double-breasted waistcoat, yellow tie, sky blue shirt, messy hair and cold hands.

He was the one all the girls noticed. They ignored the uniforms, transfixed instead by his English aristocrat's demeanour, his slight limp and his half smile. But on seeing the attention he paid to Soleá, a tanned beauty in a backless dress who wore her long hair loose, they didn't dare approach him in case the wild animal bit them. Her father wasn't there to give her away, so Berta walked into the church on the arm of the mayor, an old schoolmate. Until the day before, Berta hadn't remembered much about him except his wicked ways, his name, Anselmo, and how bad he was at dancing the paso doble. The women in the portico shouted to tell her how gorgeous she looked, the altar boy rang the bells and the inhabitants of surrounding villages were confused by the time because the main mass had always been at twelve.

Manchego was waiting at the altar. He turned towards the door so he could see Berta come in. And he gazed at her with the eyes of his soul, which don't see age or extra pounds, only the marvel of a shared heart, and he saw her as a twenty-year-old, firm of flesh, ripe of mouth, pale and radiant, his bride.

She held out her hands to him and said 'I love you' without the priest's permission. They held hands through the whole ceremony, until the time came to exchange rings, and then they cried, sighed, laughed and, after hearing the magic words 'I now pronounce you man and wife', they kissed, this time with the priest's blessing. The priest was moved as well, but he tried not to let it show so he didn't set an uncomfortable precedent that he would have to begrudgingly repeat at other weddings with couples who were less in love, lest people thought he had favourites.

Grains of rice and flower petals rained down on them as they left the church, they received hundreds of hugs and then went back into the cool church to participate in their first public ceremony as husband and wife.

The solemn procession of the Virgen del Carmen was led by the band with their piccolos and drums, followed by the dancers wearing espadrilles and coloured skirts, then the men carrying the Virgin. Last came the people of Ortigosa, following the patron saint who protects their land and families, brings together friends and couples, watches over sleep and cures illnesses, who comes in secret to watch a birth or accompany a death, and is the reason why half the girls in Ortigosa are called Carmen.

Everyone walked precariously down the steep cobbled streets towards the village square, until they reached the oak tree that towers over the bullring, and there they let the Virgin rest for a while, so the women could bring her flowers, dancers could devote to her their hours of practice, their ribbons and sticks, and their hopes. Then, on the men's shoulders once more, to the San Miguel church and the main mass and then vermouth in the square, with the band playing paso dobles, until it was time to eat.

After the aperitif, the newlyweds and their guests walked up to Berta's grandfather's allotment, across the street from the house, next to the old telegraph office. The same allotment where some naughty boys, who were no doubt present at the meal, once hid to play a trick on a dreamy girl who used to sit by the attic window.

The long table had been laid for fifty, and was a bit wonky given the natural slope of the ground, but it was very pretty with wildflower centrepieces, antique chinaware, jugs of Rioja, all under a huge grapevine dripping with fruit.

Manchego raised his glass.

'Thank you all for being here, for bearing witness to the love that Berta and I share, and for being part of our story. We never would've caught Barbosa without your help, and we never would've met if it wasn't for him either. So here's to the Pirate, I hope he comes out of prison a man, in the broadest sense of the word, and that he's lost his taste for abusing women, the son of a bitch, Christ on a bike—'

'Hey, Manchego, Mancheguito,' Berta cut him off. 'It's all over now.'

'To the son of a bitch Barbosa,' shouted Manchego before downing his wine.

There was also dancing. At nine o'clock in the square, the village made the most of the fact that the Starlight band had been hired for the fiestas. They played a mixture of paso dobles and Lady Gaga covers in a brutal mishmash of tradition and modernity until ten thirty when silence fell for the fire bull to pass through.

Berta had told her friends to come in comfy clothes and not to wear heels, because the thing with the bull was serious; she still got scared stiff when she thought about it. But they didn't pay her any attention. They waited with bated breath for Adalberto to come out carrying the fire bull, a frame covered in fireworks; they were all terrified because he couldn't see well under his costume and his arms were getting burnt. He started running, forgetting that some people were outsiders, rich kids from Madrid, and didn't know that the bull would charge and the spectators had to get out of the way – instead, they stayed stock-still, like halfwits, and he had to shout: 'Move!' before he flattened them. What a scene, five policemen and their wives, and the smell of their scorched uniforms.

Berta had gone up to the balcony of the casino and was shouting like mad from there, because Manchego had started running behind the bull, trying to wrestle him into the fountain, 'You're going to burn yourself, you plonker!' while Adalberto was trying to escape up the street.

Finally, the lads from the village rugby-tackled Manchego into the fountain. Nothing serious, just a short dip in cold water and cow spit.

'Let's get you out of those clothes,' said Berta, trying not to laugh, more relaxed now, in the big bedroom of her parents' house. 'Get into bed, go on, or you'll catch cold and we won't have a honeymoon.'

'I don't need to warm up,' he said, letting her fuss over him. 'You might not believe it, but I'm burning up inside.'

Berta undid the gold buttons of his jacket, took off his shirt, unbuckled his belt.

Manchego held her as if she was his first love, with a mixture of curiosity and fear, with closed eyes and open hands.

284

And they shared fifty years of love in a single night, with sparks that burned down to embers, like two lit torches that would never go out again.

Chapter 56

Moira Craftsman flatly refused to go back to Granada to attend the 'silly nonsense' of her son's Spanish wedding. She later found out that the most surprising things happened during those three days and nights: men tore off their shirts then danced bare-chested, the newlyweds were lifted aloft under a shower of sugared almonds, and Atticus's tie was cut off and pieces of it shared among guests.

She decided to ignore the music that echoed in her head for those three days and instead dedicated herself body and soul to the final preparations for the proper wedding, which would take place on the first Saturday of September at their house in Kent.

Fortunately, the bride hadn't shown the least interest in being involved in organizing the event because, as Atticus had explained somewhat harshly over the phone, Soleá believed they were already married, according to Catholic and Gypsy customs, and she would rather go on their honeymoon in Ibiza, where the sunsets were an incredible colour.

After that, Moira couldn't shake the sound of the springs in a beaten-up old bed in Ibiza, and the banging of a headboard against a wall. It kept her awake for ten nights in a row. When she closed her eyes she clearly saw a little whitewashed house, surrounded by pine trees and pots of flowers, furnished with wicker chairs and Mexican rugs, the coloured walls decorated with the strangest of objects. At the back, under a canopy made of coloured sarongs, she saw a bed covered in cushions, and Soleá naked on the bed, tousled hair, clinging to Atticus as if she might strangle him. He loved her in a way that made him tear, hurt and strain, because he had discovered a new way to breathe without air, and he had realized that he couldn't go on living without Soleá.

The scene was so violent that white feathers flew out from the pillows, they tore the sheets and broke the bed. But they carried on making love on the floor, not realizing that the walls of the house were starting to shake and the foundations to crumble.

The invitations had been sent out in May, inside huge envelopes lined with rose-patterned tissue paper and accompanied by elegant cards giving details of the time, place, dress code, wedding list, local hotels, a map and the announcement that there would be a special menu for vegetarians, coeliacs, and those with lactose intolerance and nut allergies.

Of course, the dress code was none other than light-coloured morning coats for the men, and cocktail dresses with hats or fascinators for the women. There was a line indicating that the mother of the groom would be in lilac so that others wouldn't wear the same colour and steal any thunder from the person whose big day it really was.

Because one thing was clear: given Atticus's disastrous choice of wife, Moira had to take the reins and do what would have been expected of a more respectable bride,

287

however exhausting the job that had fallen to her proved to be.

First she had to choose the dress, either Alexander McQueen or Stella McCartney of course, and have Grandmother Craftsman's diamond bracelet set in a silk tiara to be worn over the lace veil.

She ordered the shoes from Stuart Weitzman, even though she would have preferred something more traditional, but when she walked past the window she saw a pair so scandalously delicate that she had to go in and try them. As luck would have it her feet were the same size as Soleá's, so Moira could feel for herself how comfortable and soft they were and secretly planned to sneak into her daughter-in-law's room after the wedding and collect them, along with the tiara, the veil and the dress, because she couldn't let Soleá shove those beautiful things into her grandmother's attic. No, Moira would keep them and perhaps, if the time came, they could be used again, when Atticus came to his senses and remarried, this time to an elegant English girl, of course.

The wedding presents started arriving at the beginning of June. Since Atticus had been away for several months and the bride's address was off the map, everything was sent to the house in Kent, which allowed Moira to keep tabs on who gave what. This information came into its own when she made the table plan, because she was able to seat people according to the value of their gifts. The drawing room became a gallery with all manner of artworks, silver, porcelain, glass and other fine objects on display.

In her black notebook Moira wrote down a list of names followed by a description of the gift and an estimate of its price, as well as a note on the effort each person had made depending on their economic situations. In other words, the silver jug from the Cromwells deserved less thanks than the tray from the Snowdons, given what a bad time of it they had been having since the property market crashed.

Victoria Bestman, as always, won the prize for generosity, because she sent a Cartier box with some diamond earrings that had belonged to her mother, together with a note which said that they were a hereditary gift and should pass directly to Atticus's daughters, bypassing Soleá, who wasn't really family after all.

Grandmother Craftsman, meanwhile, took the prize for lack of common sense. She turned up unannounced one Sunday at teatime, driving a convertible Bentley, with her chauffeur in the passenger seat, and shouted that she couldn't think of a better gift for her grandson than a two-seater racing car. She had driven from London, dicing with death on the narrow lanes, with Albinoni's *Adagio* at full volume and a cigarette in a holder between her fingers. They had tea in the library, the silence as thick as hummus after Grandmother Craftsman said in passing: 'I didn't like you all that much to start with, either,' which Moira took personally despite Marlow's best efforts to convince her otherwise.

'How do you want me to take it, Marlow?'

'In the abstract, Moira, in the abstract.'

One of the biggest setbacks in the process of organizing the wedding was the church. The Craftsman family didn't often attend services at the church in Sevenoaks, even though they were generous benefactors and owned a mausoleum in the rear part of the cemetery. However, they were respected by the community and had always maintained a good relationship with Reverend Fellow, so they invited him to dinner as soon as they had set the date for the wedding, to give him the news and ask him to take care of the ceremony.

'Impossible,' he said. 'They've already been married by the Catholic Church.'

'Well, now they'll be married by ours,' replied Moira.

'The thing is, Mrs Craftsman, as far as I know, your son Atticus was baptized and received the sacraments of the Catholic Church prior to his wedding. That is to say, he has changed religion.'

Moira had an almighty fit at the reverend when he revealed that unsavoury news, then threw him out, cursing his lack of authority with regard to his flock. Then she started to weep inconsolably as she remembered her misfortune when it came to her sons' weddings: first, Holden, with a bride who was six months pregnant, and now Atticus, with a Spanish Roman Catholic.

There would be no church, what an embarrassment, but there would be an altar with flowers in the small chapel at their house, someone would recite a few verses by Keats and a choir would sing. The bride would enter on Marlow's arm and the groom on her own lilac muslin-clad arm; Moira would walk solemnly, putting on a brave face, and the guests would believe that the tears she was holding back were of emotion and not of anger. She would spread out a red carpet from the living room, crossing the hall. Soleá would walk down the stairs and Atticus would come out from the library and meet her in the chapel. It would be a bit odd, but it would have to do.

They put up a white marquee in the garden, between the rose garden and the lake; they hung eight chandeliers from the canvas roof and decorated the walls with family portraits brought out from the house. They planted real trees between the tables and the centrepieces were ordered from a famous florist in London, the same one the Middletons chose for their daughter's wedding.

Planning the menu required masterful diplomacy. Back in 1979, before his sons were even born, Marlow had promised his great friend the Count of Bradford that his restaurant, Porters, would provide catering for each and every celebration at his house. And so it had been, however much Moira cursed her luck. She preferred French cuisine to traditional English food, and would have given her life to serve soufflé and sole *meunière* instead of the overly familiar roast tomato and basil soup, terrine of smoked salmon and beef Wellington with mushrooms and brandy sauce, but when she suggested a change to her husband he went off on one about a gentleman's word and its resistance to the passing of time, the principle of loyalty, the value of honour and the British people's inevitable, inherited and deep-seated hatred of the French. Then he slammed his fist down on the table, convincing Moira that her efforts were utterly useless. In the end, her only victory was to swap the dessert and have crème caramel instead of jelly with cranberries, and she comforted herself with being able to offer menus adapted to meet the special dietary requirements of certain guests. In this way, hiding behind allergies, intolerances, religious prohibitions, orthorexia, vegetarianism or difficulties with chewing, she was able to devise a parallel and almost clandestine menu that she quietly recommended to every single one of her guests.

The final straw came at the last moment when she discovered that on top of the wedding cake there was an edible miniature of Atticus and Soleá astride one another in a rowing scull; the detail had been added by Holden, who had decorated his own wedding cake with a figure of his pregnant bride dragging him towards the altar.

And so, victory by victory, failure by failure, Moira just about managed to survive until the first Saturday of

September and appear elegant and smiling before the guests, none of whom wanted to miss the intriguing wedding of the heir and the Gypsy girl.

Chapter 57

What happened that day in the old house in Kent had no more scientific basis than elves or witchcraft. How else to explain the sun bursting through the grey clouds, or the thousands of migratory birds that flew over the garden all at once, or the mesmerizing blue of Soleá's Hemingway eyes as she came downstairs, or the irresistible power of her enchantment, the same one that had made Atticus fall in love, which made the men cling tightly to their wives so they didn't lose their heads and made all the women happy to anchor them to reality.

Soleá, looking like a vestal virgin with long black hair like a runaway thoroughbred's mane, came down the stairs like a dream from an ancient Roman temple and walked down the hallway towards Atticus, floating on the cloud of her silk dress, not touching the floor, not looking at any-one, because for her no one else existed but the blond soldier waiting for her at the altar with open arms.

No one listened to the music or the poems during the ceremony. The only thing that anyone heard all day, as clearly as broken silence, was the persistent, rhythmical beating of two racing hearts. No one tasted the delicacies that arrived at their tables, or listened to the speeches, or appreciated the quality of the champagne, or the sweetness of the meringue, because all their senses were fixed upon Soleá and Atticus; a gravitational force of supernatural proportions, a bona fide electrical charge that at around midnight was finally liberated as an explosive orthogenesis, an earthquake measuring nine on the Richter scale, a terrifying tsunami that inexplicably affected everyone there.

The only person who did know exactly what had happened was Moira, but, for all the ups and downs of the years to come, she managed to keep the secret until the day she died and feign ignorance when anyone asked her (in private, of course) what she had put in the food to make everyone experience the same orgasm at the same time. It had been particularly shocking in the case of couples who hadn't slept in the same bed for years.

'It must've been a collective hallucination,' she would reply, flustered, while trying to erase from her mind what she had seen by chance and could never get over, for all the intensive therapy sessions she went to. At midnight, bored of champagne and dancing, Atticus and Soleá had slipped away from the party under the cover of darkness and taken refuge in the library. Because they had arrived barely in time that morning, dishevelled and sweaty in the car given to them by Grandmother Craftsman, they hadn't had a chance to fully explore the house. Moira had been nervously waiting for them in the circular gallery with the hairdresser, the stylist, the interior decorator, the photographer, little Oliver dressed as a tin soldier, the hostesses dressed as nineteenth-century maids, and in such a tizzy that no forced smile could hide her annoyance. She whisked Soleá away as soon as she got out of the car and marched her up to Atticus's room, on the first floor, where the white dress was hanging from the ceiling lamp so that it didn't get crumpled, her shoes, her tiara and even her fancy underwear, bought in a well-known shop on Regent Street, awaited her. At first, Moira objected to the bride wearing the awful gold crucifix that for some reason she refused to take off, but when Soleá threatened to run away barefoot across the fields behind the house, she had to give in to the only condition imposed by the otherwise docile, resigned young woman.

'Today is proof of my love for you, Tico,' Soleá had told her husband when they were driving under the chestnut trees that lined the drive. 'I'll do anything your mother asks me, I'll be like a passive little lamb, but promise me that we'll go back to where we've come from as soon as we can, before I go crazy.'

'I promise,' Atticus replied. 'I swear by these,' he added, kissing the tips of his fingers as he had seen the Gypsies do in El Albaicín.

So, the literary heart of the house – the library containing eight thousand books, with its open fire, velvet sofa and the armchair where Atticus recovered from his rowing injury, the same chair where he learnt to love Duras, Lawrence, Miller, Nabokov and Sade – had remained closed, fascinatingly dark until that moment.

Atticus led his wife hastily down the hall, under the portraits of the Craftsman grandparents, opened the library door, settled Soleá on to the sofa and went to light the fire, which immediately burst into life with yellow flames.

She got up silently and went to stroke the leather-bound volumes. She and her colleagues at *Librarte* had always dreamt of living surrounded by books like these, some of which were hundreds of years old.

'One day,' Berta liked to say, 'we're going to get an amazing library together. We'll fill it with all the books we've read. It'll be like Borges's library, a metaphor for the universe: circular, with hexagonal walls, and infinite. And even if the world ends and the human race becomes extinct, our library will endure, "illuminated, solitary, infinite, perfectly motionless, equipped with precious volumes, useless, incorruptible, secret".'

The others would close their eyes and imagine a place that was different for each of them and yet identical: exactly like the library in the house in Kent.

While Atticus lit the fire, Soleá wandered around the room, her hands gently stroking the spines of the books, until one in particular caught her attention because its red leather was so hot.

'This book's on fire,' she said in surprise.

Atticus left the bellows on the floor and went over to his wife.

'Let me see,' he said with a strange tremor in his voice.

Among the innocent novels of Jack London an anonymous book was pulsating, as red and furtive as its five erotic siblings.

'I've never told you about my private library, have I?'

'The five books piled up on your bedside table?'

'Yes,' said Atticus. 'Well, it seems that you've just found the sixth.'

They opened it together, burning the tips of their fingers, and discovered, not the least bit surprised, that it was no less than Richard Francis Burton's translation of the *Kama Sutra*, with hand-drawn illustrations inserted into the book on creased pieces of card.

'The man who owned this collection was a talented artist as well as an avid reader,' Atticus managed to say.

'Or the woman,' whispered Soleá.

But Atticus had already ripped off her dress and let it

fall on to the carpet. And Soleá had lain down on top of it, in front of the fire, she had let her hair down, removed her shoes, peeled off her tights and adopted one of the positions catalogued by Vatsyayana in around the year 300 of the Christian era. And Atticus was trying to adapt to her movements when, unexpectedly, the library door opened and there appeared the rigid, statuesque face of Moira Craftsman. She had been looking for them everywhere, irritated at finding them missing, and, guided only by her prison officer's instincts, had found them in the library.

Soleá and Atticus were completely unaware that, that night, for the first time in her life, Moira watched a couple so entwined that it would have been difficult to separate one from the other or identify the body parts that belonged to each one. If at that moment the fire had raged out of control and they had both burned to death, the only way to tell them apart would have been with a DNA test of the charred flesh and, given the challenge presented by that task, it would have been better to put their ashes into the same urn and grieve for them together: one of life's ironies.

Moira stood with her hand on the door frame, paralysed, and looked over at the corner of the room where she saw a wise-looking man of about eighty, smoking a pipe and accompanied by a little Hobbit. The man greeted her affably, lifting his hat. 'It's been a long time, dear Moira,' he said wordlessly. 'How we've changed since those distant times when you and Marlow shared your illicit love in his room in Exeter College. You were able to reach ecstasy in under ten minutes, simply by reading passages from the six erotic books that he gave you, young and inexperienced as you were, when he realized how poorly your imagination matched your desire. How we three enjoyed those forbidden games, Moira Craftsman, and what a shame that we so quickly forget how exciting love can be when it's no longer clandestine. Now my Hobbit and I prefer these two; they're thoroughbreds, they're Formula One, they're like pressure cookers.'

Moira didn't want to stay to the end of the scene. Tolkien had lost interest in her and was concentrating on the lovers writhing on the carpet. She carefully closed the door to the library, and in the hallway, short of breath, she felt the same ecstasy as all the guests that starry night, a feeling that not one of them would be able to forget for as long as they lived, no matter how many loves and pleasures they experienced.

Atticus and Soleá, exhausted and conjoined, cemented together, lived a hundred years in a single body, a single flesh, united for ever, man and woman, just as God imagined, sculpted and breathed life into them: in his image and his likeness.

Mamen Sánchez is a deputy editor at *¡Hola!* magazine and editor of *¡Hola! México*. A bestselling author in Spain, she has published three books for children and the novels *Gafas de Sol para Días de Lluvia*, *Agua del limonero*, *Juego de Damas* and *La Felicidad es un Té Contigo*. She lives in Madrid and is married with five children.

Lucy Greaves translates from Spanish and Portuguese. She won the 2013 Harvill Secker Young Translators' Prize and was Translator in Residence at London's Free Word Centre during 2014. She lives in Bristol.